MORTMAIN

BY THE SAME AUTHOR

Tapu

Children's Books

The Wrestling Princess and other stories
Oscar and the Ice-Pick
Your Dad's a Monkey
Put a Sock in it, Percy
Porcellus, the Flying Pig
Flying Pig to the Rescue
The Cuckoo Bird

MORTMAIN

JUDY CORBALIS

Chatto & Windus
LONDON

Published by Chatto & Windus 2007

2 4 6 8 10 9 7 5 3 1

First published in Great Britain in 2007 by
Chatto & Windus
Random House, 20 Vauxhall Bridge Road,
London SW1V 2SA

www.randomhouse.co.uk

Addresses for companies within The Random House Group Limited can be found at: www.randomhouse.co.uk/offices.htm

A CIP catalogue record for this book is available from the British Library

ISBN 9780701180478

The Random House Group Limited makes every effort to ensure that the papers used in its books are made from trees that have been legally sourced from well-managed and credibly certified forests. Our paper procurement policy can be found at:
www.randomhouse.co.uk/paper.htm

Typeset by SX Composing DTP, Rayleigh, Essex
Printed and bound in Great Britain by
Mackays of Chatham PLC, Chatham, Kent

Contents

Part One 1

Part Two 81

Part Three 187

Glossary 261

Acknowledgements 263

For
Sarah Billinghurst Solomon
with affection and gratitude

Mortmain

The rain hammers on the corrugated-iron roofs of the township, sweeps over the lake, and whips the surface into waves that scour the coarse sand and shingle at its edges. Where the creek joins the main body of water, its banks are torn and washed away, the soil dissolving into mud. Further up, rivulets are cracking apart the parched soil.

Earth sluices from the sides of one of the deeper gullies as the rush of water swells and widens, dragging with it clods of clay. Something is emerging – a long starfish, its five points reaching towards the sky. Behind the star is an articulating joint inside a sodden sleeve. Rising from its hiding-place, it floats to the surface of the lake.

One

'the defence of the realm'

♖

A man has certain needs.

Wilson Castle, sleepless in the dawn summer heat, pads over creaking floorboards to the violet-scented bedroom of his wife, Rosalba.

From the depths of feigned sleep, Rosalba watches the door open, spies her husband between her eyelids and consoles herself with the thought of her vinegar sponge soaking in its ivory bowl on the night table.

Five times now, Rosalba has given birth and she has no wish ever again to endure such agonising indignity.

How stylish it has become to give one's daughters Maori names. One cannot be so frivolous with boys. But girls are different. They marry. It is not as if they must carry on the family line. Rosalba's two buds, twenty months apart, are named for birds – Huia, the elusive wattle-bird, and Kotuku. Kotuku, like her namesake, the white heron, is pale, long-limbed and graceful. Quite beautiful, her mother considers, with all that soft blonde hair. But her baby attempts at her big sister's name, 'Huhu, Huhu', and the sudden realisation that this diminutive may cling for ever to her older daughter, propel Rosalba today on a rare visit to the nursery.

'Atkinson!'

Atkinson appears, slack-bosomed, behind the perambulator. From its interior, two sets of large blue eyes stare up at Rosalba, mesmerised by the glittering lights of the beads on her boned cream bodice. Four hands stretch up. 'Mama, Mama.'

Rosalba moves adroitly out of reach of dribbly fingers.

Little wooden Edward-Wilson clutches the iron perambulator handle. So much more sensible to give a boy a good English name.

Edward-Wilson knows better than to grab at Mama's lovely gowns. Behind his stolid gaze, he is listening to the swish of her bombazine skirt, inhaling her cool smell of violets, which he will later attempt to ingest, possess, from the violet creams in the flowered Charbonnel boxes that arrive from Home, from Dear-Great-Aunt in Oxford. Each chocolate is covered in a soft white bloom like Mama's lacy shawl.

'Huhu must go, Atkinson,' orders Rosalba.

Atkinson glances at the offending child.

'I'm afraid, in the native tongue, it means something quite . . .' Rosalba searches. 'Quite . . .'

Po-faced, Atkinson waits.

Stupid unhelpful woman, thinks Rosalba. She fumbles, struggles, then captures the wanted word. 'Inappropriate,' she brings out triumphantly. Though, in her cambric gown and bonnet, little Huia does bear more than a passing resemblance to a large white huhu grub . . .

'She is to be called Huia. No diminutives. Ever. Hoo-ee-yah.'

Atkinson's eyes narrow. She knows perfectly well how to pronounce the child's name.

'Hoo-ha,' echoes Kotuku.

'Hoo-ya,' chides Edward-Wilson.

'Hoo-ah,' says Huia herself.

'I do hope,' Rosalba confides to her husband later, 'Huia isn't unlucky.'

Wilson Castle, elegant, Byronic, looks up from his paper, puffs on his pipe. 'Why the deuce should she be?'

'Oh, owls, you know,' says his wife vaguely, patting at her hair.

Permitted to broach the sanctity of the drawing room to

bid Papa and Mama goodnight, mute Edward-Wilson, hidden in a corner, lays down visions of chocolate cream buns.

'Nonsense,' says Papa. 'The huia's a wattle-bird. Nothing like the native owl. Call's similar to a flute. The owl sounds like this.' He puts aside his pipe, cups his hands round his mouth and calls forlornly through them, 'More-o-pork, more-o-pork.'

Edward-Wilson's eyes widen. He stores up more pork in a secret chamber of his earnest little head. He steps forward.

Tonight Rosalba is feeling maternal. She enjoys being part of the charming tableau of mother and child. She blesses her son with a smile. 'Come, my lamb.'

Edward-Wilson shudders. On Sundays, lamb comes roast on a large china platter, but he has seen it before, naked and pink, suspended on the iron gambrel in the cool house, its half-detached head lolling, its eyes glazed, black swarms of flies buzzing and clamouring at the wire muslin covering the window. With roast meat comes gravy, brown, brimming in the boat, and a bowl of mint sauce, green and shiny like the paint on the front door.

From the front door erupts a lion's head, its top lip split by a golden ring. Though its mouth is toothless, Edward-Wilson has never yet dared to put his hand inside. The lion's eyes bore into him, even when he can no longer see it, so that, in the relative safety of the nursery, while Atkinson bathes his sisters, he is obliged to transfer his collection to a new hiding-place, just in case the beast has seen right inside his head. Suppose, as Papa opens the front door with his key, the lion should roar, 'EDWARD-WILSON KEEPS HIS TREASURES IN THE DOLLS' HOUSE'?

Then Papa would stride along the verandah, go directly to the dolls' house and there discover the miraculous ostrich feather painstakingly extracted from Mama's boa, the coloured silks filched from her work-basket, the stolen bottle of her almost-empty Parma violet scent. The scent is Edward-Wilson's most precious possession. When he pulls out the glass stopper, Mama comes drifting from the bottle.

Edward-Wilson is six. Older than his sisters. He can barely remember his brothers, Charles Willoughby, twin to Huia, and baby John Marchmont, though he recalls two separate times of small white coffins and long black lamentations. And the horses. He remembers the horses very well. Grey as cinders, and on their heads dark plumes dipping and prancing.

Charles Willoughby and John Marchmont live now with God in Heaven, but also spend time under the earth in the churchyard where, sometimes, Edward-Wilson, Mama and Papa visit them. Fortunately, his brothers are unable to return: a large angel with beautiful wings is standing on top of them, blocking the way. Edward-Wilson is glad of this. If they were to come back, Mama might not notice him at all.

Even now, he remembers her scooping him up in her black arms, clutching him to her, sobbing, 'My little chicken, my sparrow, my duck.' For he, too, had had the fever; delirious nights when the door-knocker lion had stalked him, raging and roaring through his fiery dreams. But he had not died. 'The Lord has spared us this one, at least,' Grandfather Castle had said. 'The Lord giveth and the Lord taketh away.' And Mama had jumped from her chair and run from the room. Behind her, on her plate, her roast lamb and potatoes had slowly congealed below their slippery spinach and gravy glaze. Edward-Wilson, nursery bread and milk barely fingering the edge of his perpetual hunger, had watched them set.

Among Edward-Wilson's treasures are three wooden whistles, each one given to him by Giant Wretch. He is not permitted to blow them, but from time to time he breathes into the squashed end of the largest one and captures a thread of sound. And, if he puts the other end by Ku's ear, then sighs into it, she screams magnificently, her little white lozenge teeth glittering in the light.

Edward-Wilson himself rarely screams, but occasionally, when he is managing not to cry, blood blossoms at the base of his right nostril, flowers suddenly into a gush and trickles down his lip, across his teeth, to splat onto his knickerbockers, the nursery floorboards and once, memorably, onto the Turkey carpet, mingling for ever with all the other wounded blood-brown swirls and whorls.

He finds these bouts of nasal stigmata terrifyingly satisfying: the salt-metal taste in his mouth, the bloody deforming trails across his face, the sticky jelly feel of it tightening his skin as it sets. Last time, the gore had slipped like candle-grease onto the planks of the verandah. Today, surveying the spot, Edward-Wilson gloats secretly over the indelible farthing-size blotches that immortalise him.

Here fell the blood of Edward-Wilson Castle,
January fourteenth, in the year of our Lord,
nineteen hundred and seventeen.

Just like the photograph of Great-Grandfather Castle's tombstone in the Crimean War.

♘

On the far side of the paddock where the horses, Kaiser and Kruger, placidly graze, the chimney stacks of the Castles' next-door neighbours are barely visible through the towering macrocarpa trees. In the shambling eyesore of a house, with his wife, Lavinia, their children, and Lavinia's mother and brother, lives Euclid Wrench.

Under normal circumstances, given the condition of the house and its occupants, Rosalba Castle would eschew all contact. But Euclid Wrench is an M.A. (*Cantab.*) and an Hon., the younger son of an earl, with a family crest and motto, *Dare to Win to Win to Dare to Win Another Day.*

'One does not judge the Wrenches by the usual standards . . .' says Rosalba to Wilson. And Wilson invariably answers, 'Deuced fine chess-player. Man's a genius, that's the problem.'

A man has certain needs. Euclid and Lavinia Wrench share a bed, an insanitary habit, in the view of Mrs Emily Younghusband, Lavinia's mother. Small wonder Lavinia has so many children. For Euclid Wrench has begotten upon his wife five sons and a daughter. And between them has arisen what began as a splinter of discontent, but has swollen over the years to a huge bone of contention.

Lavinia, an only daughter, cherishes an only brother, Bertie. Called to account for Queen and Country, Bertie emerged from the Boer onslaughts decorated for his valour. An un-espoused man without issue may always dare to win to win to dare to win . . . observes Euclid tartly from behind his ten-week-old copy of *The Times*. At which, Lavinia compresses her already thin lips, not her best feature, and occasionally even sweeps from the room.

For Bertie's life, almost lost from a shot to the throat, was saved in the field hospital by the performing of an emergency tracheotomy. The small pursed mouth this has left in his neck is normally concealed by a casual scarf or a well-placed cravat. Sisterly Lavinia has forced herself to look at the orifice and even to applaud Bertie's party piece, 'Pale Hands I Loved Beside the Shalimar' whistled through the ghastly hole. The crowing glory of his repertoire.

Invalided from the army, Bertie has adopted the appalling habit of tobacco. Not stout manly pipes or even thick exotic cigars, but narrow tubes of nicotine, constructed from transparent papers and tresses of shredded plug, the shreds laid reverently along the centre of the wafer papers, one side turned onto the other, the top line passed along the tongue, wetted, pressed onto its fellow and sealed: the resulting white worm inserted at the mouth's corner. Degradingly hoi polloi.

And Bertie has an even more ridiculous piece of exhibitionism. Having ritually prepared the filthy weed, then joined it up with unhygienic spit, he ostentatiously inserts it in his tracheotomy vent and savours it to the fag end. How many, many times has Euclid had to steel himself to watch the smoke billowing from his brother-in-law's mid-neck?

Another thorn pricks Euclid's sensibilities. The six young Wrenches are not ethereal butterflies wafting from flower to flower, sustained on nectar alone. Like their mother's forebears, they are solid yeomen who take a great deal of feeding and clothing. And Bertie has a pension. Modest, but, as Euclid is forced to concede, a help.

Euclid himself has impeccable taste in dress. Though he no longer maintains a valet, appearances are important to him: he prefers the feel of silk to calico against his crêpey chest. Decayed his shirts may be, but silk is always silk.

As with clothes, so with nomenclature. Euclid is a classicist, fluent in ancient Greek. In the first week of their marriage, he and Lavinia had agreed that he should have the styling of any male offspring while she would have the choice of female naming. So, when the first little Wrench appeared and his exhausted wife, clutching him to her bosom, murmured 'Bertie' over the infant's head, Euclid was astounded to discover he had a battle on his hands.

At the sight of his dome-headed, wrinkled son, he had whispered in a swell of pride, 'Perseus.' Perseus it must be. And one cannot put a Bertie, an Edward or a George – stolid, stalwart, reeking of England – as bedfellows to a Xerxes, an Agamemnon or a Paris. Euclid's entire being revolted against it. An excellent woman, Lavinia. Drew milk from a cow's udder like an Arcadian milkmaid. Splendid in the conjugal rights department. Even seemed to enjoy it. But, in the matter of pure classical form, like most women, she was a barbarian. Yet the eldest Wrench has been baptised Perseus Albert, and Euclid still winces at the sound of it. As soon put a Grinling Gibbons border on the friezes of the Parthenon.

The twins, Hector and Hercules, then Lysander, swiftly followed Perseus and, finally, the long-desired daughter. 'Penelope,' cried Euclid, over the cradle. 'Parthenope, Niobe, Cassandra.'

But on this child's name, Lavinia stood four-square and unyielding. No amount of pleading, sulking or threatening, not even a spectacular tantrum that left Euclid exhausted and feverish, could persuade her to budge. Obdurate. That was the word for her. And there is nothing more obdurate than an obdurate Northamptonshire woman. For three long weeks, Euclid dared to try and tried to win to try to win again. In vain.

Lavinia clung to her rights. This baby was a girl and she, alone, would choose her name. And what had his wife decided to call their only daughter? Ethel. Plain and simple. Nor would she agree to her husband's final desperate attempt to claw back some remnant of his classicist's dignity. 'At least,' he had pleaded, 'Æthel?' But he was repulsed.

Even now, nine years on, when he looks at ungainly red-haired Ethel, visions of Persephone, Calliope, Antigone rise to haunt Euclid. For this slight against his taste and judgement, he will never quite forgive his wife. A merciful piece of fortune that the last child was another boy. In a spirit of malicious revenge, Euclid named him Orpheus Ulysses Archimedes Xenophon, and Lavinia knew better than to comment.

Wilson and Rosalba Castle refer privately to Orpheus as 'the Orful Wrench' and to his older brothers as Parse, Hic, Haec and Hoc.

Monday is Greek day when the family speaks only in classical Greek – excepting Bertie, who is unable to speak intelligibly, and Lavinia and her mother, who know no Greek. Tuesdays are Latin days, but for the rest of the week Euclid randomly quizzes his offspring in either tongue. Perseus, Hector, Hercules, Lysander and Ethel have buckled down to their father's regime, but young Orpheus is a rebel. In him, Euclid sees a reincarnation of himself.

Though Lavinia is now fifty-two and he rising sixty, she still seems to enjoy Euclid's overtures, emitting gasps and sighs of what he takes to be pleasure. In his fantasies as he lies atop her, he is Zeus, the lightning bolt, cleaving the soft Hellenic earth, the great swan ravishing his Leda. Assuming the mantle of Amphitryon, he descends upon Lavinia in a shower of gold, attacks her Trojan ramparts and thrusts with his thunderbolt lance. Always in heroic nudity, but without the accompanying classical helmet. Euclid is a purist, but he has *some* sense of the ridiculous.

At the pa, the nearby Maori settlement on the river that leads to the wild Pacific Ocean, it has been the fashion for over two generations to give one's children names commemorating English missionaries and monarchs. Te Mara's grandson, Eruera, celebrates Edward, his king; and his granddaughter, Wikitoria, the late Queen Victoria, queen of the Pakeha, queen of the Maori, paramount chief among paramount chiefs.

'Mokopuna!' Te Mara calls his grandson. He sees Eru looking about for a hiding-place. Too late. He knows he has been spotted.

'Aie, Koro.'

'Go to your kuia,' says the old man, 'and tell her to stop gossiping over there and come back to her own whare. Say your koro is hungry. He needs his kai.'

Te Mara watches his grandson run off, then settles himself on the ground in a patch of shade. A man has certain needs and women are quick to snatch an advantage.

In the wide lobby behind the Wrenches' front door stands a huge brown mastiff, its drooping eyes and hanging jowls closely resembling its master's. This is Argus, ears eternally cocked, eyes forever fixed in waiting, immortalised by Euclid during his taxidermy phase. Above Argus's head, a barn-owl soars from the ceiling, a mouse impaled on her claws. Taxidermy proved messier than Euclid had anticipated. The mouse, though small, had been difficult to reconstruct to a recognisable shape, and its first two tails putrefied before disintegrating.

Stopping now to caress Argus's head, Euclid considers himself in the lobby mirror. This vile summer heat has shrivelled and sucked out colour from his skin. His face looks as if it has been fashioned from wax that has melted, then re-set two inches lower. He is a lean man, but empty jowls swing on either side of his jaw, his fleshy lower lip droops above the cleft in his chin, the bags below his eyes have fallen onto his cheeks. The eyes themselves rest like faded blue billiard-balls in moist red-veined pockets. His central bald pate is softened by a ragged remnant craftily slicked across its front. Grey, sadly. Even his intimate hair is grey now.

Though Time and Gravity are allied against him, Euclid is not dismayed. For years, unknown even to Lavinia, he has studied Aristotelian, Neoplatonic, Gnostic and Stoic texts, and the writings of Archimedes of Syracuse. From these, he has elicited that, hidden in the fabric of the universe, lies Clavicula, the Little Key that will turn the lock on the Gate to Eternal Existence. Gunpowder, Euclid knows, was accidentally discovered by the Chinese in their attempts to find the Elixir of Life. In his wool-shed laboratory, he is honing his own distillation skills – unexpectedly useful when the pear tree fruited so abundantly last year.

Still contemplating his face in the mirror, Euclid reflects that the theory that alchemy is concerned with turning base metals into gold is simplistic, appealing to the Croesus in ordinary men. The transcendence of death depends first on the finding of the fabled Philosopher's Stone: another decoy for the naïve, since the Philosopher's Stone may be a powder or liquid and not a solid at all. The true answer, Euclid knows, lies in transmutation. And here, in New Zealand, banished from his native land, Euclid has at last brought his long quest for the Universal Panacea almost to fruition. Poised on the brink of discovery, he sees his name shimmering, the ultimate in a noble line – Hermes Trismegistus, Plato, Thomas Aquinas, Roger Bacon, Nicolas Flamel, Paracelsus, Newton . . . Wrench.

Bestowing a final pat on Argus, Euclid sets off for Castle's house where he and his two adversaries are engaged to participate in their fortnightly three-man chess match.

As he strides towards the gate, Euclid looks with satisfaction at his smallholding. All the vegetables for the household are grown in the mediaeval manorial manner. Each spring, Hector, Hercules and Lysander haul down the huge wire-netting hen-cage and re-erect it over the remnants of last season's garden. Then Ethel and Orpheus shoo in the fowls to begin their new year's work of fertilising the soil. Perseus works long hours in the cowshed with Io, Pasiphae and Europa, but he, too, helps to dig over the ground which, pecked bare by the hens last year, will be left to lie fallow for twelve months. Then comes the planting of the garden where the hens have been two years before. This involves all hands. Even the indolent Bertie, throat scarfed tightly against flying grain, assists in broadcasting seed.

Beneath the pomegranate tree, Euclid examines a fruit he has extracted from its nest of spikes. Strange about the Persephone myth: one seed per month. Far more than twelve seeds in this specimen. Could there have been an ancient twelve-seeded variant of the modern pomegranate? Unlikely. As is the existence of centaurs. But, he reminds himself, nothing is impossible. Catherine the Great, Tsar of All the Russias, was reported to have been serviced by her horse.

Euclid recalls his pilgrimage to the Parthenon. Marvellous sense of aesthetics, the Greeks. Athletic chaps, cultivated, constantly searching for truth and form. He shudders as he remembers the seething swarms in the Plaka, every one a Phoenician or Syrian. No question about it, your ancient Greek has passed down his lineage to the British torch-bearer. The modern English gentleman is the embodiment of an ancient Greek. Look at Lord Elgin. Bally incredible that shipping back of the Marbles. Saved them for ever. Byron, too. Realised that Greece was too precious a heritage to be handled by the Greeks.

Euclid envisages a new monograph: *Passing on the Diadem: Britannia via Elysium. An exposition of the Greek Heritage of the True English Gentleman. By the Hon. Euclid Wrench, M.A. Cantab.*

This last qualification is not strictly accurate, Euclid having been rusticated two terms before presenting his tripos, but in Castleton two years and a term is enough of a part to stand for the whole.

♜

A small owl stands blinking at the Castles' door. Such a dull square box of a child, thinks Euclid. He pats the cardboard-brown head, feels in his pocket for a farthing. Comes instead upon one of his whittled whistles and presses it into the boy's hand. 'Mind you don't blow it too close to Mater.'

Edward-Wilson's eyes shine within their wire frames. *Another* whistle from Giant Wretch. He darts the treasure into a pocket. Just in time. Here comes his father, holding out a hand.

'Said your how d'you dos to Mr Wrench, Edward-Wilson?'

'How do you do, Mr Wretch.'

Papa opens his mouth. Mr Wretch flicks a hand. 'No matter, Castle. Board ready?'

Papa smooths his coat. 'Awaiting only our other worthy contestant.' He turns to his son. 'Run along, my boy.'

'Yes, Papa,' says Edward-Wilson, his hand clinging to his trophy.

Castle has set up his chessboard on a fine Pembroke table which Euclid has admired before: 'Twin to the one we had at Home at Gawminsgodden.' On that occasion, Rosalba, her impeccable taste confirmed, had instructed Atkinson to serve chocolate shortbread fingers with the chess-players' tea.

Te Mara, having deposited his grandchildren in the Castles' kitchen, takes from his flax kit his own board and chessmen and lays them out beside Castle's ivory and ebony ones.

Te Mara's pieces are all of carved bone, the board inlaid with opposing squares of totara and kauri. This splendid set has come down from his grandfather who taught him to play chess when he was a child. With these pieces, his koro had played against Governor Grey and beaten him again and again. Grey, said his koro, had longed for this chess-set, had offered large sums of money, land even, in exchange. But the great chief would not yield it up. Instead, he had ordered his personal carver to create another – similar, yet not too much the same – and had given it to Te Kawana Grey as a gift worthy of his mana.

For Te Mara's chessboard contains a secret.

'Mokopuna,' whispered his dying grandfather, as Te Mara had sat guard over his departing spirit, 'fetch me the chess game from my waka huia.'

And Te Mara had felt along the crossbeams of the whare and lifted down the sacred box, carved like a small canoe, in which lay the pawns and the castles and the knights and the bishops and the queen and the king . . .

'And the board, Mokopuna.'

And when Te Mara had put them beside Koro, the old man had lifted his grandson's hand and placed it on the bundle. 'Yours. Win always. But, if you should suffer defeat, reconsider your strategy in time for the next battle.' He had covered Te Mara's hand with his own.

'Give me a pawn.'

Te Mara had pressed a pawn against the limp palm.

'These pieces have special power, Mokopuna. Do you know why?'

'No, Koro.'

'Because they have been fashioned by a tohunga carver to the sound of a sacred chant. From human bones he cut them, the bones of our enemies: the pawns from the thigh bones of a Tainui chief, the castles and knights from the bones of a tohunga of that butcher, Te Rauparaha, the bishops from an Arawa warrior . . .'

'And the king and queen?'

Astounded, Te Mara had heard the old man's sudden rasping laughter and seen the delight that leapt on his wasted face. 'From a Pakeha. They were shaped from the jawbone of a lieutenant of General Cameron's Scottish regiment.'

Te Mara remembers how he had struggled to pull away his hand. And how the old man had leant towards him, eyes still blazing. 'Utu,' he had whispered. 'Revenge.'

Wrench picks up one of Te Mara's knights and examines it.

'Amazin' workmanship. Superb carvin'.' He peers harder. 'Some kind of native ivory?'

'Yes,' says Te Mara. 'Very rare. Impossible to obtain now.'

Chess with three players poses problems. Over time, a system has evolved: the host plays by himself with the white pieces; his guests, playing black together, may confer only in sign language.

For several hours now, they have been settled at the Pembroke table and play has been frustratingly even. Then Te Mara signals a potential move to take Castle's knight. Wrench shakes his head and tries to convey his own preferred tactic. Disagreeing, Te Mara pantomimes a series of following moves. Wrench, unable by the rules to consult him in speech, remains wordlessly adamant.

'Come *on*, you two,' complains Castle, and Te Mara, remembering he has promised not to be late home, yields the point.

Triumphantly, Wrench moves their piece and captures the opposing bishop.

'Aha,' cries Castle, and, as Te Mara glowers at Wrench, he sweeps his rook through the resulting gap in the defence and shouts, 'Checkmate!'

Sorenson, the Castles' handyman, is not a Scandinavian. He is a Russian, very possibly from a noble family – as Rosalba is always at pains to explain – who, for unknown reasons, has taken a Nordic name. This is of little consequence since he is discreet, hard-working and, above all, trustworthy. The chopping of kindling and firewood, the tending of the fire under the copper in the wash-house, the blacking of boots and shoes, the mending of spouting and gutters, the yard-sweeping, the digging and planting of the vegetable patch, the wiring of the chicken run, the thousand and one little jobs that a household generates – even the beheading of chooks that have recklessly gone off lay – all fall, as Wilson likes to put it, within Sorenson's jurisdiction.

Whatever the weather, he arrives punctually at seven every morning on his old bicycle. Barring Christmas and New Year's Day, he takes no holidays, nor does he want any. He has been employed at the Castles since Wilson successfully defended him on a vagrancy charge. Following his acquittal, Sorenson arrived every day at Beaumont, Castle and Partners ready to work in order to pay off his bill. Beaumont and any former partners being long dead, it fell to Wilson, sole practising occupant of the chambers, to reiterate, without success, that no money was required now or in the future.

Morning after morning Sorenson reappeared, pleading for employment in broken, almost unintelligible English until, in desperation, Wilson offered him a trial post as general handyman at his own home. In doubt as to whether Sorenson had understood him, Wilson, opening the door to an early-morning knock, discovered the chap standing on the back verandah, bicycle propped by the side of the garage. Securing his pyjama cord, he had directed the fellow to the first job he could bring to mind – wood-chopping. By the time Wilson had dressed and readied himself at the breakfast table, Sorenson's flying axe had filled the wood store.

Atkinson does not approve of Sorenson, though she is forced to concede he is a hard worker. Foreigners upset her and, since she counts as a foreigner anyone who is not a native-born Castletonian, Sorenson is merely one of the many people with whom she holds no truck. Rosalba's initial misgivings, however, have been entirely overcome and Wilson now counts the hiring of Sorenson as one of his more inspired decisions.

But even trustworthy and hard-working Sorenson is not permitted to touch Wilson's Model T Ford. The Ford lives in the wool-shed, opposite the shearing stands where Arkie Montgomery and his fleece-o clip the ewes. Its space is a shrine to modernity. Full benzine tins are stacked in the corner and the spare crank-handle is suspended from a hook on the wall, above the shelf for the polish and buffing chamois. Much of Wilson's weekend is spent washing and glossing his Beloved, bringing the shine on her brass headlamps to mirror pitch. A self-taught driver, he is a familiar sight as he splutters along Main Street.

Rosalba has a mixed view of the Ford. While it is certainly a symbol of superiority and progress and is faster and more comfortable than the stagecoach or the trap, its fumes and erratic jerks and its downhill speed make it more unpredictable than any horse.

If Euclid Wrench were not a thoroughly committed Hellenist, he would be a Sinologist. Busy behind the wool-shed, where he has amassed a collection of brass and cast-iron bedsteads, he considers the achievements of the Chinese race. Bronze-casting, the wheel, silk production, porcelain, poetry, exploration: an impressive list.

Euclid unscrews the ball knob of a child's iron bedstead, seizes the rod inside and extracts it like an arrow from its double-barred quiver. Laying it aside, he starts on its neighbour. One barley-sugar-twist finial is rusted into place. He smears a dollop of orange-stained goose grease onto the stubborn metal, working it around the joint.

Armour: another remarkable Chinese invention. The emperor's warriors wore mail tunics of overlapping squares, which, unlike their clumsy European counterparts, were highly flexible. Amazing, thinks Euclid, how the Greek soldier had no need of armour, only a helmet to protect that most vital of man's organs – his brain. Heroic nudity: the ultimate way to wage war. Though there must have been the occasional irresistible temptation to swipe quickly and cleanly . . .

Euclid compresses his thighs and returns to his contemplation of the Chinese. Physically stocky and muscular, according to Marco Polo – exactly like the New Zealand Maori who, Euclid is convinced, are their direct descendants. Migration is a perfect possibility: to Hawaii via the islands of southern Japan, from there across the Pacific Ocean in junks. Dragon prows: the carved Maori taniwha on the headboards of their canoes. Consider the general central flatness of the face in each race. Euclid jiggles at the greased finial. He has submitted his new monograph, *The Maori: Sons of China?*, to *The Journal of the Polynesian Society*, but no editor has had the breadth of vision to publish it. *The Times*, too, has rejected it. A pity, as Euclid would have relished the correspondence on the *Letters* page. And, both races have brought warfare to a pitch of perfection: General Cameron's letters Home were full of praise for the natives' sophisticated deployment of jade clubs. Jade! By Jove, thinks Euclid.

Unfortunately, the only Chinese specimen in Castleton is the pigtailed man who comes weekly with a handcart to collect and deliver laundry for Mrs Younghusband and Bertie. This wizened yellow creature will hardly convince Te Mara to claim him as an ancestor. Nor will his fellow countrymen, who haunt the docks and back-street opium dens in Wellington. Euclid pulls at a rod. The last one. And it comes away easily, leaving a rectangular outer frame.

'Pater!' Ethel flaps into view, the sun catching her frightful ginger hair. She rocks towards him like an awkward giraffe. 'Luncheon will be served in fifteen minutes.'

Euclid wishes he could feel some sort of attachment to this gosling daughter. If she were only a little . . . smoother . . . at the edges. She is not . . . maidenly, he thinks, has none of the rounded softness of her mother. She is too much of a Wrench.

♛

Auntie Kereru has sent Wiki and Eru to collect cress. Wiki has a kit slung across her back and Eru clutches a sharp shell for cutting. They paddle along the edge of the stream, scouting for green clumps.

Eru points to the tiny leaves by their feet. 'Why can't we take these ones?'

'You dumb or something?' says Wiki, wading into deeper water. 'For all you know, some dog or cow's done a mimi there.'

They splash on upstream towards the bridge.

'There's a whole lot over there,' says Wiki. 'Give me the shell and I'll cut it. You see if you can get some freshwater crays.'

Eru steps among the stones in the shallow water, turning over the larger ones and peering into the spaces left below. The crays are so transparent they are really hard to spot. He pokes with a stick and is rewarded by seeing the ripples made by scuttling legs. Plunging in his hand, he withdraws three fat crawlies, each about four or five inches long. Within ten minutes he has enough for a feed.

Wiki is still hacking away at the cress.

'I need the kit,' shouts Eru. 'I've got tons and they're pinching me.'

'I need the kit, too. Use your shirt.'

Eru has just taken off his shirt and secured the crawlies in it, when he hears the sound of an approaching motor. It must be Ed's father: no-one else out here has a car. He is straightening up, ready to wave, when something catches him in the back and knocks him forward into the creek.

'Get down,' hisses Wiki, hunching behind him, her head almost touching the water. 'Quick. Hide your face.'

On the bridge above them, Mr Castle's Ford rattles on the gravel, blowing dust clouds behind it.

Eru is furious. 'What did you do that for? You want to drown me?'

The car is out of sight now. Wiki scrambles up. 'You got no shame or anything?' she shouts, flinging down the kit. 'You want those snooty Pakeha seeing us getting our food out of the creek?'

The Wrenches' house has two eyes and a nose, thinks Edward-Wilson, as Papa steers the motor up the bumpy drive. And a wide verandah mouth. On top, where the attic windows are, it has a crooked hat with a balcony brim and a jaunty chimney-pot for a feather. Its casual untidiness, its general air of neglect, remind him of easy-going Mrs Winters, their occasional mother's help, who lets the children eat sugar cakes at luncheon, paddle in their underwear, play with mud, and fish for tiddlers while she reads her *Ladies' Companion* under a shady tree. Mrs Winters has not looked after them for a long time now, not since the day Ku fell into the pond, but Edward-Wilson eagerly anticipates her return.

The Model T pulls up and Edward-Wilson shrinks back into the leather upholstery as boys loom and surround him. His father is barely out of the car before Lysander and Hector are pushing at the sides of the bonnet, folding them up to gaze at the engine, and the Orful Wrench is fiddling with the crank-handle. Mrs Wrench appears, cool and pale as a blancmange. Edward-Wilson examines her wobbly, gelatinous shape struggling to slip from its knitted grey mould. Her head is a cottage loaf, her hands dear little sausages. 'Boys!' she admonishes in her soft-syrup voice.

Wilson Castle pulls out his watch. 'Morning, Mrs Wrench.'

Lavinia struggles to recover her rusty social graces. 'Mr Castle, how delightful to see you again.'

Ethel flurries towards them. 'Pater says he'll be along in a jiff.'

Huia and Ku, frilled and curled, each clutching a wax doll, take in every detail of Ethel's clothing, most of which is hidden behind a sack apron. She is wearing a black and white frock, cut down from one of her grandmother's old day-gowns: it has neither shape nor style and has been fashioned with the sole idea of decently cladding the body. A pathetic attempt has been made to beautify the apron by the application of chain-stitch daisies. This excites Ku's particular scorn. 'Look at her apron,' she hisses to her sister.

But Huia is made of kinder stuff. It is she who allows Edward-Wilson to nurse and dress Amelia, her doll; she who knows the hiding-place of Edward-Wilson's treasures but will never, ever tell. She feels the rolling waves of Ethel's shame. 'Your apron's very nice,' she says. 'Did you embroider it yourself?'

Ethel nods, mute with the sudden knowledge of her own inferiority. Surrounded by brothers, she has barely been aware she is any different from them; but, confronted now with the ringletted, pintucked, white-muslined Castle sisters, she is overwhelmed by the cruel realisation that her dress is ugly, her apron – which this morning seemed so pretty with its daisies dancing through the tiny holes of sacking – is coarse and rough. And wrong.

'You're very good at chain-stitch,' says Huia. 'Mama has to unpick mine over and over.'

This generosity only increases Ethel's agony, as does the sight of the Castles' dolls. Amelia and Dorothy have come from Sydney, though you could not call them Australians. They are dressed like small petted English children: Dorothy has a frock of white ruffles and a tiny hoop and stick of her own, while Amelia is a baby with a long lawn gown, a lace bonnet and a bottle and shawl.

Ethel, too, has a doll, made for her by her grandmother from a knitting pattern and blue and white yarn. Dressed in one of Orpheus's old baby smocks and a knitted bonnet, she has, until now, seemed beautiful.

Huia, conscious of Ethel's scrutiny of Amelia, thrusts her darling at the bigger girl. 'You can hold her, if you want. Have you got a doll?'

Ethel gazes at the wax rosebud lips, the blue eyes fringed with real hair lashes, the curls beneath the bonnet. She hesitates, then shakes her head.

Pity overwhelms Huia. No clothes to speak of and no doll, either. 'Look under her gown,' she whispers. 'She's got real combinations.'

As Huia and Ethel lift Amelia's lacy hem, Euclid strides onto the verandah. His hair is slicked neatly over his bald patch and he smells of carbolic and limes. He extends a hand to Castle, a jovial greeting to Castle's daughters. Then he catches sight of his own brood, still surrounding the Ford. 'Custodes!' he bawls. 'Abite ad stationes! Testudinem facite!'

The effect on his sons is startling. As one, they straighten up, scatter and reassemble in front of their father in a five-point formation, backs to one another, fronts facing outwards. 'Old Roman manoeuvre,' explains Euclid. 'The tortoise. *They* held their shields up in front of them, like this, of course. Bally nearly impenetrable.' He frowns at Ethel. 'Spoils it a bit havin' an odd number, but couldn't contemplate usin' the girl.'

In the distance, a lone figure enters the driveway. 'Ah, there's Te Mara,' says Wilson.

'So we're a quorum,' says Euclid. 'Gentlemen, to your tasks. Orpheus and his sister to see to our guests.' He turns to Castle. 'Didn't bring your young chap, then?'

Wilson realises that Edward-Wilson is still huddled inside the Ford. 'Get out, at once,' he commands.

Edward-Wilson slides his leaden feet onto the running board and plods across to the others, aware that Orpheus is sizing him up through mean black eyes.

'Better come in,' says Orpheus, watching their fathers disappear into the house.

The lobby of the Wrenches' house is dark after the harsh light outside: it is some moments before Edward-Wilson's eyes adjust to the gloom. Beside him is a hallstand and, on the far wall, he can make out a coat-rack. Suddenly, lurking in the shadows opposite, he spies a huge beast, poised to attack. He lets out a shriek and blood gushes from his nose as if he has been mauled.

Hastily depositing Amelia in Huia's arms, Ethel undoes her apron. 'Lie down,' she orders Edward-Wilson, kneeling and placing the apron under his head. She turns to Orpheus, 'Fetch Mater. Quickly.'

In the study, having heard his son's cry, but being reluctant to draw the attention of an upper-class fellow like Wrench to his boy's cowardice, Wilson decides to let things take their course. Unaware of the blood seeping across his host's lobby floor, he marvels again at the shelves of leather volumes, the marble portrait busts, the framed engravings of the Parthenon. He points to an ornate casket with coloured stones encrusted in the silverwork. 'I say, deuced fine box you have there.'

'Came down from the mater's mater,' says Wrench. 'Frenchie-style. Or Italian or some such. Prefer the more classical stuff, m'self, but it's a fine piece of its type. The mater used it for her tiara.' He expands his bottom lip in a ghoulish smile. 'Tiara went to Brother Archibald's wife and I got the casket. Use it for my papers. Ideal size.'

A rap at the French window announces Te Mara's arrival. 'Quite a party in your lobby,' he remarks. 'Couldn't hear me knocking for the din they were making.'

'Admirin' Argus,' explains Wrench.

Te Mara, who considers the stuffing of Argus a dismally amateur effort, nods politely.

In the lobby, the girls hover anxiously around Edward-Wilson's prone figure. The front-door key has had no effect and Ethel's sack apron is ruined.

Orpheus reappears. 'Mater isn't in the dairy.'

'Do you think,' says Ku, 'he might bleed to death?'

Ethel dabs at the red tide around Edward-Wilson's head. 'He's still breathing.'

'Ice might stop it,' says Huia.

'We haven't any ice.'

Huia is amazed. 'But how do you keep your butter?'

Shamed again, Ethel is about to explain that they make it fresh every second day and that, with so many brothers . . . when Edward-Wilson gives a groan.

Orpheus regards him with interest. 'It looks,' he remarks, 'exactly like when Perseus stuck the pig.'

In the breakfast room, Bertie Younghusband rolls himself a delicate finger, inserts it in his neck vent, lights it and has just turned back to his newspaper when he realises there is a hubbub in the lobby. Better see what's going on, he decides.

Ethel appears to be hunched over something on the floor. 'Oh, Uncle, thank goodness.' He can hear the relief in her voice.

Of all Lavinia's offspring, Bertie considers the girl Ethel the most disturbing. That wild mass of vulgar ginger hair. But now beside her floats an ethereal female, white-clad, with soft fair ringlets.

'It's Edward-Wilson from next door,' says Ethel. 'His nose won't stop bleeding.'

Bertie leans over the boy.

Edward-Wilson, pleasurably aware of the scrutiny, and smelling smoke, opens his eyes.

There are times when, in the excitement of the moment, Bertie forgets he can no longer speak properly. 'Quite a bloodbath you've made' is what he intends to say.

But Edward-Wilson, exhausted, surrounded by murky shadows, hears only a furious gobbling, opens his eyes fully and looks up into the top half of a hideous gargoyle with smoke pouring from its neck. He gives a scream of terror, and blood gouts from his nostrils.

Stepping over the boy, Bertie stalks off.

Ethel stands up. 'We . . . we'll have to get Pater.'

Orpheus stares at her. 'You can't. He's playing chess.'

'*Dare to Win to Win to Dare to Win Another Day*,' she intones. 'I'll go.'

She sees that, despite himself, Orpheus is impressed.

Clutching at the memory of the Spartan boy with the fox gnawing at his vitals, Ethel taps nervously on the study door.

'Come!' cries her father.

Ethel stumbles into the room. It is Tuesday. What can she say to explain what has happened?

'Salve, o Pater,' she begins.

From the side of the board where they are playing together, Castle and Te Mara gaze in astonishment.

'Pater . . .' falters Ethel. 'Pater . . .' She is seized by sudden inspiration. 'O misere . . . sed . . . sed animus relinquit puer Castelli.'

Te Mara leans forward. 'What did she say?'

'She said,' replies Euclid, neatly capturing one of their

opposing pawns, 'that Castle's young chap's gone out of his mind.'

'Come, Wikitoria,' says Te Mara. 'Read to your koro.'

Wiki takes up her primer. '*Dog Tray*,' she reads, '*is wicked today, And poor Mistress Slop is missing a chop.*'

Te Mara laughs as he pinches her cheek. 'And why? Why is this old lady without her dinner, eh?'

Wiki pummels his stomach. 'I don't know.'

'Because her naughty mokopuna ate it.' Te Mara ruffles her hair.

'Not her mokopuna, Koro. The bad kuri.'

Koro tickles her. 'No. It was her mokop . . .'

'Wikitoria,' calls Auntie Kereru. 'Help me set the table, now.'

'Leave her, Kere. She is reading to me.'

Kereru appears in the doorway, her large figure encased in a floral print dress. Her hair is drawn back into a horse's tail. 'You spoil that girl,' she says crossly.

The old man smiles at her. 'She is like her kuia, this one. So like.'

Kereru refuses to return the smile. 'Looking like her kuia isn't going to get the table set.'

Since the day of the Castles' visit, Ethel has changed. She is aware of herself as a separate entity. Like a calf newly born from its mother, she staggers on barely unfolded legs, blinking at her expanded horizons, uncertain of what lies around her now that she knows she is on her own. How will she manage to fend for herself in this wider world that is encroaching upon her? I am ten years old and I am not good enough, she thinks. I do not measure up.

Yes, she can sow seeds and milk a cow, but she can never make her hair stay down in the sleek, classical mode she knows her father admires. Even when she smooths it flat with water, it springs out around her head again in seconds. 'Just like Medusa's snakes,' says Pater.

This is why Edward-Wilson Castle never talks to me, Ethel tells herself. Whenever he looks at me, he thinks of the Gorgon.

♖

Sorenson has hobbled a steer in the shed where he does his slaughtering, then stunned it with a mallet before cutting its throat. Edward-Wilson has heard the sickening crunch of wood on bone and the protesting roar of the doomed animal.

'Purely a reflex,' says Papa, catching sight of his son's stricken face. 'One blow and it's all over. They don't feel a thing, I promise you.'

'But what if . . . what if they do?'

'Haven't I just told you, old boy, that they don't?'

Edward-Wilson steels himself to pass the meat-cage and the huge side of beef, flayed and stripped, hanging inside. He won't, he mustn't, look. He will keep his head down and stare at the ground.

A black clot quivers on the earth. Edward-Wilson stamps his foot and the clot heaves and explodes into a swarm of blowflies, clouding briefly round his head. As he swats at them, he sees the earth is matted with setting blood that has seeped from the cage and pooled on the soil in front of him.

'I must say, Rosa,' remarks Papa, 'our own animals have the edge on the butcher's beef.'

'We did long division this morning,' announces Ku, 'and I got all mine right. Except one, but everyone got that wrong.'

'Don't talk with your mouth full, Kotuku,' says Mama.

Ku swallows. 'And Myrna Bertram's run away.'

'Myrna wouldn't run away,' says Huia. 'She's a Brethren.'

'She's probably playing truant,' says Mama.
'Myrna never plays truant,' says Huia.
'And she hasn't been in school for three days,' says Ku.
'If I have to tell you one more time, Kotuku . . .'
Papa leans forward. 'Bertram, did you say?'
'Please, Wilson, don't encourage her.'
'No, this is important,' says Papa. 'Where does she live, this . . . what did you say her name was?'
'Myrna,' says Huia. 'Her sister's in my class. They live out at Boundary Line, Papa. All the Brethren do.'
'She's a copper-top?'
Huia nods.
'That'll be one of Hec Bertram's girls,' says Papa. 'He's a client of mine. I was out there last Monday. Cow stood on his foot and he hasn't been able to put it to the ground since, so I took out some papers for him to sign. I wouldn't have thought he's the sort whose daughters would go gallivanting.' He turns to Mama. 'I'd better nip over to Boundary Line after pudding.'
Edward-Wilson, sitting in his usual place at table opposite the girls, catches sight of the half-carved joint, its crusty edges and gently oozing pink centre . . . Concentrating fiercely on his plate, he pushes the hysteria of the bluebottles out of his mind. He bisects a slice of beef, closes his eyes and . . .
'*Edward-Wilson*,' says Mama, 'leave the table at once. Your nose is . . .'
'Bleeding all over the cloth,' says Ku.

♛

Te Mara leads his grandchildren along the side path of the Castles' house to the kitchen verandah. Wiki drags her feet and glowers mutely. She hates these enforced visits.
As they pass the wool-shed, Eru nudges her. 'Look at their car.'
Maybe, thinks Wiki, we can manage to sit inside it without any of the grown-ups noticing. 'Looks like a pretty dumb car to me,' she says aloud.

Koro stops. 'Behave yourself, Wikitoria. Show respect for your elders.'

'I *am* behaving myself,' she mutters.

Te Mara raps on the kitchen door. Atkinson lets him in. 'Kia ora,' says Te Mara politely, but Atkinson, without answering, slams off to fetch Mrs Castle to deal with him.

This evening Wilson, briefly detained at his office, has telephoned Rosalba asking her to deputise for him. Flinching at the sight of one pair of dusty shoes and two pairs of bare feet in contact with her clean linoleum, she offers apologies and refreshment.

Three acceptances. Three pairs of brown hands that have been Heaven only knows where, thinks Rosalba, and are now clasped around her kitchen glasses, which will have to be thoroughly scoured after they leave. And that will put Atkinson totally out of humour. Decency forces Rosalba to offer chairs and to steel herself as the chief lowers himself onto one of them, and that grubby little girl – so sullen – plonks herself down on another. Only Eru is left standing, clutching his blackcurrant cordial.

'I'll call Edward-Wilson,' says Rosalba.

There is no need for Te Mara to bring his grandchildren with him every time he comes to play chess. No-one could accuse me of being a snob, thinks Rosalba, but there are limits. No matter how often she and Wilson have terse words about it, Wilson stubbornly refuses even to approach Te Mara. 'Bad form,' he had said yesterday, when she had broached the subject again. 'You'll just have to make the best of it.'

'How are you, Wikitoria?' she asks now, for civility's sake.

Wikitoria politely lowers her eyes. 'Very well, thank you, Mrs Castle.'

Shifty, says Rosalba to herself. Can't even meet my eye. Probably wondering what she can help herself to while my back is turned.

Wiki knows she is distasteful to the older woman. She has seen Mrs Castle's involuntary grimace as she handed Koro his glass.

She has noticed how Mrs Castle always avoids coming too close to them.

Wearing her meekest expression, Wiki stands up and sidles as near to Mrs Castle as she can. 'Excuse me,' she whispers demurely, 'can the girls come and play?' Observing the way her hostess discreetly recoils from contact with her, Wiki moves closer. She breathes onto Mrs Castle's glass, watching with satisfaction as the Pakeha does her best to suppress her revulsion. Secretly exultant, Wiki expands the success of the little diversion she has created for herself. She wanders about, fiddling with objects in the kitchen.

'Ah,' says Rosalba tensely, 'here comes Edward-Wilson, so you two boys can run along.'

Correctly judging that anything silver will be particularly precious to Mrs Castle, Wiki picks up a teapot from the dresser, lifts the lid and inspects the inside. Putting down the pot, she picks up a pepper-holder shaped like a hat with little legs below it. 'Pretty,' she says. The salt dish has a tiny silver spoon in it. For extra effect, Wiki carries this to show Koro, who reaches out and holds it in his hand to admire it. 'Very fine, Mrs Castle,' he says gravely.

♖

Wilson puts down his whisky glass. 'He needs toughening up. He's too much with his sisters.'

'He's too much with his little Maori friend.'

'What the devil do you mean by that?'

'There's no need to glower. You're the one who encourages that old man to bring those children here.'

'For Heaven's sake, Rosa, keep to the point. It's Edward-Wilson I'm concerned about.'

'Boarding school will sort him out.'

'He'll be massacred at school if he starts screeching like a girl.'

'You're being theatrical, Wilson. I've never heard him screeching.'

'You weren't at the Wrenches' last month. He's nine years old. He ought to have outgrown all that babyish nonsense.'

'He ought to have more suitable friends.'

'And what, exactly, is wrong with Te Mara's grandchildren?'

'Don't be obtuse, Wilson, you know very well. Perhaps, when the children were small, it didn't matter quite so much, but now . . . What happens when they're older? You surely don't expect them to mix then?'

Wilson gulps down the rest of his whisky. He stares truculently at his wife. 'I don't see why not.'

'If you don't see,' says Rosalba coolly, 'I certainly can't explain it to you.' She lays aside her petit-point. 'I'm off to bed.'

♘

Now he is so near his great discovery, thinks Euclid, it is time to introduce his theory to some other party. Not Lavinia: not the sort of thing the female mind can grasp. Nor Te Mara. Excellent chap in his way, but the native intellect is not rigorous enough. Castle, however, is a possibility.

'The pater, of course,' begins Euclid as Wilson's Ford chugs along Main Street, 'was a Cambridge man. Like m'self.'

'As were my own father and grandfather.'

'Really? I don't recall your sayin' so.'

Wilson, who has told Wrench this at least a dozen times, is annoyed. 'Christ's College.'

'My own alma mater. You didn't follow the family tradition?'

'It was on the agenda, but the old man had a dicky heart and *if* I'd gone Home for . . .'

'Pity,' says Euclid. 'Simply no substitute for an Oxbridge education. Nothin' like it. That, of course, is where I first developed my own interest in . . .'

'Still,' says Wilson stiffly, 'going to Vic doesn't seem to have hindered me. Or Brother Charles. Charles is a silk, you know.'

'You mentioned. As I was sayin', to expand the mind's horizons, there's nothin' like a thorough groundin' in Greek.'

'Possibly.'

'Indisputably. The ancient texts are where one encounters the foundations of all intelligent thought.'

'Fascinating.'

'If you've got a minute, I'd be happy to show . . .'

'Afraid I'll have to pass on that,' says Wilson. 'I've got to take a document over to Fisher so he can sign it before I go to Wellington next week.'

♖

It is Atkinson's day off and Rosalba is finding her children a trial. 'Time to feed the hens,' she calls in what she hopes is an inviting tone.

'Not yet, Mama,' says Huia. 'It's too hot. Atkinson does it later.'

Edward-Wilson says nothing, but Rosalba sees him shudder. The shudder ignites her smouldering resentment. 'Nonsense,' she says briskly. 'It makes no difference at all when the hens are fed.'

They get up reluctantly, limbs heavy with the heat.

'Come, Edward-Wilson, you are the eldest. Let your head save your legs. Take the basket.'

'There won't be any eggs,' says Huia. 'Atkinson says it's so hot, they're all off lay.'

The huge wire cage at the far end of Home Paddock is filled with the squabble and scurry of brown and white feathers, darting red beaks and skinny, scaly legs flashing tiny swords on the backs of their high-stepping claws. Edward-Wilson looks away. He hates the hens' swift, sharp movements, the vicious dots staring cross-eyed at him from either side of their scimitar beaks.

But Huia loves the plump, puffed fowls clucking warmly in their dustbowl beds, digging for worms with their pretty red beaks, rooing in their throats to each other in the heat of the day as a dreamy white film swims up and across each dear little eye. 'Stupid things,' she coos.

Edward-Wilson does not think the hens at all stupid. He knows they are clever, calculating, quick with their unexpected puncturing thrusts, always watching for a chance to attack. He looks compassionately at the corner cage where a sad White Leghorn is pining in Splendid Isolation, most of her feathers ripped out, her beak cruelly torn to half its size, a great gouge next to her eye.

Dipping his hand into the grain tin, he feels the hard seeds slide through his fingers, leaving their dust on his palm. He proffers a handful through one of the diamonds of the netting. The Leghorn approaches, lowering her head. Then, with a sudden dart, she strikes at his offering, leaving, on his outstretched palm, a small, painful gash.

Rosalba brushes an imaginary thread from Wilson's sleeve.

'Problem, Rosa?'

'Atkinson's demanding another domestic.'

'Not live-in, I hope.'

'No, no. She's going on about things being too much for her, how she can't get down on her knees properly because of her rheumatism. That kind of thing.'

'I dare say it'll blow over.'

'Well, if she *were* to take umbrage and go, we'd be in rather a pickle. She's not the best, I grant you, but the idea of finding, then breaking in, a new cook-general . . .'

'How old is Atkinson?'

'I've no idea. Middle-aged, I suppose.'

♛

Seated on the verandah, Wiki squashed between her large knees, Kereru brushes her niece's hair and gathers it into a tidy braid. 'There. That's better.'

Wiki tilts back her head. 'Ow, you're pulling.'

Kereru winds a piece of string round the end of Wiki's pigtail to secure it. 'Lovely hair, you've got. Just like your kuia's.'

Wiki rests her cheek against her aunt's knee. 'You know my mum . . . ?'

Kereru stiffens. 'What about her?'

'What colour was *her* hair?'

A moment's silence. Then, 'Brown,' says Kereru. 'Mouse-brown. And straight.'

'She was pretty, though. Wasn't she?'

'Pretty enough.'

'That's why my dad fell in love with her.'

'Could be.'

Wiki pokes at an ant foraging on the silver-grey planking. 'D'you think she might . . . you know . . . come back sometime?'

'She won't be back. In Australia last I heard.'

'Might be she'll send for us.'

Kereru puts her arms round Wiki. 'You want to leave your old auntie? Your kuia? And your koro, what would he do without his little mokopuna, eh?'

Wiki snuggles into Auntie's ample warmth. 'I just wondered, that's all . . .'

♖

'I can whistle, Papa.'

'Jolly good, old man.'

'Do you want to hear me?'

'Why not? Away you go.'

Edward-Wilson scrunches his mouth as Eru has shown him and produces a reedy but recognisable sound.

'Splendid, old chap.'

'Can *you* whistle, Papa?'

Papa purses his lips, blows loudly and produces such a rude sound that Edward-Wilson can't help laughing.

''Fraid not. You're one up on me already, my boy,' says Papa. 'I can manage a bird-call any time you like, but I've never mastered whistling.' He winks, screws up his mouth and produces another fart. 'Not a word to Mama, mind.'

'Come on, Edward-Wilson. Dive in there for that catch,' bellows Wilson, as Huia smacks the cricket ball in a wide arc.

The ball is red and hard and delivers a nasty thwack. Edward-Wilson makes a tentative grab at it and is relieved to hear its soft thud on the ground beside him.

'Duffer!' cries his father. 'Show resolve, old man. Don't give those girls any quarter.'

Evening after evening Wilson bowls slow balls at Edward-Wilson. And his efforts are paying off. Gradually, but perceptibly, Edward-Wilson is developing a style, the steady stance of a decent, handy batsman. A bit more work on his bowling, thinks his father, a bit less flinching from the ball, and when he gets to school he may even make the Claybourne Junior Eleven.

♛ ♗

Te Mara's house sits in the pa, backing onto the river. Wrench strides confidently through the Maori village, looking neither left nor right. Wilson is diffident, almost apologetic, waving to a gaggle of boys arguing about turns on a rope swing and stopping to shake hands with a young man who steps out of the bushes to greet him.

'Shake a leg, Castle,' bellows Wrench, picking his way along the path through the kumara patch.

Wilson stares at the house, steeling himself to go inside. One end of the verandah sags, giving the building a drunken air: a kuri-dog flopped by the steps raises first an eyelid, then its hackles, growling in its throat as Wilson approaches.

From the dark of the hall, Te Mara appears. Reproaching the dog, he ushers in his guests.

Wilson keeps his gaze politely lowered as they enter, but Wrench pauses in the hallway in front of an object hanging on the wall. It is a bag made entirely of feathers. 'Native birds?' he booms, reaching out and stroking them.

Wilson notices Te Mara's flicker of dismay. The bag must be

special. Funny, these Maori. Set great store by the most mundane things. And Wilson would swear the bag has never been hanging there before. Why now?

Then he realises. It has been placed there instead of the photograph. But why? And where *is* the photograph?

Discreetly, he scrutinises the walls of the sitting room. Yes, there it is. On the wall that leads to the kitchen, Manu, Te Mara's only son, looks pensively from his studio portrait into a future all too soon to be lost to him. His dark hair curls on his forehead. His aquiline nose emphasises his large, brown eyes. Wilson feels a familiar pain. Deuce it, the boy, Eru, is the living image of his father.

'Kia ora.'

Wilson quickly averts his gaze, but too late. Kereru, Manu's sister, has been watching him. 'Kia ora,' he replies.

She has Manu's eyes and the same thick glossy hair, but, in the manner of many Polynesian women, Kereru has run to fat. Somehow, though, thinks Wilson, this suits her. It gives her a presence, a gravity almost, that was lacking before. Shame she's never married: she must have had suitors. Could it be that . . . ? Surely not. And then, of course, she's had Manu's children to raise. Her broad forearms protrude from her flowered house-dress, and her feet overflow her leather slippers.

'You're looking well,' ventures Wilson.

'Father's ready,' she snaps and vanishes into the kitchen in a cloud of hostility.

'We're waiting, Castle,' cries Wrench, and Wilson, seating himself at the chess-table, is relieved to find he has his back to the photograph.

Wilson lingers after the game. 'I was wondering,' he says cautiously, watching Wrench disappear along the river bank, 'if there's any chance we might be able to come to some kind of amicable arrangement about Fisher?'

Te Mara shrugs.

'He's keen to buy. He's willing to offer you a considerable amount more.'

Te Mara shakes his head.

Wilson flourishes a piece of paper. 'The agreement's right here.'

'No, I am sorry, but until I get my koro's land back, I cannot sign any other Pakeha document.'

Te Mara's grandfather's land lies further upriver: forty acres of prime sheep-farming country on which the Church Commissioners have been grazing four breeding ewes to the acre since Te Mara can remember.

Wilson frowns. 'Mind if I take a seat again?'

'Please.' Te Mara settles on a chair opposite. He regards Wilson steadily.

'Look, Te Mara, we're friends. You know you can trust me. Let's go over this business of your grandfather's land again. What, exactly, is the problem?'

'You *know* the problem. My koro gave that land to the Bishop of Wellington.'

'Indeed he did.'

'The bishop himself promised to build a Maori school there. That is why Koro gave the land.'

'Quite.'

'I see no school.'

'Dash it, Te Mara, we all know why.'

'If there is not to be a school, that land must come back to our people.'

'Utterly impossible. I've told you before. Legal precedent. *Prendergast CJ, 1877*. I'll paraphrase it for you. When the Pakeha arrived here, Maori society had no legal system, hence the Maori had no rights of property to grant land to the Church in the first place.'

Te Mara leans forward. 'Deceitful Pakeha scheming. That land is ours. Like the land by the river for which your Mr *Fisher* is *fishing*. And my answer to him is, "No".'

♙

It is a freezing July morning. As she wakes, Huia instantly

smells the hoar-frost – cool, glittery, breath-snatching. Feeling the sharp edge of the air, she burrows back under the eiderdown, dreading the moment when she will be forced to fling back the covers and jump out, shivering, to grab her clammy clothes, laid out overnight on the chair.

Frost lies on the puddles in fine thin crusts; ropes and bands of it sparkle all over the hedges. The air is full of anticipation. On their way to school, the children shout and sing, cracking the puddles, devouring the rime on the bushes, their cheeks flushed, their gloves woolly-wet.

Now, before school, in the icy playground, they skip together with a long, long rope, all the girls – *salt, mustard, vinegar, pepper* – while the boys play British Bulldog. From time to time, the boys whistle and the girls make sheep's eyes back at them.

Eru gazes a moment too long at Huia.

'Who's in love?' shout the boys. 'Woo, woo, woo.'

But Eru is not bothered. He smiles at Huia, then runs back into the heaving mass of boys tagging and pushing one another round the edges of the playground. Yesterday, at playtime, Eru wrote I LOVE YOU on a scrap of his blotter, ran up to Huia and pushed it into her hand while she was playing hopscotch. Maybe, thinks Huia, he'll kiss me later behind the bike sheds. He's done it before. Huia has not told a single other soul, not even her best friend, Gwennie Fraser. Glancing down at her new tartan skirt, she raises her feet just before the thick cable of the rope slams onto the tarmac below her. Every time she jumps, her hair lifts up and her breath puffs out in a cloud of mist.

A small knot of boys detaches itself from the mass of grey and maroon jerseys and comes wrestling and fighting towards the girls.

'Oh, oh, oh!' sigh the girls. Jump, skip, jump, skip!

The boys shout raucously, pushing and pecking at one another like crows.

'Take no notice of them,' says Gwennie. 'They're just skiting. Trying to put us off.'

The girls ostentatiously ignore the shoving, scuffling ruffians.

'Are they still there?' asks Joan Mason, who has her back to them.

''Course,' says Ku. 'Stupid things.'

'All boys show off,' says Evelyn Simpson.

'*Skite, skite, you dirty skite, you kissed your girl on Friday night,*' shouts Marie O'Malley and the other girls join in.

Abashed, the boys slither away.

'Honestly,' says Gwennie, fiercely turning her end of the rope, 'they've got a cheek, bothering us like that. What are you up to, Huia?'

'Ninety-eight,' puffs Huia.

'*Ninety-nine, one hundred,*' chant the girls.

Huia glances up at the arc of the rope above her head, judges it exactly and races out beyond its orbit as it crashes down behind her. She slides in behind Gwennie, places her hands next to her friend's on the heavy knot and swaps places with her without a second's interruption in the rope's insistent slapping rhythm.

Eru runs close to Huia as she works away with both hands – turn, turn, turn. He smiles, then veers away. Over his shoulder, he blows her a kiss.

'Eru's nice,' says Dolly McInnes who has seen, 'but he couldn't ever be your boyfriend you know, Huia.'

Edward-Wilson is not popular, but his sisters are and so is Eru. Because of them, he is allowed to join in some of the playground games, but school playtime is still an ordeal to be endured every day. Now, the August holidays have just begun and he savours the pleasure of being allowed to play with Eru whenever he likes, hunting, tracking, stalking, sneaking illicitly to the dam or the river, snooping on the girls doing the washing in the stream at the pa. Last holidays, concealed in the toe-toe bushes, they watched while one of the girls lifted her skirt and did a mimi almost next to where they were hidden.

'I'm going to call for Eru,' he tells his mother after breakfast.

'Not today.'

'But he's expecting me.'

'I'm sure he'll manage without you. You're spending altogether too much time with Eru. You need some other friends.'

'I don't want any other friends.'

'That's not for you to judge.' She hands him the trug. 'Off you go now and get some vegetables for Atkinson.'

'But Sorenson . . .'

'Tell Sorenson I said you were to have them.'

What the Ford is to Wilson, the vegetable garden is to Sorenson. Beneath the pepper tree he has excavated a large rectangle and lined it with clods of rotted-down horse manure from the stinking barrel behind the wool-shed where the blowflies constantly hover and whine.

Separated by a no-man's-land of crushed shells, Sorenson's vegetables march up and down the plot in military rows: a battalion of leeks, a company of lettuces, platoons of feathery carrots, several squadrons of silver beet. Foot patrols of radishes edge every path, with detachments of onions to each side.

Under no circumstances is Atkinson allowed to pick any of these vegetables. She must accept whatever munificent bounty Sorenson chooses to bestow upon the trug on the back verandah.

Edward-Wilson sets off to find Sorenson. Please, please, please, he begs an indifferent deity, don't let him be in the meat-cage.

♛

'I see the Prince of Wales is coming on a Royal Visit,' says Wilson. 'Travelling on the same train his parents used twenty years ago.'

'You sure?' says Wrench. 'Nothin' about it in *The Times*.'

Wilson just manages to stop himself reminding Wrench that, if he *will* rely on a ten-week-old paper for news . . .

'Where will he travel?' asks Te Mara.

'All the main centres and Rotorua. For some kind of Maori conference, the article says.'

'I do not think,' says Te Mara, 'that the Arawa will be so happy to greet this prince.'

'Dammit,' says Wrench, drawing himself up, 'of course they'll greet him. They're his bally subjects. He's their future monarch.'

Te Mara gives Wilson a sly glance. 'Precedent,' he says. 'When the last royal prince came to Aotearoa, though he waited two whole days in Rotorua, the Maori king refused to meet him.'

Myrna Bertram's disappearance is on the front page of *Truth*.

'How distressing for poor Mrs Bertram,' says Rosalba Castle to Dulcie Bickford, whom she has met in Main Street.

Huia stares at the *Truth* noticeboard and its grainy picture of Myrna taken from last year's school photograph. Someone else's arm is visible at her side. The headlines above it say: RIMUTAKA POLICE SEARCH YIELDS NO TRACE OF MISSING SCHOOLGIRL.

'What I can't understand is how the Bertrams ever allowed a scandal-sheet like *Truth* to get hold of that photo in the first place.'

Rosalba moves closer to Dulcie. 'They didn't. In the strictest confidence, I happen to know it was . . . acquired.'

'Acquired?'

'Ssh. Yes. I'm afraid there's always someone ready to profit from the misfortunes of others.'

'You mean . . . someone . . . *sold* it to them?'

'I was thinkin' of gettin' back to a bit of taxidermy,' remarks Euclid. 'Light starts goin' early now it's winter.'

'Very ripping,' says Te Mara. 'But what of your other works?'

Like the rest of the inhabitants of Castleton, he considers Wrench's agglomeration of old beds and gates behind the wool-shed to be the outward sign of some inner derangement.

'Almost at completion point.' Euclid expands his bottom lip. 'Any moment now. Pai bo kai kino tan gan.'

Pai bo kai kino tan gan? Te Mara catches a familiar word. Can Wrench be trying to speak to him in *Maori*? 'Kai?' he repeats.

'Archimedes of Syracuse.' Euclid allows himself a moment of pleasant reverie. '*Give me a place to stand and I will move the earth*.'

'Checkmate!' shouts Te Mara. They are playing today as single opponents, Castle having been detained by the drawing up of an urgent will to prevent old Franklin from dying intestate.

Euclid, like any English gentleman, is a good sport, and a good sport is always gracious in defeat. 'I'll trounce you next time, Sir,' he promises, shaking hands.

'But for this time,' says Te Mara, who sees nothing but humiliation in defeat, 'I have terrownced you.'

'Somethin' I've been meanin' to ask you, by the way,' says Euclid. 'About taxidermy.'

Te Mara nods.

'I gather you chaps are pretty skilled at that. Ever tried any yourself?'

The chief shakes his head.

'Be interested to see the Maori version, I must say.'

'We do not keep our animals this way. I have none of these stuffings.'

'Oh, not animals,' says Euclid blithely. 'Heads. Human heads, y'know. Read about them in *The Journal*. Army fellow wrote it all up. Apparently you chaps used to chop off one another's heads and smoke 'em. White men, too. This Major Robley had a few sketches he'd made. Bloodthirsty stuff.'

Te Mara is outraged. How dare this Pakeha desecrate the sacred? To speak of these things at all is forbidden to any but chiefs and tohungas, and then only at the appropriate time and in the proper formal manner. Outwardly, however, he betrays no sign of his horror.

'So I was wonderin',' continues Wrench, oblivious of his offence, 'whether you might arrange for me to take a look at one or two. Thought I might write 'em up for *The Journal of the Polynesian Society*.'

The trouble with the Pakeha, Te Mara tells himself, is their lack of respect. Would I be asking Wrench or Castle to display their departed parents and grandparents? Never! And look at how they march across the grass in front of the meeting-house without a single thought that they may be offending the gods, or me, by lack of reverence. Yes, in their churches they are pious, but how often do they go to the graveyard to speak to the dead and keep them informed? And does not Castle sometimes sit on the edge of his own dining table, placing his backside right where the food is served every day?

'So, what chance d'you think?' asks Euclid.

'These . . . things . . . do not exist. What we do not have, we do not have.'

'Good Lord.' Euclid rubs his hands together. 'So the whole Major Robley stuff's a sham, eh? Some kind of hoax.' He smiles. '*The Times*, I think, must know of this.'

♗

On the round table in Mama's bedroom stands a cluster of silver-framed photographs. Mysterious John Marchmont, in his Honiton lace christening gown, lies in the crook of his mother's arm as she gazes tenderly down at him. There are only two other snapshots of Baby John: before any more could be taken, he was Called Home.

Huia cannot remember John Marchmont, who died after only ten weeks of life; but, worse, she cannot recall anything of Charles Willoughby. She gazes at the photograph of the two of them together. Twins. Solemn in her white organdie frock and bonnet, she sits beside a smiling child with a mop of blond curls. His white top is buttoned to his shorts, his baby feet – like hers – are bare.

This is Mama's favourite photograph. Huia knows because Atkinson has strict instructions always to replace it at the front after dusting. Two other large photographs show the whole family. The biggest silver frame curls around an oval in which sits Papa in a high-backed armchair, with Edward-Wilson beside him in his Eton suit and Ku on his lap. Mama, in an armless chair next to his, her skirts trailing sideways, holds John Marchmont, and in the gap between Mama's skirt and Papa's trousered leg stand Huia and Charles Willoughby, hand in hand, the smocking on her dress matching the stitching on the top of his shepherd suit. Together they smile into the circle of the draped black box that Huia knows must have been in front of them. But why can she remember nothing of that day, of the plump curling hand clutching her own? Again and again, Huia has tried to will herself to bring back the moment, to feel once more the soft flesh of this shadowy small figure.

Atkinson has told her – well out of the hearing of Mama – that for three years she and Charles Willoughby shared a cot. If they were parted, even for an hour, they would droop and weep. Yet she, Huia, then so much entwined with him, now – just six years later – cannot muster even a fragment of memory of him. How can she have so cruelly forgotten him?

This dereliction of love troubles Huia. Today, permitted in Mama's sanctum while Atkinson does the room, she stares at the only other photograph in which the family rests entire. At one side, on a carpet of grass strewn with improbably large daisies, crocuses and poppies, rests Mama, her elbow propped on her raised knee, her chin cupped in her hand as she watches her children. Behind her, one hand lightly brushing her head, stands Papa; and beside her, on a cushion, lies Baby John. Barefoot, Edward-Wilson, Charles Willoughby, Huia and Ku occupy the centre of the magic lawn. The girls, wearing identical flower wreaths on their heads, are holding up daisy chains, Edward-Wilson is pulling the handle of a toy dog on a wheeled platform and Charles Willoughby offers a plush rabbit to his twin sister.

Huia remembers the dog. It is still in the toy cupboard. But of the day itself she can summon up no recollection at all.

She scrutinises the other photographs. Her favourite is the small boy in a girl's smock and boots. It is Papa. Four years old and not yet trousered. And now, today, for the first time she realises what he is clutching. 'Look, Atkinson. See what he's holding. It's the rabbit, the exact same one that . . . that . . . Charles Willoughby is trying to give me here, in the big photograph.' She thrusts it at Atkinson. 'You can tell it is. Look at the buttons on its trousers. And the way its ear falls over. It was Papa's, wasn't it?'

Atkinson nods.

Huia is overwhelmed by the same surge of exhilaration she feels when she successfully manages to race from under the crashing weight of the playground skipping rope. If she has the rabbit – if she actually holds it, examines it carefully, stares for a long time at its buttons, its bent-over ear, strokes its fat plush body – maybe Charles Willoughby will start to emerge from wherever it is she has hidden him.

It is pointless to question Mama. She refuses to allow either his name or John Marchmont's to be mentioned, though occasionally she will volunteer a tiny piece of information. 'A more angelic child never lived.' 'In three years, not a storm-cloud crossed his little face.' So Huia knows that, of all her children, Charles Willoughby is the one Mama has loved the most.

May the eighth is the birthday of John Marchmont. Even now, Mama often weeps on that day. 'What day was Charles Willoughby's birthday, Mama?' Huia had asked once, when she was younger. She still remembers her mother's furious response and the sting of the angry slap, and how Edward-Wilson had explained later, in the sanctuary of the nursery bedroom, that – twins always being born on the same day – Charles Willoughby's birthday had been the same as Huia's own.

Every year, on their birthday, Huia secretly chooses one of her presents for him. 'This is Charles Willoughby's,' she tells herself, 'but he has lent it to me.' Last year, he got a double-layered pencil case with a hole for a rubber and little grooves to hold the pencils. Because it is really Charles's pencil case, Huia is especially careful whenever he lets her borrow it.

She replaces the photograph of Papa.

'Don't you make fingermarks on that table, now,' Atkinson warns.

'Atkinson?'

'What?'

'The rabbit. Papa's. Where is it?'

Atkinson, shaking the duster out of the window, has her back to Huia. Huia hears her sigh.

She tries again. 'Is it in the toy cupboard?'

'No,' says Atkinson. 'Give over about that rabbit, will you?'

'But I'd like to just see it.'

'You'd have some job, I'd say,' says Atkinson. 'They buried it with little Charles, God rest his soul. The only thing the two of you ever fought over was that blessed rabbit and so, when he went, your ma said, "At least he shall have the rabbit." She placed it in his poor baby hands herself. Then, of course, we had you howling and crying for it for days, the wretched thing. There was times I thought of digging it up myself, I really did. Just to get a bit of quiet. So you'd better give up on that rabbit. It's twelve feet under, what's left of it. And for the Lord's sake, don't mention it to your ma.'

The dirt on the driveway is so compacted that Te Mara's shoes leave no imprints in it. From Wrench's house floats a thin wailing. Screwing up his face against the pain of this screeching, Te Mara knocks on the door just as Wrench, conducting, appears from behind it.

'Kia ora,' bellows Te Mara.

'Galli-Curci,' shouts Wrench, leading the way into the study where a scratchy needle revolves on a spinning black disc. The horn from which the noise is blaring faces them. The chief sighs as he notices the needle has completed barely half its circuit.

His left hand still conducting, Wrench picks up a sheaf of papers from his desk and waves them at Te Mara. 'Got somethin' here which'll interest you.'

Te Mara is not a reading man. As an orator, he has no equal, but for things written he relies on Kereru or, occasionally, Wikitoria. 'Undoubtedly,' he says politely. 'But I must, of course, take it home to read with most proper care.'

Galli-Curci gives another screech.

Te Mara winces. But he is saved.

'There's Castle comin' up the drive now,' says Wrench, peering through the pane. 'Pity. Not enough time to hear the whole side. Castle's got no ear for music, y'know. None whatsoever.'

♙

Mama is out with the girls and Papa is playing chess. Apart from Atkinson, busy in the kitchen, Edward-Wilson is alone in the house.

Heart thudding, he slides into Mama's bedroom, opens her drawers, her wardrobe, feels the stuff of her frocks, the silk of her underwear, breathes in deeply at her dressing table where her mysterious potions and ointments lie exposed, lifts the lid of the ivory bowl on her night-table and replaces it quickly as the acrid smell of vinegar bites his nostrils.

Listening out for Atkinson or the sound of the returning trap, he eases the stopper from the crystal bottle and drowns himself for a moment in waves of violet. Then, careful to leave nothing open, nothing undone, no trace of himself, he slips out and down the hall to Papa's study.

Surrounded by the manly whiff of pipe tobacco, lucifers, leather and ink, Edward-Wilson examines each of Papa's desk drawers in turn. He pokes among the files tied with pink tape, the dusty papers, memo pads, bills. In the bottom right-hand drawer is a wooden box of dominoes, lying on top of a pile of coloured picture postcards. Seizing the postcards, Edward-Wilson scans their backs for secret messages, but there is nothing. The one of Ayers Rock has been sent by Aunt Poppy – he recognises her writing – but the others are from people of whom he has never heard.

Disappointed, he tries the bottom left-hand drawer. It is locked, but there is a key lying in the pen-and-wiper tray.

Sneaking to the door, he checks for any sound, but the only noise is of Atkinson clattering bowls.

The key slips easily into the lock and turns at the first attempt. Edward-Wilson's spirits lift. Surely, here, he will discover something new? As he pulls out the drawer, he feels his heart racing and a thrilling sense of guilty anticipation.

Inside, there is only one object. Edward-Wilson recognises it at once. Grandfather Castle's wig-box with his name written on it in golden letters. He rattles at the lid, but this, too, is locked, and a thorough search reveals no sign of its key.

Wig-boxes are certain to hold only wigs, but why is it here at home and not at the office?

He is pondering this when he hears the unmistakable sound of horses' hooves. Hastily, he replaces the box, locks the drawer, puts back the key and, heart hammering, speeds outside in time to greet Mama and the girls.

The young Wrenches have gone into town for a few necessities. Most of what they require is made, grown or slaughtered at home, but exotics such as sugar, tea, barley, thread and candles must be purchased in Castleton.

Ethel is entranced by these rare visits to the grocer's with its silver-lettered sign: Maples General Stores. From the outside, the shop front is deceptively tall, like the haberdasher's and the photographer's studio with which it shares a corrugated-iron overhanging verandah roof, and a decorated front two storeys high. It is only when you go round the back and view the building from Victoria Street, or walk inside and look above you, that you see that the lettered front is a façade and that all the buildings are really only of normal height.

The interior of Maples General Stores is a dark cavern of enticing smells and of shelf upon shelf of mysterious tins and bottles – Black Strap Molasses, Camp Coffee and Chicory, Carnation Tinned Milk, Colman's Mustard, Bird's Eye Custard Powder – their colourful labels shining through the gloom of the shop. But Ethel's favourite packets sit stacked in tidy rows behind Mr Maples's head: Creamoata, Cream o' the Oat, with Sergeant Dan holding a packet of Creamoata on which there is a smaller Sergeant Dan holding a smaller packet of Creamoata, on which a minute Sergeant Dan holds an even more minute packet, on which a minuscule Sergeant Dan . . . Ethel never tires of examining this model of Infinity.

On the floor sit large sacks, tops folded neatly back to display their rice, sugar, split peas, pearl barley and sago. Preserved eggs float in the deep tin of isinglass on the counter.

There is no-one else in the shop. Mr Maples, in his apron, hands on his hips, half-rolled sleeves showing his corned-beef forearms, is waiting for her. 'Well, young lady?' Ethel blushes under his scrutiny. His corpulent body and thinning hair make it difficult to guess exactly how old he is. He winks at her. 'What'll it be today, then?' He raises a fat forefinger. 'Let me guess. A large box of chocolates. Am I right?'

Ethel turns even pinker. Exotic drifts of mace, ginger, nutmeg, allspice, cinnamon, vanilla and sticky raisins engulf her. She shakes her head. 'Two pounds of sugar, a packet of salt, a sack of plain flour and a pound of dried peas, please,' she gabbles, struggling to make out her mother's pencilled list. 'And . . . one packet of tallow candles.' She hesitates. 'Pearl barley, one pound, a pound of tea and . . .' she looks up, 'and half a pound of broken biscuits, please.'

The broken biscuits are a treat.

Mr Maples hands Ethel a brown paper bag and a tin scoop. 'Like to choose them yourself? Four scoops should do it.'

Ethel has bought broken biscuits before. She knows he is

being generous. 'Thank you, Mr Maples.' She must try not to be greedy by overfilling the scoop.

'Take one,' offers Mr Maples.

Ethel hesitates, then selects the larger portion of what was once a cinnamon biscuit with a crown stamped on one side. Three-quarters of the crest remains. Saliva already forming in her mouth, she sniffs up its spiciness. It crunches and cracks deliciously as she chews. Sometimes, in the same purchase, there will be several jigsaw pieces that can be fitted together to make complete biscuits. As soon as she gets home, Ethel will spread out the broken bits looking for match-ups. With their distinctive decorations, cinnamon snaps and cocoa fancies are quite simple; ginger nuts are the hardest. Pater, who does not approve of baking shards, will eat the reconstructions without complaint, so Mater relies on Ethel to patch them together for him.

'Your brothers picking up the flour later, then?'

Intent on the biscuits, Ethel nods.

'That be all, Miss?' Mr Maples wipes his hands on his ticking apron.

Is there time, thinks Ethel, to sample just one more piece? Her hand hesitates over the biscuit bin.

'Anything further?'

Ethel colours. She looks down at the wide-planked floor. 'Mater says, "Do you have any spare sugar bags, please?"' she mutters.

'Right,' he says kindly. 'Got the odd one or two out the back. Flour sacks do you?'

Ethel nods. As he disappears into the storeroom off the shop, she has time to cram into her mouth a nearly complete cocoa fancy and half a malted milk wafer.

Mr Maples reappears. 'Found these.' He holds out two flour sacks, a sugar bag and a tea sack stamped with a smiling Indian maiden waving her hand towards a bag of Mazawattee tea. 'This one any good?'

The tea sack will make a beautiful apron. Maybe even a skirt for the dairy. 'That's lovely, thank you.'

'Bit of a change,' says Mr Maples heartily.

Mater's tea has come from one of the dear little boxes with sliding lids and silver paper lining. Emboldened by his kindness, Ethel hears herself asking, 'Does the bop tea come in sacks, too?'

'Bop tea?' Mr Maples looks puzzled. Then he throws back his head and laughs.

Ethel is mortified. What has she said wrong?

Mr Maples pulls down the box from the shelf behind him. 'Not bop tea,' he says. 'Them's just initials. Broken Orange Pekoe, that's what it's real name is.' He laughs again, 'Bop tea, eh?'

'I'm sorry,' says Ethel.

'No call to apologise,' says Mr Maples. 'No harm in a good laugh.' He passes the box to Ethel. 'You see there, that's its name. Smell that.' He pulls back the lid and Ethel inhales the sharp black, foreign smell.

She fits her finger into the groove and slides back the wooden cover. 'The box is pretty,' she says.

'Here,' says Mr Maples, suddenly, handing it to her. 'Nothing much left in it. Why don't you take it? Save me throwing it out.'

'Could I? Are you sure?'

'A pleasure to give it to you, Miss. I never could resist the charms of a redhead.'

♖

Wilson slides into his place at the head of the table. 'Shocking business.'

Rosalba looks up. 'What is?'

'Wretched affair, the whole thing.'

Feigning interest in their plates, the children listen attentively.

'They've found a body. Well, most of it. In the river, a mile or so upstream from the pa. A young girl, so Sergeant Reilly says.' Wilson pauses. 'They think it's Hec Bertram's daughter.'

'Myrna,' cries Huia. 'It can't be. She's from our school. We *know* her.'

'But if her body was in the river . . .' says Rosalba.

'It hadn't been there long. It was dumped there in the last few days.'

'Was she . . . I mean, had he . . . ?' Rosalba breaks off, aware of her children's attention.

'Impossible to tell.'

To tell what? wonders Edward-Wilson. Aloud he says, 'Won't there be fingerprints?'

'A bit late for that now, old chap.'

'I'm uneasy about you and the girls being out here on your own,' says Wilson.

'We've got Sorenson.'

'True enough, but I think a few sensible precautions wouldn't go amiss. And at night now, until this chap is caught, I want all the windows shut and locked. Are you children quite clear about that?'

♛

Te Mara has placed a tapu on the river.

The rope-swing dangles from its branch and the banks are deserted: there is no sign of the girls who usually do their washing in the stream.

'But you can paddle in it, can't you?' says Edward-Wilson.

Eru shakes his head. 'Not even skim stones. But you don't have to worry. This is only for Maori, not Pakeha. You can go in the river if you want to.'

'I *don't* want to,' says Edward-Wilson.

♖

Flossie McPhee's wardrobe is astonishing; remarkable in its awfulness, its inappropriateness, its astounding audacity.

Exactly like Flossie herself. Immediately on Flossie's arrival, her new employer has intimations of trouble to come.

'Florence,' says Rosalba. 'A classical name.'

'No-one never calls me Florence.'

Rosalba seizes the high ground. 'Which is why we shall use it.'

'I don't like it. I can't do me work if I don't feel good about me name.'

Rosalba realises her hands are clenching involuntarily. 'If you're serious about wanting this position, you will have to resign yourself to being called Florence.'

Flossie shrugs. She is wearing a long-bodiced frock, buttoned down the front, with a fringed uneven hem.The nap on each leg-of-mutton sleeve lies in a different way, making one green and the other muddy-brown. It seems to have been cut from an old tablecloth.

'Perhaps you have something a little more . . . suitable to wear?' says Rosalba.

Flossie shakes her head. 'Only got this one and me best black.'

Rosalba is saved from further discussion by the arrival of her children. 'Master Edward-Wilson,' she says, 'Miss Huia and Miss Kotuku. And this is our new under-parlourmaid, Florence McPhee.'

'Flossie,' says Flossie, holding out her hand. 'Pleased to meet you.'

So incongruous is Flossie's sense of dress that Rosalba is obliged to buy her a uniform.

Flossie is by no means grateful. 'Common, that's how I look now,' she says, gawping in the looking glass at her reflected self in its black frock and stockings and white pinny, with the small starched, pleated cap that Mrs Castle considers sets off the whole outfit. 'She's made me into a real guy and no mistake.'

'Classic redhead, that new domestic,' says Wilson. 'Temper to match, I shouldn't wonder.'

♘

Bertie Younghusband conceals himself behind a macrocarpa tree on the boundary between the brother-in-law's land and the Castles' property. The contents of the parcel he is clutching are so whiffy he fears the old half-blind Labrador dozing on the verandah will catch the scent and give him away. There is nobody about, not even the bad-tempered housekeeper.

Bertie steps from his hiding-place. Advancing towards the verandah, he extracts a couple of gobs of gristle from the parcel and tosses them to the dog. No response. Then, gradually, its eyes open, its nostrils twitch and it hauls itself up and lumbers towards the scraps.

'Good dog,' gobbles Bertie, moving nearer.

The animal ignores him.

It occurs to Bertie the creature may be deaf. He lobs a stone onto the wooden planks. No response. Splendid, he thinks to himself, throwing a few broken biscuits from Ma's morning-tea plate. Now, he is within touching distance. 'Good chap,' he croaks. The dog stands still, snuffing at the verandah floor, tail very slowly wagging. Time to take a chance. Still wary, Bertie sidles towards it and, finally, reaches out a hand and caresses its solid head. Couple more visits like this, he tells himself, and I'm quids in. No doubt about it.

♙

It is Edward-Wilson's birthday: he is eleven. Next year, he will go to Claybourne. He has received a magnificent bicycle, half a crown and a penknife from Papa and Mama and a box of coloured pencils from his sisters. Papa's godmother in Christchurch has sent a book. Of poetry. Edward-Wilson has been forced to read aloud the first verse of 'What Can a Little Chap Do?'

What can a little chap do?
What can a little chap do?

He can fight with his might
For the good and the right
That's a very good thing he can do.

'Bit more feeling, old man,' said his father.

So Edward-Wilson had to stumble through the verse again, then Papa stood up, straightened his back, cleared his throat and, embarrassingly, in a strange throbbing voice, read it, too.

Edward-Wilson is on his second slice of cake when hooves are heard. It is Williams, the carrier. Kaiser and Kruger whinny and stamp in their paddock as his old mare, Gertie, shakes her tethered head, flicking the foam from her gums. She clomps her fringed white feet on the gravel, rattling the cart. Perched on its surface is a large slatted box.

Williams and Papa lift the crate from the cart. Edward-Wilson's heart begins to thump. He has seen his own name printed in heavy black letters: MASTER EDWARD-WILSON CASTLE, CASTLETON HOUSE, CASTLETON, NORTH ISLAND, NEW ZEALAND.

'It's something alive,' says Ku. 'It says: WATER REGULARLY.' Ku is a good reader.

A tiny cluck, a rattle of agitation, feathers fluffing, claws scraping. Dread seizes Edward-Wilson. Then he sees the other lettering stencilled into the wood – AUSTRALIAN APPLES. BALLARAT.

'Is it apples?' he quavers.

The adults find this very amusing.

As Papa and Williams prise up the slats, a net of chicken wire is exposed. Tied to the wire is an envelope marked, like the box: MASTER EDWARD-WILSON CASTLE.

'Better undo it,'says Papa, handing it to him.

Inside is a card, showing a boy in a green knickerbocker suit whipping a red top, with WISHING YOU A VERY HAPPY BIRTHDAY coming from his mouth in a bubble. Edward-Wilson opens the card, revealing a message and a ten-shilling note. A ten-shilling note! He snatches it quickly.

'*Ten shillings*. What on earth is Poppy thinking of?' cries Mama.

'Read what it says,' urges Ku.

The note is for Edward-Wilson to buy himself something special and the present in the crate is for all the children. As it is Edward-Wilson's birthday, he is to choose which he wants and the girls may share the other.

'Go on, Edward-Wilson,' cries Ku. 'Open it. Quick! Quick!'

But where? Edward-Wilson stares at the crate.

Williams bends over, unhooks the wire at the edges and rolls it back. 'There you are,' he says.

Edward-Wilson peers into the depths. Below is a tiny, exquisite pair. The miniature rooster glitters and glimmers as the sun strikes his scarlet crest, his shining purple and flaming orange feathers. He cocks his head, fixes Edward-Wilson with his bright black eye.

Williams strips away the cladding from the sides, revealing it to be a cage, lined with straw at one end and crushed shells at the other. A miniature water-trough and feed-trough are secured to the wire.

The rooster shakes his head, arches his claws, struts back and forth and fluffs out his feathers. Then, without warning, he lets out a mighty cock-a-doodle-doo. The sound is so large from such a small bird that everyone laughs.

'Well, I'd better be off,' says Williams.

Papa digs in his pocket, presses something into Williams's palm.

Ku skips round and round the cage. 'Look, Mama, look at the rooster. Can I hold him, please, Mama? Please?'

'Steady on,' says her father. 'It's Edward-Wilson's day.'

'Are they peacocks?' asks Huia.

'Gracious, no,' says Mama. 'What a funny idea. They're bantams.'

'Will they get bigger?'

'No,' says Papa, 'they're fully grown.'

The bantam rooster is the colour of the spilt benzine on the wool-shed floor. Iridescent purples, greens, oranges, reds, scarlets and blues rainbow among his feathers.

'So,' says Papa, 'shall I lift out your cockerel for you to hold?'

Edward-Wilson shakes his head. He turns to the bantam hen, a dumpy pile of brown feathers, drab shadow of her glorious mate. But Edward-Wilson has seen how comfortably she squats in her corner, how calmly she has responded to new faces, new surroundings, new light. He notices her dear little butter-yellow beak, her friendly charcoal eyes.

'Well, Edward-Wilson?' Mama sounds slightly exasperated. 'What will you call your rooster?'

Edward-Wilson imagines himself tucked up beside the bantam hen. 'I want the hen.'

'The hen?' Papa looks at him strangely. 'Think about it a bit longer, old boy. Once you've made your decision, you must stick by it. No turning back. You understand?'

'Yes, Papa.'

'He's a fine fellow, that rooster. Quite the master of the coop. He's your man.'

'I don't want the rooster. Huia and Ku can have him. I want the hen.'

'Then the hen you shall have,' says Papa and, reaching down into the coop, he scoops up the docile bird and places her in his son's outstretched hands.

She is warm, underneath. Hot, almost. And she sits contentedly on Edward-Wilson's palms, allowing him to hold her against him. Where she nestles by his chest, he feels her warmth transferring to him, oozing through his shirt into his skin. She puts her head on one side and peers at him. Tentatively, he touches her beak. On either side, it has tiny holes that open and shut as she breathes. She rubs her beak affectionately against his finger and a flush envelops Edward-Wilson. She likes me, he thinks.

Ku clutches at the rooster. He squawks and scolds as he struggles to free himself.

Huia watches her brother press his face against his hen's silky feathers. 'Why didn't you want the rooster?'

Edward-Wilson inhales the smell of straw and heat. 'Hens lay eggs,' he says with simple logic. 'If I take her, I get the eggs. And, later on, I get the chicks.'

Papa stares at Mama in surprise. Then he smiles. He ruffles Edward-Wilson's hair. 'That's my boy,' he says.

Edward-Wilson's heart soars. Gently, he strokes the dowdy feathers. She is magic, this tiny bird. An enchanted princess. She has been his for only a minute and already she has made Papa proud of him.

♖

'Te Mara's asked me to bring the children with me on Wednesday.'

Rosalba stares at Wilson. 'To the pa? Surely not?'

'Why not? It's less than a mile away.'

'Distance has nothing to do with it, as you very well know. It's quite impossible. I can't allow it.'

'I've already said they'll come.'

Rosalba turns away from him. 'I am not having them picking up Heaven knows what at . . .'

Wilson catches her shoulder. 'You're a snob, Rosalba. Do you know that?'

'How dare you call me names? Don't touch me. Do you think I don't know why you want to hang around that old man and his family?'

Wilson flushes. Steady, he warns himself. Don't give anything away.

'Obvious, isn't it?' he says coolly. 'I've been playing chess at the pa for the last five years . . .'

'If it wasn't chess, you'd have had some other excuse.'

'. . . not to mention the fact that I'm the solicitor for the tribal lands. Which pays for most of the clothes on your back. And for everything else in this house . . .'

'The children,' says Rosalba icily, 'have already accepted another invitation for Wednesday, so they will *not* be going to the pa.'

♗

Ethel and Orpheus stand on the boundary watching Huia help Ku cut out paper dolls on the verandah. Huia flourishes the scissors. 'Come over.'

Ethel hesitates, but Orpheus is already clambering through the fence.

'You can cut this one,' says Huia to Ethel. 'Lend her your scissors, Ku, and take the Orf . . . Orpheus to see the bantams.'

Edward-Wilson is reading and Huia and Ethel are dressing their cut-outs when there is a scream from the garden. Down by the fowl-run, two figures are tussling together, the smaller one beating at the other with her clenched fists. 'Come quick!' shrieks Ku. 'The Orful Wrench is stoning our bantams.'

Huia, torn between indignation and embarrassment, glances at Ethel. Has she heard this reference to her brother?

But Ethel has broken into a run. She seizes Orpheus by the ear. 'Stop that, at once.' She looks anxiously at Edward-Wilson. 'Are they all right?'

The bantams have fluffed themselves out to twice their normal size and are clucking and fussing. Edward-Wilson reaches in and lifts out his hen. As the bantam settles against him, Ethel strokes her with a forefinger. 'She's so soft.'

Embarrassed by Ethel's proximity, Edward-Wilson stands mute.

'Could I hold her? Just for a minute?'

He passes over the small warm body.

'She's much nicer than an ordinary hen. Does she lay eggs?'

'Yes,' says Huia. 'She's had two lots of chicks.'

Ethel looks at Edward-Wilson. 'Might she have some more?'

He shrugs. 'Maybe.'

'Could I . . . I mean, if nobody else wants one, do you think . . .?'

Edward-Wilson shuffles from foot to foot.

'Next time,' says Huia helpfully, 'I'll tell you and you can choose one.'

'We've got a baby calf,' says Ethel. 'Would you . . . would you like to come and see it?'

Ku's blonde hair has escaped from its band and swings forward over the wooden rails of the stall where Io, with her astonishingly long pink tongue, is licking her calf, Minotaur. 'It's the most dear, darling baby,' she squeals. 'Is it a boy or a girl?'

Ethel shifts uneasily. 'A boy.'

'When did the stork bring it?'

Ethel glances at Huia.

'She means the baby-stork,' explains Huia.

'He didn't come with a stork,' says Ethel slowly. 'He got born.'

'Which one's his father?' says Ku.

Orpheus smothers a giggle. He kicks a bit of dried manure across the wool-shed floor. 'The bull.'

'Which one's he?'

'These are all cows,' says Ethel, frowning at Orpheus who is grinning. 'The bull's out in the paddock.'

'Wouldn't you think,' says Ku, 'he'd want to be in here with his wife and baby?'

♟

Squatting on the back verandah, Wiki lobs a stone into the river and watches it plunk to the bottom. Her grandmother's voice carries clearly from the kitchen. Kuia is talking to Auntie.

'Why does he come here at all?'

'You'll never get your father to tell him not to come any more.'

'Aie . . .' Auntie's voice is bitter. 'An old man doesn't see what he doesn't want to see.'

Kuia sighs. 'How many times have I warned him no good can come of mixing with the Pakeha?'

'I know. But we can't avoid it. We all have to mix sometimes . . .'

'You think I'm old and stupid? Of course I know that. But there's mixing and mixing. In my father's day, it was formal, dignified, ceremonial. None of this house to house, playing chess, taking tea . . .'

Wiki shifts on the wooden planks. If she can sneak off unobserved, she can escape the scolding that will surely come if they know she's been eavesdropping.

Rolling into a ball, she somersaults over the verandah's edge and crawls below the wooden planks, emerging in the gap beneath Auntie's bedroom window.

♘

Euclid hums to himself as he arranges his laboratory shelf in the wool-shed. Beside his bottles of vinegar and sal ammoniac sit a cardboard cylinder of sulphur and a packet of salt. The necessary splashes of urine Euclid will provide fresh, as required.

In the dairy, Lavinia smooths back her grey-streaked burnished hair. 'Whatever's Pater up to?' she asks Perseus, who is seated on the milking stool, hauling on Pasiphae's teats.

'He's got some more bedsteads. From Mr Morley. The Morleys are getting six new wooden ones with wire-woves and horsehair mattresses.'

'Goodness,' says Lavinia, contemplating the luxury of six new beds.

There is only one trouble with dear Euclid, she reflects. He is a genius. Were it not for his jealous elder brother, undoubtedly he would have prospered. Lavinia recalls the old earl, his admiration for Euclid's theories, Euclid's monographs, how gladly he financed his brilliant younger son. And then he had died and Archibald had succeeded.

The fifteenth earl, devoid of appreciation of his younger brother's intellectual talents, has grudgingly settled on Euclid a yearly pittance, conditional on his quitting England for ever. Exiling his own flesh and blood! The recollection of it brings an angry frown to Lavinia's placid features. How the old earl must long to rise from his grave to avenge his favourite, she thinks, pinching Iphigenia's udder in her indignation.

Iphigenia bellows, lifts her tail and lets loose a trail of liquid manure which splashes into the milk pail.

Leaping to her feet, Lavinia smacks the animal hard across the rump.

From behind her comes Perseus's slow, deliberate voice. 'She didn't do it on purpose, Mater. She's only a cow.'

Lavinia gazes at Perseus, his troubled frown, his large raw hands, his plain freckled face. Poor boy, he is too like her. Another peacemaker. 'Sorry, Perse,' she says. It is Tuesday. 'Mea culpa, Iphigenia.'

♙

Edward-Wilson, chewing grass stalks with Eruera in the paddock, watches his friend watching Huia on the verandah.

'She's all right, your sister, eh?'

Unconsciously emulating Kaiser in the next field, Edward-Wilson spits out the fibrous, cutty part of his stalk and rolls the green matter round his mouth.

'Like that bantam you got off your auntie.'

Edward-Wilson looks at him, puzzled.

Eruera presses on. 'Like your bantam, here.' He describes a semi-circle in front of his chest. 'And little and fat.'

He intends this as a compliment, as Edward-Wilson clearly sees. And sees, too, that his friend, his only friend, is ignoring him in favour of his sister. A dagger stabs beneath his heart. 'She's not as pretty as Ku,' he says disloyally.

'Aie, that Ku.' Eruera shrugs. 'Mean, like Wikitoria.'

♖

Haunted by dark dreams, Wilson wakes in the early hours. No point in trying to get back to sleep. He winds his dressing gown round him, tiptoes along the passage to Rosalba's door and gently turns the handle. Locked.

Wilson pads back to his own bed. Well, he has tried. Tried to do the right thing. On Rosalba's own head be it. No-one could call her a loving wife. She spends too much of his money. Snubs his friends. Locks her door against him.

♙

Every month, business obliges Papa to spend three or four nights in Wellington.

Edward-Wilson is waiting impatiently for the next trip when, with Papa away, he will have another chance to examine the locked wig-box in the study drawer. In the meantime, he has been searching for hiding-places where the key might be secreted.

The kitchen drawers have yielded nothing, nor has the tallboy in Papa's bedroom.

♖

Wilson heads homeward. His business has gone smoothly again, thank Heaven. He is never at ease on these trips until he knows everything in Wellington is safe and secure. And, last night, after pulling off yet another adroit transaction, he had rewarded himself by driving back past the cemetery. He had parked the car and gone in. On a whim. And . . . Well, best not to think of that.

Ahead of him soar the crests of the Rimutaka ranges, the tops of the higher peaks shrouded in mist. A pall of dust rises behind him as he drives, loop after loop, up and up, the air chilling as he climbs, the rising wind starting to shake the motor. The Ford's wheels skid slightly in the loose metal as he negotiates the first double-hairpin bend: on either side, the road falls sheer into the ravine. '*I'm sitting on top of the world,*' bellows Wilson, in his passable baritone, '*singing a song* . . . Christ Almighty!'

Rounding the corner, he has almost driven straight into a horse and cart. Wilson hauls on the wheel, edges past the animal and pulls into the next tortuous turn. Suddenly, with the cart swaying behind it, the horse breaks into a trot, overtakes him on the bend, cuts in front and slows to a measured plodding just ahead of the Ford. Wilson is in a quandary. If he continues at this pace, the engine will stall, but if he parps the horn, the horse may bolt and plunge the cart over the side. The carter shouts inaudibly, his voice lost in the now-howling wind.

Slowly, the Ford grinds its way behind the horse and cart up towards the summit. The horse's foaming mouth points skywards. Wilson puts his foot down a little, edges forward and attempts to pass. No luck. At the last minute the blasted creature blocks the way again.

Round the next bend they proceed in their cortège. The Ford begins to sputter, and steam oozes from the bonnet. Dust and misting vapour are reducing his visibility so much that Wilson can scarcely see the cart's tailboard. Unexpectedly, it looms up in front of him and he realises with relief that it has stopped. He steers past it: he has managed the last of the bends. Now, if he can get up enough speed to get a run at the final slope . . . He accelerates and the car shoots forward. Then, with an abrupt judder, the engine dies. Wilson applies the handbrake as hard as he can and jumps out. The cart is drawing level. If the carter manoeuvres a bit, there is just room for him to pass. Instead, the man pulls up. 'Mr Castle?'

'Good Lord, it's you, Williams. Didn't recognise you in that cap.'

'Keeps off the dust. Overheating, is she?' He climbs down from the cart and secures the reins to the Ford's door-handle. 'Don't worry,' he says, noting Wilson's expression, 'she'll not pull on it.'

Wilson shivers in the gale. 'Starting her again on this slope's going to be a problem.'

'I'd not give a lot for your chances.'

'Not much option. Even with help, I'd never manage to push her up to the summit.'

Williams is silent; then, 'Could be there's a way,' he says. 'If

I take Dolly on to the top, uncouple the cart and bring her back down, she'd likely be able to pull up your car.'

'Surely she couldn't manage a motor-car on her own?'

'She's half Clydesdale – very strong – and I'd push behind. You'd be having to steer.'

As he watches the cart disappear, it occurs to Wilson that Williams may change his mind, but after nearly half an hour the sound of hooves floats towards him.

Freed from the shafts of the cart, the mare is picking a path down through the loose metal. 'Hello there!' calls Williams.

'Hello! Good of you to come back.'

Dolly does not like the car: she shies away. Scenting a coming rival, thinks Wilson.

'She doesn't seem too keen.'

'She'll do.' The carter pats her neck, soothing her as he uncoils the hitching reins. 'She's a great horse. One of Gertie's. The mare that delivered those bantams to your young lad.'

'I remember.'

'Well, I put Gertie to the Clydesdale, and Dolly's the result.' Williams kneels down in the dust. His muffled voice drifts up to Wilson, 'If you'd hand me down those hitching reins . . .'

'Will you walk beside her?'

'No, she can't be turning hitched like this, she can only go forward. But she knows her way. Once a month we go over to Wellington: she knows the road better than I do. Best you get in behind the wheel now, Mr Castle.'

Gradually they advance up the road, Dolly pulling, Williams pushing and Wilson fighting to keep the Ford in a straight line. The flat ground at the summit of the Rimutakas is now visible. Wilson can make out the shape of the cart and, beside it, other horses and several standing figures.

'Hoy!' bellows Williams's disembodied voice. 'Lend a hand, will you?'

'I'll be cranking her for you,' says Williams.

The engine coughs and dies, then, on the next turn, starts. Wilson slides the ratchet into advance and, nerving himself for the descent, releases the handbrake and depresses the accelerator pedal. 'Now!' he shouts. Williams and his helpers give the Ford a great shove and Wilson feels it roll gently forward, then rapidly gain momentum. The first hairpin bend is in sight. He slows down. The car judders and the engine dies again. The road is steep, the bend tight. No chance now to get out and crank her. No choice but to freewheel down. The Ford lurches right, then left. Wilson brakes. Too hard. The nose spins sideways, the body of the car slewing behind it, and Wilson realises he has made a complete half-circle and the Ford is now facing up towards the summit.

Keeping her well against the earth wall of the cutting, away from the gully side, Wilson allows the car to slip backwards until, by degrees, he rounds the next curve. Now he faces the dangerous manoeuvre of another 180-degree turn on the coming corner. Heart thudding, he slowly turns the wheel. The car veers from side to side. Despite the icy cold, his gloves and hatband are sodden.

'Right!' he cries aloud as the Ford speeds up and swings neatly round the next bend.

Wilson feels suddenly exhilarated. I'm starting to get the hang of this reversing, he thinks. Bit like the old how's-your-father. All in the thrust and the rhythm.

♙

Flossie has discovered Edward-Wilson's treasure hoard.

Coming into his bedroom unexpectedly, he is horrified to see her clutching his precious bottle of Mama's violet scent. He snatches at it. 'Give that back!'

Flossie holds the bottle out of his reach. 'I only wants a dab.'

'I'll tell.'

'And I'll tell your ma what you've got in that old dolls' house.'

'Leave it alone.'

'A dab's not much.'

Edward-Wilson has a sudden inspiration. 'If you put that on,

Mama will smell it and you'll be in trouble. She'll think you've been in her bedroom, stealing.'

'You been stealing yourself, Master Edward-Wilson,' says Flossie hotly, but he sees that she is considering the sense of this. 'All right,' she says finally, replacing the stopper and handing the bottle back. 'Pinch me a feather off of that boa of hers, and I won't say nothing about it if you don't neither.'

The grass is so scorched that in places it has burnt away entirely. The river trickles between baking stones and the trees loll against the fence-wires, drooping over the barren graveyard of the dam. Edward-Wilson is too hot to bother to scuff his feet in the dust, too listless to consider walking to the pa to call for Eru. A mynah bird hunches on the corrugated-iron roof, its beady eyes hooded against the harsh light. Edward-Wilson squints his own eyes against the glare of the sun's reflection.

For two months there has not been a drop of rain and the water tanks are almost empty. Flossie no longer rinses out the chamber-pots every morning, but tips their contents behind the wool-shed, then scours them with sand. 'Pooh,' she says, wrinkling her nose as she passes Edward-Wilson. 'Your Pa's po stinks.'

Edward-Wilson can see Flossie now, by the copper, stirring the sheets with the thick, smooth copper-stick. She prods and digs angrily, every so often raising a piece of linen on the stick's end, then poking it back into the steaming water. In the drought it takes Sorenson until midday just to draw and cart water from the river. When she finishes pounding them in the soapy copper, Flossie will feed the sheets and pillowcases through the rubber rollers of the mangle into the waiting tub of clean water on the other side, where Atkinson will dunk and wring and twist them with her lobster hands until they are ready to hang on the line.

Flossie and Atkinson have their backs to him, but, at any minute, one of them may turn and spot him and demand he help with the wringing. In winter, Edward-Wilson loves to hover in the steamy warmth, but today . . . He slips through the gate and out into the paddock. A heat-haze shimmers over its surface and the dead stalks of the grass-clumps stick up like tiny fence-posts from the black-curled mounds beneath. Lying on the arid earth in the far paddock by the boundary, Edward-Wilson stares up at the endless blue sky. Not a wisp of cloud smudges it, but suddenly a tiny dark shape appears, dropping down and down, right towards him. Can it be a Flying Saucer? No. As it gets nearer, he hears its warbling and the vibrating trill that makes his ears tingle. He watches as it hurtles earthwards, then swiftly turns upwards again, still singing. A skylark. Whistling just for him. But now it has vanished again, lost in the wide arc overhead.

Rolling onto his front, Edward Wilson follows the progress of a ladybird along the stem of a desiccated grass stalk. She splits open her hard shiny back, fans out her surprising gauzy wings for a moment, then closes them and inches on tiny legs towards the dried-out seed pod.

'*Ladybird, Ladybird, fly away home*,' chants Edward-Wilson.

'*Your house is on fire*,' says a voice. '*Your children are gone*.'

The carrot hair and tomato face of Ethel Wrench appear from behind the macrocarpas.

While Edward-Wilson has been spying on the ladybird, Ethel has been spying on *him*.

♘

Somewhere in New Zealand, Bertie Younghusband tells himself, there is a nice, steady girl who will be able to see past his injuries to the real Albert. But how is he to meet her without an entrée into Castleton society? 'Couldn't you invite Mrs Castle, Lavvy?' he pleads, today. 'Only for tea. Not luncheon.'

'Invite the Castles? Oh, Bertie, no, I couldn't possibly. I . . . I don't have a matching tea-service. And Euclid would never allow it.'

Nothing for it, decides Bertie, but to continue scouting on his own account. From his earlier recces, he knows Mrs Castle is fond of flowers. Her garden may be a good starting point. And now, when the old deaf Labrador dozing on the verandah catches his scent, it thuds its tail on the boards, but neither barks nor makes a move towards him.

Dashed good-looking woman, Mrs Castle. Bertie, examining her from behind the macrocarpas, feels a stirring in his groin.

She leans forward to snip some roses. Bertie can see the outline of her breasts beneath her muslin blouse, the swell of her hips, her ankles . . .

'Mum!' shouts a raucous voice and the pert ginger-top comes out from the kitchen.

Mrs Castle straightens, her breasts swinging as she moves. 'What is it, Florence?'

'It's Atkinson, Mum. She needs her vegetables for tonight.'

'Then she must ask Sorenson.'

'She has, Mum.' The girl winds a curl round a finger. 'He says she can't have no onions today. And she's got to have onions. For the corned beef.'

Mrs Castle sighs. 'Can't she manage without?'

The girl shakes her head.

'Tell Atkinson I'll see what I can do. And Florence . . .'

'Yes'm?'

'Do stop fiddling with your hair. It's most unhygienic.'

♖

Wilson stares blankly at the papers strewn over his desk. He reaches for the whisky bottle, pours himself another finger and gulps it down. The exhilaration he felt after his Wellington trip has been replaced by wretchedness. The thrill of freewheeling backwards down the hairpins of the Rimutakas has been cancelled out by the humiliating knowledge that he is now a local laughing stock. And, worse, what if someone in Wellington has recognised him? Why, he asks himself yet again, did I take such a stupid, such an idiotic, risk?

He feels the old ache in his chest. He hesitates, then, slowly, opens the drawer and lifts out his father's wig-box.

♟ ♙

Anzac Day. The bitter funereal pang of autumn chrysanthemums weights the air of the Assembly Hall.

'*God of our Fathers, known of old,*' sings Mr Joblin, the headmaster. Next to him is the mayor with his golden chain. On Mr Joblin's other side, the president of the Returned Services Association stands like a ramrod, his chin jutting forward as he bellows out the words of the hymn.

Beneath whose Awful Hand He holds
Dominion over palm and pine.

Why, wonders Huia, standing clutching her side of Standard Six's wreath, has God got an Awful Hand? Feeling Mr Joblin's eyes on her, she opens her mouth wide for the final refrain, '*Lest we forget, lest we forget.*' She steals a sideways glance at Joan Hopkins. Everyone knows that Joan's real father died in the Great War just before she was born and that her mother's new husband has adopted her. Does Joan remember her father? Momentarily, Huia reflects on the glamour of having a dead father who, like Eru's, is a War Hero. Billy Bradshaw gives a tug on the wreath from the other side. Standards Five and Six must lead off with the wreath-laying ceremony and the piano has fallen silent.

Huia and Ku are always chosen to be wreath-bearers. *Their* mother can be counted on to send them in wearing clean clothes and shoes and socks. Eru and Mereana are clutching the wreath for the Pioneer Battalion. Eru is in shoes, but Mereana is barefoot. On Anzac Day!

Huia knows the drill. Clinging to the wreath, she and Billy clump up the Hall's central aisle. Approaching the makeshift altar below the dais, they lay down their offering, take exactly three steps back and bow their heads. They are meant to say a silent prayer, but Huia counts under her breath to twenty, then opens her eyes and raises her head. Billy who has been squinting through his eyelids waiting for her cue, snaps his head back into position, they wheel outwards, turn and march together to their bench. The Standard Three and Four wreath-bearers, one of whom is Ku, pass them on their way back.

After Assembly, the whole school will set off in crocodile, the wreath-layers at the head, and place their offerings on the town Cenotaph where the stone soldier, leaning wearily on his rifle butt, gazes at the words carved below his feet: PRO PATRIA. Then Mr Joblin will dismiss them, right there in Albert Square, and they will have the rest of the day off.

♘

Bertie Younghusband remembers the chaps in his battalion speculating on the worst injury that might befall them. The shooting off of his privates; that's what every soldier feared most. To wake up from one's injuries to find one was not a whole man any more . . . And yet, thinks Bertie, I may as well not be a whole man, for all the chance I have of meeting a marriageable girl. He inhales deeply, forces himself to pull himself together. He will take a stroll to the Castles' boundary. Might even bump into that saucy little redhead, Flossie . . . Funny how she seems to have taken a shine to him. Mind you, the odd florin's a great easer of pathways.

♟ ♙

Eru has many more skills than Edward-Wilson. Koro has taught him how to weave eel traps out of flax strips, hang them in the stream and wait until eels undulate into their open jaws. He can call up birds by imitating their cries and even make a wood-pigeon snare.

Today, they are heading for the cool muddy waters of the reservoir dam. Though there is no tapu on it, the dam is strictly out of bounds to both of them. Last year a boy drowned there, caught among invisible water-weed.

As they slap about in the mud at its sides, skidding and squelching, Eru spots a frog in the nearby rushes. 'Ssh.' He glides silently up to it and snaps his hand round it, trapping it. 'Hey? You want to see something funny?'

Edward-Wilson nods eagerly. He can tell it is going to be a secret. His friend's voice holds the promise of things forbidden.

'Got to get rid of that plurry Wikitoria. She's got the hots for you. She was following us most of yesterday.'

'She wasn't!'

'You didn't see her. Me neither. But she told Koro all about us swimming down the dangerous bit of the dam. Said she stalked us through the Domain. So she must have been there all right.'

'What a snitch.'

Eru blows softly on the frog's face. It stares at him with protruding eyes, the pulse in its throat thudding.

'See that hollow grass over by the fence. Go and get us some. A good bit, eh? One like a straw inside.'

Edward-Wilson roots around in the clump and breaks off several long sticks.

'Not too big. About that size. Yeah. Nice and juicy, but strong.'

Holding the straw in his hand, Eru spits on one end of it. The beat in the frog's neck hammers beneath the thin layer of its skin. Its terror is comic and the familiarity of its fear makes them both laugh too loudly as they watch it trembling in Eru's grasp. Edward-Wilson feels his own breath quicken as he is swept by the excitement of anticipated power and cruelty. 'Stupid bloody thing,' he jeers.

'You dumb frog,' says Eru, spitting on the straw again. 'Okay.' He turns to Edward-Wilson. 'Look at this.'

Deftly, he flips the frog upside down so that its round, fat bottom is upended. Its backside is green and yellowish with a cleft between the buttocks. Pushing them apart, Eru works the wet end of the straw into the tiny hole. Edward-Wilson gazes in guilty fascination as his friend puts his mouth over the straw's other end and, holding the frog between his two hands, begins to blow gently down the grass.

The frog's eyes bulge larger and its stomach begins to puff out. Eru's own cheeks and eyes are popping, too. On and on he blows, the frog swelling in his hand. 'Hey, stop!' yells Edward-Wilson. 'The bloody thing'll explode.' Clutching his arms round himself in excitement, he laughs aloud . . . at . . . what exactly? Is it the bloated ball of the frog's belly that is making him double over now in amusement? Is it the straw sticking out so rudely? His own bold swearing? Or the hilarity of relief at being the torturer, not the tortured? Now the frog is so distended it looks like a bug-eyed balloon dangling two stubby arms and two waving web-footed legs.

'Ready?' Eru spits out his end of the grass straw and, leaving it still poking from the frog's behind, sets the creature down on the murky surface of the dam.

'Watch him go!' he shouts, whipping out the stalk and giving the frog a shove.

Bubbles spurt out after it as it spins crazily, propelled across the water by the air escaping from its anus. Already, its scrabbling legs are beginning to paddle through the little rough waves around its slowly deflating abdomen.

Lying on the bank, Edward-Wilson and Eru snigger and giggle helplessly.

'Your koro showed you that?'

'You mental? Koro knows I did that, he'd skin me.'

Edward-Wilson describes the arc of an imaginary inflated belly above his own. 'When you were blowing . . .' he starts to splutter but is forced by his own laughter to stop.

'Yeah, yeah.' Eru rolls onto his stomach, snorting at the memory.

'Pretty dumb frog, eh?'

'So plurry dumb. Just sat there in my hands.'

Abruptly, Edward-Wilson sits up. 'Look now.'

Eru rolls over and sits up, too.

The frog, almost back to its normal size, its rear legs hanging diagonally below it, is making its way to the far side of the dam. The spots and ridges on its back have dwindled, its tiny front legs stroke through the water. With a sudden leap, it arcs through the air and disappears in a clump of water-weed.

'I hate frogs,' says Eru.

'Me, too.' Edward-Wilson skips a stone across the water. 'You found your dad's medal yet?'

Eru's father was a war hero, fallen for his country in the fields of France. '*In Flanders' fields the poppies grow*,' they recited in class at Castleton Primary. Eru's father, Edward-Wilson knows, died in no-man's-land bearing a wounded comrade on his shoulders. '*Greater love hath no man than this*,' intones Mr Joblin each Anzac Day, '*that a man lay down his life for his friend.*'

Would I lay down my life for Eru? wonders Edward-Wilson. He suspects that, when it came to it, he might not do the manly thing, that cowardice might overcome him as it has done so often before. 'How come your dad's name's not on the Cenotaph?' he asks.

'They don't always put Maori on.'

'George Tamahere's uncle's there.'

'He never got a medal, though.'

Edward-Wilson knows from Eru that his grieving koro has put away Eru's father's Military Medal in his sacred huia-feather box, not to be touched now or ever until Eru himself is a grown-up.

'You ever look in the box?'

Eru is shocked. 'That's tapu. Not for me to touch. There'd be big trouble if I looked in that.'

'You got any of your dad's war stuff? His bayonet or his tin hat or anything?'

Eru shakes his head. He plaits three grass-stalks into a pigtail and holds it out to Edward-Wilson. '*Pull the Chinkie's hair.*'

Edward-Wilson gives it a hard tug. '*Chinkie-Chinkie Chinaman velly, velly sad*,' he intones ritualistically. '*All his cabbages velly, velly bad.*'

'*Pooh, pooh, pooh*,' shrieks Eru.

They are floating in the dam, faces to the sky, when Edward-

Wilson spots the figure darting from the stand of bush. Wikitoria, secret and silent, with her wooden rifle and her dangerous outlaw air, has been stalking them.

'Plurry Wiki,' he screeches.

Eru has seen her, too. 'She's going to steal our trousers.'

They race up the bank. 'Wait till I catch you,' roars Eru, reaching Wiki as she snatches up Edward-Wilson's underpants. Grabbing her by the arm, he wrestles her to the ground.

Wiki goes limp. She begins to shake with laughter. 'Look at you,' she jeers. 'Poor little boys, eh?' She points at their shrunken penises, dangling forgotten in the rough and tumble. 'No point any girl bothering with either of *you*.'

♞

Nowadays, whenever Ethel goes into Maples General Stores, it seems the proprietor has a present for her. There are whole cocoa fancies saved from the broken-biscuits box, twists of tea in brown paper and, today, an almost full bottle of Camp Coffee and Chicory with a beautiful label on which a desert sheikh is taking coffee outside his tent. 'Makes you wonder,' says Mr Maples, 'how they keep 'em clean.'

'The cups?'

'No, dear, the white robes. No water and all that sand and everything. Which reminds me. Excuse me a minute.' He marches ponderously into the darkness of the room behind the counter and returns holding a small white gauze-wrapped cylinder. 'Spare Reckitts. Fell out of the big box. Expect your mum blues her wash, doesn't she?'

'Yes, she does. Thank you. You're very kind.' And he is.

He bends across the counter towards her. 'Now what's on your list today? Pass it over, dear, and we'll see what we've got.'

Each time it seems to take longer to assemble the things on Mater's list. Last week, Mr Maples had asked if Ethel would mind if he went ahead and served these others who had come in after her, seeing that their lists were so much shorter. In fact

Ethel had noticed that, though one of the lists was even longer than her own, Mr Maples had dealt with it at far greater speed. 'Better thank the little lady for giving up her turn,' he had told that particular shopper as Ethel blushed puce in the corner by the flour sacks.

And that's another thing. Every time she comes in now, he has at least two best flour sacks saved for her, the loose flour brushed and shaken off. He really is generous. All the same, even though she is fourteen and practically grown-up, Ethel feels somehow better when she sees one of her brothers looming in the doorway ready to carry the heavier provisions.

♙

Edward-Wilson spots a farthing lying among the small stones in the road. He seizes it. Luck! This must be a sign that boarding school is going to be all right. His hand curls over the coin in his pocket. It is warm from the sun and he can feel the raised picture of the king on its face. He won't spend it: he will hide it somewhere safe where no-one else will ever find it and where it will go on bringing him luck. And he will tell nobody. Not even Eru.

But no place in the house is safe from Flossie's snooping: he will have to bury it in the garden. Edward-Wilson examines the bushes lining the roadside fence. Too difficult to find it again. The roses by the side boundary are large and prickly and Mama is always snipping there with her secateurs. He goes round the back where the pepper tree is soughing and dipping in the breeze. At the side of the vegetable garden, a rough piece of its trunk sticks out, making a step up into the branches. Under there – that's the place, he tells himself.

'Why're you wandering round the garden like a sick chook?'

Edward-Wilson starts, then recovers himself. 'Why're you?' At least Flossie hasn't seen his lucky farthing. 'Atkinson'll give you what for.'

She shrugs. 'It's her half-day. And your ma's out, too.' She gives him a calculating look. 'You up to something?'

'No.'

Flossie squats down at the edge of the vegetable patch, whistling a strange little tune through her teeth. She looks pertly at Edward-Wilson. 'Clever, eh? Bet you can't whistle like that.'

'Bet I can.'

'Go on, then. Copy us.'

Edward-Wilson whistles.

'Not bad. You're quite a good whistler, you are. Me beau learnt that tune to me.' She whistles on for a minute or two, then, 'Don't suppose you'd have a spare thruppence?' she says.

Edward-Wilson shakes his head.

'I'll show you something if you give it to us. Something special.'

'I haven't got threepence.'

'Something you never seen before.'

'Like what?'

'That'd be telling. Gimme the money first.'

'I told you, I don't have threepence.'

'A copper then.'

'Not if I don't know what it's for. Anyway, I'm busy.'

'Oh, busy,' mimics Flossie, scathingly.

Edward-Wilson fingers his farthing.

'Your dad's a good 'un,' says Flossie. 'Gave us a tanner last week.'

Edward-Wilson is stabbed by jealousy.

'But I spent it.'

'What on?'

Flossie touches the bridge of her nose with her finger. 'No telling.'

'No telling.'

'Promise?'

'Crossmyheartandhopetodie.'

'Fags,' says Flossie.

'You . . . smoke?'

'They wasn't for me. They was a present.' She pauses. 'For me sweetheart. Didn't know I had a beau, did you? He usually smokes roll-ups, so I bought him packet ones, for a treat. But I kept two for meself. You want one?'

Edward-Wilson shakes his head.

'I'll give you one if you like.' Flossie fishes in her pocket and withdraws a battered white roll. 'Don't let your ma see it.'

A silence falls. Flossie breaks it. 'Why're you going off to school, then?'

'I just have to, that's all.'

'You want to?'

'Not much.'

'Why don't you say you won't go?'

'They won't listen to me.'

'Tell you what,' says Flossie, 'seeing you're going and everything, I'll make it a ha'pence.'

Rummaging in his satchel for the halfpenny, Edward-Wilson is aware of Flossie in the hall.

'You got it?'

'Yes. Here.'

Flossie slides the halfpenny into her apron pocket. 'Right-oh, then, stand there. With your back to the wall. Ever see a girl before?'

Edward-Wilson feels his legs dissolve, his face turn red, his throat tighten.

Flossie laughs. 'Don't look like that. It won't bite you.'

Edward-Wilson knows he should turn away, walk quickly outside, tell Flossie not to . . .

'Open your eyes, then.'

She has lifted up her skirt and stands with her legs planted apart. Where Edward-Wilson has what Papa refers to as his 'equipment', Flossie has nothing but a small triangular bush of golden-red curly hair.

She seizes his hand. 'Go on. You can touch it.' And before he can snatch it back, she has thrust his hand into the bush. Among the hair are two lips on either side of a long split. Struggling to free his hand, he feels his fingers pushed deeper into a warm, damp stickiness.

His struggles cease. Of their own accord, his fingers seem to be probing into the wetness inside Flossie. She squeezes her thighs round his arm, trapping his hand inside her. He is waiting for her to shout at him, tell him to leave her alone, but she seems to like what his fingers are doing. Moaning and wriggling, she rubs herself against him and, with her free hand, reaches down between his legs . . .

'No,' gasps Edward-Wilson as she grabs at his crotch.

'I'm not gonna hurt you,' croons Flossie, working her hand down inside his trousers.

Suddenly, she unclasps her legs and snatches away his hand. 'Oh my Gawd. Someone's coming.' She pushes him. 'Quick. Get youseself straight.'

Edward-Wilson's body is shaking, his hand seems to belong to someone else, his equipment is stiff and red and something is oozing from the end of it. He can hear Flossie in the breakfast room, protesting loudly. 'It ain't my fault, Mum. It's Atkinson's half-day and I'm all on me own here.'

It is the last week of Edward-Wilson's holidays. In one more week, he thinks, with rising panic, I'll be at Claybourne.

Huia and Ku are playing chase round the end of the verandah, Kaiser and Kruger are stamping in their paddock. The comforting smell of sheep drifts in the air. What will they do when I'm not here? thinks Edward-Wilson. Will they even notice that I'm gone? He can feel shameful tears prickling under his eyelids.

'Come *on,* Edward-Wilson,' screeches Ku, flying towards him. 'Huia's It. Don't let her tig you.'

Edward-Wilson runs, heavy-legged and dispirited, and is tigged within minutes.

'Now *you*'re It,' cries Ku. 'Catch us, catch us.'

A sudden fury seizes Edward-Wilson. Racing after her, he seizes her and pounds her against the wire.

'Ow!' howls Ku. 'Let me go, you mean pig.'

Serves her right, thinks Edward-Wilson. *She* isn't being sent away to school.

Papa is talking to Sorenson by the meat-cage.

Biting the inside of his top lip, willing his nose not to bleed, Edward-Wilson approaches.

'Papa?'

His father looks up. 'What is it, my boy?' He turns to Sorenson. 'Well, that's settled.'

Sorenson nods and strides away.

'Now then, Edward-Wilson . . . ?'

'It's about school, Papa.' He hesitates. 'I . . . I'd rather not go.' He looks desperately at his father. 'I could stay here. I could go to Boys' High in Masterton. With Eru. You said yourself it's a good . . .'

His father frowns. 'I'm disappointed in you, Edward-Wilson,' he says. 'Very disappointed. Your mother and I are making considerable sacrifices to send you to Claybourne.'

'But, Papa, all the other boys in my class . . .'

'You're not "all the other boys". Duty, Edward-Wilson. You know what "doing your duty" means?'

'Yes, Papa.'

'At Claybourne you will do your duty. Just as I did. As Grandfather Castle did.' His face is stern. 'I expect great things of you, my boy.' Edward-Wilson sees his expression soften. 'By the end of your first term, you'll love the old place. Be wondering why you ever funked going.' He grips his son's shoulder. 'Chin up, old chap. You're a Castle. No cowardy-custards in *this* family, eh?'

Two

'under pain of forfeiture'

♙

Each morning, when Edward-Wilson opens his eyes, he prays he will find himself back in his bedroom at home. Instead, he sees two rows of white-counterpaned iron beds, stretching along either side of the dormitory. Another day at Claybourne to endure.

He does his best to remain invisible. Though he has learnt to accept the daily torments, the cold baths, and the random cuffings and slipperings meted out by the older boys to the younger, he still lives in dread of a beating. The impenetrable systems of friendships and clubbability are as baffling and foreign as French. '*Sneak, pig, blancmange, Castle-parcel, Castle-arsehole*' ring in his ears as he shrinks from his marauding, jolly fellows.

Claybourne is cold. Permanently cold. Two regulation blankets are permitted per bed and no eiderdowns, not even in winter. The bathwater is always icy and only Sixth Formers are allowed a fire in their common-room. If it is very frosty, the junior common-room has a fire on Sundays but no more than five or six boys can get near enough to warm themselves and Edward-Wilson does not dare push his way to the front.

Then, there is the food. '*Good, nourishing, plain food,*' says the prospectus, but there is never enough of it. At mealtimes, clutching his plate, Edward-Wilson steels himself to line up with the rest of his form and pass, first by the cook, Mrs Jenkins, then by her assistant, Cynthia, in order to have dumped on his plate a portion of whatever miserable stew or dried-up casserole is on the day's menu. Though the gristly meat, the white tubes in the kidneys and the over-boiled cabbage revolt him, Edward-Wilson, like the other boys, is so hungry he would gladly fill up on the cabbage water if it were available.

The fastest eaters can gain a refill by rejoining the queue. The Sixth Formers, always served first, wolf down their food in minutes. And, if treacle tart or spotted dick and custard are being served, there is a riot to claim a place in the line again.

So far, Edward-Wilson has never managed a second helping. He wakes inhaling the imagined smell of food. Some nights, he dreams he is at home gnawing on the carcase of the Sunday lamb, pale pink blood dripping from his jaws, his hands thick and greasy with congealing fat.

But, finally, after nearly a term of miserable loneliness, he has made a friend. Mulholland, though overweight, pimply and hopeless at games, has already spent three years at prep school before coming to Claybourne and has an enviable knowledge of how to survive.

Edward-Wilson, seeing him struggling with his Latin prep, had offered him his own book to copy.

'I say,' Mulholland said, 'jolly d. of you, Castle. You sure?'

Edward-Wilson nodded.

'Better put in a few sentences of my own,' said Mulholland cheerily, 'or the Doctor'll be suspicious. Wouldn't do to get the whole thing right.' Blots from his nib dropped onto the page. 'You're lucky, Castle. No-one in my family's ever been blessed with brains.'

Today Mulholland has had a fruit cake from his grandmother. All tuck is kept in Matron's cupboard from where she rations out portions on Sundays, but Mulholland is an expert at wheedling extra slices.

'I want to share it with the others in my dorm,' he says, winking at Edward-Wilson as soon as Matron's head is safely in the cupboard.

The thick smell of cake floats from its tin. Edward-Wilson

feels saliva collecting in his mouth as he anticipates the dense spiciness crumbling on his tongue, the juicy raisins, the tangy fruit peel, maybe even the sticky sweetness of a glacé cherry. Before he takes a piece, he will scan the slices for one with a pale blotch embedded in it.

Mulholland has shown him the secret of lasting in the wash-room flannel-hanging contests. 'Get your people to send you some Colman's Mustard in your next tuck parcel, but I'll give you some for now. Rub it on your Ernest about ten minutes before, especially underneath. And make sure you don't get any on the end.' The pain almost brought tears to Edward-Wilson's eyes, but he has out-hung the other five participants in the last two contests, even when the flannels were wet. And Mulholland has told him he is 'pretty impressive in the size department'.

'Right, old chap,' says Mulholland, who has just been commended by Matron for his generosity, 'off to the locker room to pig out. Three decent slices each, if no-one spots us.'

♜

Huia, up earlier than everyone else and filling the hens' grit-tin in the wool-shed, jumps as Eru's sister appears beside her. 'Oh. Hello.'

'I thought I'd come over and see you.'

'It's . . . early for a visit.'

Wiki peers in the tin. 'That for the hens?'

'Yes. Grit for their egg shells.'

'We use smashed-up beach shells for our grit.'

'You've got hens?'

'My auntie has.'

'Is . . . is Eru with you?'

Wiki shakes her head. 'He doesn't know I'm here. No-one does.' She digs in her pocket. 'D'you like cress?'

'I think so.' Huia notes Wiki's expression. 'Yes, I do.'

'I brought you some. Fresh picked this morning.'

'That's very kind of you,' says Huia, who knows her mother's views on eating cress from the river bed.
'It's good with pork.'
'I'm sure.'
'Ed off at school, then?'
'Yes. We . . . we had a letter last week.' Huia casts about for something she can give Wiki in return. What on earth does she want? Why is she here? If Mama sees her, there'll be trouble. 'Would you like a couple of our eggs?'
Huia will have to pretend that the hens are off lay. Glancing over her shoulder for Mama, she leads the way to the hen-run.
Wiki stares at the Rhode Island Reds, the Buff Orpingtons and the White Leghorns scratching around with the bantams. 'I've got Pakeha blood, myself,' she says. 'On my mother's side.'
'Oh,' says Huia.
'My mother's koro was the governor.'
'Really?'
'Yes. Te Kawana Grey.'
'Gosh.'
'That's why my dad's Military Medal is going to come to me.'
'But what about Eru?' asks Huia.
'When my dad died,' says Wiki firmly, 'he said it had to go to the eldest. That's me. It's a tradition.'
'Yes . . . well. Look, here're two lovely brown eggs. Still warm.'
'If you don't mind,' says Wiki, 'I'll take those white ones over there.'
Back at the pa, she will slip them under a nesting hen. That'll be one over Auntie.

♞

'Mr Wrench?'
Euclid starts. So engrossed is he, he has not noticed the approach of Lavinia's mother.

'A word, if you please.'
What on earth can the old trout want? ''Fraid it'll have to wait.'
'It can't wait.'
'Bally awkward.'
Emily Younghusband is not deterred. 'I insist you tell me, Mr Wrench, what it is you are doing with these . . . these . . . bedsteads.'
'Ah.' Euclid hesitates. Then, why not? he thinks. After all . . . any day now . . . And soon, the whole world will know.
'I'm waiting.'
'Bit tricky . . .' says Euclid, 'but you're familiar, no doubt, with the ancient Greek texts?'
'Of course not.'
'You'll have heard of Hermeticism?'
'No.'
'Paracelsus, perhaps?'
'No.'
'The Philosopher's Stone?'
'No.'
Euclid ponders a moment; then, 'Since you ask,' he says, 'I . . .' He leans towards her conspiratorially. 'I . . . am turnin' base metal into gold.'
'Are you sure you feel quite well, Mr Wrench?'
'Never better.' Euclid points to the bedsteads. 'Now, in ancient times, you had people believin' it was possible to turn all these into gold. Literally. But it's a cypher, of course. The Ultimate Great Secret.' He pauses. 'Pai bo kai kino tan gan,' he booms suddenly.
His mother-in-law starts.
'*Give me a place to stand and I will move the earth.*'
She stares at him.
'Eternal life,' says Euclid. 'That is the true secret of the alchemists. And, any day now, I shall be openin' the Door to Eternity with Clavicula, the Little Key.' He looks at her proudly. 'There. Now you know.'

My poor Lavinia, thinks Mrs Younghusband. Aloud she says, 'I see.'

Wrench appears delighted by this. 'Excellent. Capital.' He places a hand in the small of her back and propels her into the wool-shed. 'You observe those bottles and retorts?'

'I . . .'

'Chemicals. All purchased for the same purpose.' He pauses, expands his bottom lip, then says in a confidential whisper, 'I shall shortly become the first person in the world to harness cosmic rays.'

♛

Te Mara, walking into Castleton for tobacco, his grey hair partly covered by his favourite sailor's cap, is not his usual self. His shoes slap down the tussocky grass by the roadside. Something is brewing with Wikitoria. Te Mara's warrior blood senses impending battle. Wikitoria has a toss of the head, an animal wildness in her eye that Te Mara has not yet managed to curb . . .

How much simpler it was when she was still a child. He remembers how she ran to him, lifting her arms to be picked up, how she snuggled against him as he told her stories of Maui, the hero. 'My koro, my koro,' he hears her call as she hid behind the nikau palm, jumping out and crying, 'Aie, here I am.' How she laughed, begging him to find her again. And her soft, small body sleeping against him on the nights when she had woken and cried for her mother . . . her father . . . And now, she has gone. Replaced by this sullen, moody creature in whom Te Mara cannot recognise even a vestige of his beloved Wikitoria.

Oh, for the time of my boyhood, thinks Te Mara, when the Pakeha were a little-known curiosity of Wellington, Auckland and the Bay of Islands, when our mokopuna were respectful and obedient, when our sons and daughters married someone of their own tribe, approved by both sets of parents.

'Why do you blame the Pakeha?' says his wife, Tiatia. 'Like

blaming the earth for turning, the sun for shining. Here they are. Here they will stay.'

But, thinks Te Mara, as he tramps towards the town . . .

A cloud of dust envelops him.

Castle leans out of his Model T and beckons with a gloved hand.

Leather gloves in this heat . . . Te Mara shakes his head.

'You don't want a lift?'

The chief sees Castle has misunderstood the gesture. He nods.

'Sorry,' says Castle. 'Is that a yes or a no?' He leans over and opens the door. Te Mara sees him staring across at his shoes as he clambers onto the running board. 'My word,' Castle says, 'all that walking barefoot in your youth must have splayed your feet.'

Te Mara, tactfully, does not ask about Castle's last trip to Wellington. All Castleton knows about his experience on the Rimutakas. At the pa, it has already become the stuff of story-telling. 'But, surely,' Tiatia had said, through gales of laughter, 'he was driving *backwards* into his *future*!'

Castle parps the horn needlessly at a Pakcha passing in a horse and trap and waits for a compliment on his treasure.

Te Mara, though grateful for the ride, considers the motor-car vastly inferior to the horse – to any horse, but most particularly to Kingi, his own black stallion. The rigidity of the steering wheel, the crank-handle, the general detachment of the vehicle and the division between conveyor and conveyed combine to make it a paltry thing. 'Because it has no wairua, no spirit,' decides Te Mara as they jolt into Main Street and turn towards Empire Avenue. No, Kingi is to be preferred in every respect, especially the smell. 'Ah, Queen Wikitoria's statue,' he cries, flinging open the door as the Ford surges on. 'Here is where I must dismount. Thank you, my friend, Castle.'

And Castle is obliged to apply the handbrake so suddenly they both lurch forward.

Te Mara laughs. 'High-spirited, this one,' he cries. 'See how he bucks.'

‘Your little sister’s a real looker,’ Mulholland says as they wait for their trunks to be carried out to their respective family cars.

Mulholland’s father’s chauffeur has come to collect him, but, to Edward-Wilson’s horror, Huia and Ku have accompanied Papa. Worse, the girls have rushed up and kissed him, in front of the entire Lower School. Edward-Wilson almost died of shame, but mysteriously the presence of his sisters seems now to elevate him in the eyes of the other boys.

‘I say, Young Castle,’ Perham says, supervising their departure, ‘better make sure you bring that kid sister of yours to visit in Napier over the Christmas holidays.’

A prefect speaking to a junior bug like that!

Edward-Wilson walks uncertainly through the pa looking for Eru. Standing awkward and alone, he has just decided to leave when a familiar figure stalks towards him.

‘Why are you hanging round here?’ demands Wiki.

‘Not to see you, anyway,’ retorts Edward-Wilson.

‘Stuck-up,’ says Wiki. ‘That’s what you are. Mr Stuck-up Boarding-School Boy. Think you’re someone because you go away to school and your father’s got a car.’ She puts her hands on her hips. ‘If you’re so high and mighty,’ she challenges him, ‘why’ve your sisters got Maori names?’

Behind the fury in her tone, Edward-Wilson can hear something else, something he recognises. But what is it exactly?

‘I don’t know,’ he says.

‘Your dad might have a car,’ says Wiki, ‘but my dad was a war hero. The Military Medal, that’s what he won. Better than any old car, any day.’

‘I know. Eru told me.’

‘And when Koro’s passed on, that medal’s coming to me.’

Though he knows this is untrue, since Eru has told him the medal can pass only to a son, Edward-Wilson does not feel inclined to dispute it.

‘So there,’ says Wiki.

'Hey,' cries a voice and Edward-Wilson sees Eru running towards them.

Sticking out her tongue, Wiki slides away.

'She bothering you?'

'Nah,' says Edward-Wilson. 'You know what she's like.'

♞

Ethel glances into the lobby to be certain that Pater has left, then tiptoes into his study. Yes, there is the tiara box, on top of his desk. Ethel fingers the stones set into the lid. With an ear cocked for Orpheus, she picks up the box and carries it into the sunlight shining through the window. The stones glitter green and red and the dark-blue ones reflect a sheen like birds' plumage. Perhaps, thinks Ethel, carefully setting the box back in exactly the same position, they *are* real, after all.

♙

Sorenson has brought Edward-Wilson's trunk into the house again. Edward-Wilson watches miserably as his mother, Atkinson and Huia pack his clothes into its gaping interior.

Even the prospect of a laden tuck-box cannot assuage his fears of returning to school. Baxter and Mulholland are the only ones in his form who refrain from calling him Arsehole. Simpkins, who made his life such a misery last term, will not be returning, but Compson and Brown will still be there.

'Arsehole'll do it,' Compson had said, whenever there was a particularly nasty job.

And, 'Come on, Four-eyes,' said Brown, lifting up his foot where the dog mess was stuck under the sole. 'Scrape it off.'

And then there had been the shameful time when, elated because he had made the cricket team, Edward-Wilson had mentioned that Papa had been capped for cricket at Claybourne.

'Papa!' Simpkins had sneered. 'Don't you know, Arsehole,

that, after the age of eight, only weevils – or girls – call their old man Papa?'

Mr Evans, who used to be a prop forward, has huge shoulders, no neck and a twice-broken nose, which spreads considerably over his craggy face. Apart from on speech days or in chapel, he wears shorts and a rugby shirt all the time. His legs are like hams and, when he bends to do up his laces, he has a back like one of the steers on the Crosbys' farm – two ranges of mountains running on either side of a narrow, sunken valley. The boys call him Old Thundercloud.

All those games of cricket at home, all that terrifying bowling from Papa, has paid off. Edward-Wilson is not a stylish bat, but he can be counted on for a solid innings and is unflinching at the crease, even when facing a fast bowler. And his own bowling is consistent enough for him to have been chosen to represent Claybourne in the match against St Leonard's.

The match is an away fixture. Edward-Wilson, lagging behind his team-mates, is alone in the changing room when Mr Evans calls him. 'Over here a minute, Castle.'

Edward-Wilson slinks towards him.

The coach grasps Edward-Wilson's chin, raises his face to the shaft of sunlight from the cloakroom window and examines first one cheek, then the other. Edward-Wilson's awkwardness turns to anxiety. Can the master be about to kiss him? Please God, no. No-one has ever said anything about Mr Evans being 'like that', though everyone knows not to be caught alone with Mr Sherritt.

'How old are you, now, Castle?'

'Fourteen, Sir.'

'Right,' says Mr Evans, releasing him. 'Hang on a minute.'

'I'll be late, Sir.'

Mr Evans looks at his wristwatch. 'Plenty of time yet.' He disappears, returning with a white object. 'Better wear that,' he says, tossing it over. 'Don't want you ruined before your time.' And he strides out of the changing room.

Edward-Wilson stares at the criss-crossed pad and straps.

'Wear that.' But how? And where? He tries it on his right hand, the pad to his palm, the straps swaddling his wrist. That can't be it.

Time is getting on. He buttons the flies of his cricket flannels, puts on his cap and turns back to the mysterious piece of clothing. It is definitely not a leg-pad, not long or thick enough. Then, suddenly, he realises. He dons the garment, picks up his bat and gloves and sets off.

As he comes out of the pavilion and crosses the grass, a ripple of laughter floats from the stands, rapidly swelling to a roar. 'Castle,' bellows Mr Evans, across the guffaws, 'what the devil d'you think you're playing at? Put that confounded jock-strap *inside* your trousers.'

'Castle,' hisses Baxter Minor. 'You still awake?'

'Yes.'

'Want a bit of toffee?'

'I'll say.'

'Coming over.'

Something small and hard lands on the pillow.

As he slips it into his mouth, Edward-Wilson remembers Baxter Minor's remark yesterday. 'Matron is an utter, absolute dog,' he had said. And, Perham, the duty prefect, who had been in earshot, had beaten him for speaking about a woman – any woman, even Matron – in such an un-British way. 'It may be decent for Wogs or Wops to speak about their women like that,' Perham had said, bending the prefects' cane across his knee, 'but no Englishman ever insults the fairer sex.'

It is rumoured at Claybourne that Matron, who has a huge, solid one-piece bosom on which rest her nurse's cross and spectacles, frequently has a woo with Dr Cunningham, the terrifying senior Latin master. Dr Cunningham wears pink deaf aids, which push out his already large ears. The boys hiss a little jingle as he passes:

Oh, Doctor Woo,
What shall I do,

Matron says I have
A nasty dose of flu . . .

'Listen to this, Castle,' Baxter Minor had said this morning. 'New Latin verb to conjugate for the Doctor. *Woo, was, what, wamus, wantus, wham, bam, thank you, Matron.*' Edward-Wilson had laughed so hard he had almost brought on a nose-bleed.

Today had been one of his best days at school. Baxter, saying he knew Edward-Wilson, too, to be a bit of a japer, after that business with the jock-strap, had chosen him to be the first to hear his clever new rhyme. The idea that he might have been being amusing on purpose was a delightful one and soothed the creeping feelings of humiliation that Edward-Wilson had been nursing since the match. 'I just . . . thought it might be bit of a wheeze,' he had stammered.

The tart, treacly sweetness of the toffee trickles now across Edward-Wilson's tongue and down his throat. 'Thanks, old man,' he whispers.

'Pater?'

'Tell Mater I'll take my tea in half an hour.'

'Yes, Pater, but Mater didn't send me. I . . . I came myself.'

Euclid pours a little sal ammoniac into the retort he is holding.

Ethel coughs, hastily covers her nose and waits.

Silence. He swills the liquid gently against the glass walls.

Ethel tries again. 'I was wondering, Pater, whether – whether . . . I mean, if you thought, perhaps . . .'

Euclid peers into the flask. 'The mark of the educated man, Ethel, is his ability to state his opinions lucidly and succinctly.'

'Yes, Pater. And it's education I've come about . . .' She runs her hands down the sides of her sack apron. 'I thought . . . I mean, I'm fifteen now and I wondered if . . . if . . . you might let me go to school. Like Huia Castle. Next door. Just for a year. Till I'm sixteen.'

A deeper silence.

'Huia and her sister both go. She says they learn about all sorts of things.'

'Greek?'

'Well, no. But . . . I already know Greek.'

'Latin, perhaps?'

'No, Pater. But, you see, I have Latin, too. Huia says they do Nature Study. And story-writing. And poetry. And geography.' She has an inspiration. 'And arithmetic. Think how helpful I could be to Mater with the accounts if I studied arithmetic.'

Her father shakes his head. 'You disappoint me, Ethel. How can you contemplate so selfishly leaving Mater and your brothers to do everything while you gallivant the day away at school?'

'But I wouldn't be there all day, Pater. I could still work hard when I got home.'

Euclid thumps the retort onto the shelf. 'As you very well know, there is no substitute for a classical education. "Pai bo kai kino tan gan . . ."'

'Give me a place to stand and I will move the earth, Pater.'

'Exactly.' He peers onto the shelf and consults his watch. 'May as well take a break now I've been interrupted. Tell Mater I'll be ready for tea in ten minutes.'

♟

'I'm warning you, Wikitoria,' says Auntie Kereru, 'this kind of behaviour can't continue. You're upsetting your kuia and your koro, people are talking about you and your wild ways. You're fifteen and a half. Nearly grown-up. So put your mind to your schooling and being a good, grateful mokopuna. Where would you be without your family, eh?'

Wiki stares at the floor.

Auntie Kereru sighs. 'I'm losing patience, Wikitoria. What is it that you want? Answer me, now.'

'Nothing.'

'It must be something. A chief's granddaughter, and you're hanging around town all day, missing your schoolwork, shaming your family.'

Wiki suppresses a snigger.

'Now your poor koro's had another complaint. From Mrs Castle.'

'That stuck-up P . . .'

'You mind your tongue! She says you've been hanging round their place. Three times she's spoken to you and had nothing but rudeness from you. How do you think your koro feels about that, eh?'

'I wasn't rude. I didn't say anything.'

'That's not what she told Koro. So what were you doing at their place?'

'Koro takes us.'

'You weren't with Koro. She said you were by yourself, outside her bedroom window, peering in at her. You gave her a terrible fright.'

'I only wanted to see . . . to see . . .' Wiki thinks back. What was it she had wanted to see? How Mrs Castle did her hair? The lovely silver brush and mirror on her table?

'How would you like Mrs Castle's girl coming here, peering in your kuia's window? Crazy, that's what you'd call a girl who did that.'

'I'm not crazy.'

'Go on doing that kind of thing and people are going to mark you out as a crazy one, for sure. And you know what happens to crazy people?'

Wiki raises her eyes briefly to Auntie's, then hastily drops them again. 'What?' she mumbles.

'They get sent away.'

♙

Flossie seats herself comfortably on Huia's bed. 'I got a beau.'

'Oh, that's nice.'

'Bought us a locket and says he's buying us a ring.'

'You mean . . . you're getting engaged?'

Flossie shrieks. 'Nah, course not. I ain't old enough. And he's too old, an' all.'

'What's his name?'

Flossie cocks her head. 'That's mine to know and yours to guess.'

'Does he live in Castleton?'

'He might. Or he might not.' She leans forward to examine herself in Huia's looking-glass. 'Bet you wishes you had curls yourself.'

'Yes,' says Huia. 'Even when Mama puts mine in overnight rags, it still falls out by lunchtime.'

'We're walking out next Sunday.' She looks defiantly at Huia. 'Got to get us some jewellery somehow. Me mam's got nothing to give us.'

'Yes, well . . .'

'I'm going to wear me best black velvet. That me auntie made. I told you about it, remember?'

'Yes, it sounds very pretty.'

'More smart, really. Black's me colour. On account of me hair.' She hesitates. 'You wouldn't have a spare white hanky you could loan us, would you? Just for going out. I'll bring it back. And I won't use it or nothing.'

Huia looks at Flossie's skinny little body, her stained crooked teeth and rough hands. 'I could give you one to keep, if you want.'

Flossie shakes her head. 'Just to loan.'

'No, it's all right. Really. I've got lots.' Huia opens her drawer. 'See. You can have this one, if you like. It's got pansies in the corner.'

Flossie stares at it. 'That's lovely, that one. Pansies is for thoughts. You sure?'

'Quite sure.' Huia digs about some more. 'You can have this, too, if you want. I never wear it any more.'

It is a cheap glass bangle, shot through with green and pink. Flossie's eyes light up as she slips it on her wrist.

♜

Wilson strops his razor, lathers his face and slices through the white cloud, revealing a smooth strip of pink cheek. He shakes the foam into the china basin, dunks the razor. This business in Wellington is getting harder and harder to manage. Nowadays, his life seems to be nothing but a juggling act. Only day-school fees for the girls, mercifully. But the boy must have his chance. And that costs money. Still, vows Wilson, exposing another slice of cheek, if he shapes up well on the academic front, by Jove, the lad's going to get his chance at Cambridge. Hang the expense. The money will simply have to be found. And then he can come back here to Castleton and take over the firm.

His hair is beginning to recede at the temples and a paunch is developing round his waist. It was dark in the cemetery at Thorndon, too dark for such details to be noticeable, too dark for his features to be recognisable. But what if someone had seen him? Had recognised the Ford? What is it that compels him to take these stupid risks? And afterwards . . . He feels the familiar swell of self-loathing.

The razor slips and gouges a tiny notch of flesh from his chin. Wilson dabs the wound with a styptic pencil, but blood continues to stain the foam.

He empties the dirty water into the slops bucket, pours fresh water from the jug into the basin and splashes his face. Next time he goes to Wellington, he will resist.

Brushing his hair, he notices the dark circles under his eyes, the wrinkles at their corners, round his mouth, creasing his forehead. The dead have one advantage over the living, he reflects. They are eternally young.

♞

Whenever Euclid allows himself to think of Gawminsgodden, he is forced to stifle bitter pangs of loss. The idea that never again will he see the dear old place, the grounds, the woods . . .

But, he reminds himself, there is no doubt that the lives of certain men are predestined. True, he has been banished from his native land by the ludicrous laws of primogeniture and flung upon foreign shores to fend for his family on a pittance, but that same Destiny which has singled him out for greatness has ensured that his path be bent towards New Zealand. For, by virtue of his friendship with the Maori chief, Te Mara, a sign has been vouchsafed Euclid.

Before coming to safe harbour in Castleton, the Wrenches, on arrival in New Zealand, struck camp for a dismal six months in Reefton, a coal-stained icy port on the west coast of the South Island. Reefton is distinguished for one thing alone: being the first place in the world to have electric lighting.

Euclid has never mentioned their short sojourn there, but only yesterday Te Mara chose to relate to him this particular legend: 'In order that his people might have perpetual light, Maui, our hero, set out to ensnare the royal sun, bind it with ropes and anchor it to the earth.'

Remarkable, thinks Euclid, that although the Maori had never known gas or electric lighting, the concept of perpetual light was recognised by the hero of this ancient legend.

At the very moment Te Mara had finished his account, Euclid had heard himself involuntarily cry out, 'Eureka!'

♛

Children, thinks Te Mara. A blessing and a burden. A hope for the future and a constant reminder of the past. Eru so much resembles his father, Manu, that there are times when Te Mara can scarcely bear it. Even his placid, gentle disposition is his father's. Whereas, to her grandfather's fear and dismay, Wikitoria has – as Te Mara sees all too well – developed a wildness, a wilful promise, a look of sexual invitation that he must do his best to curb before she brings down on her head some shaming, terrible fate.

'Why are you surprised?' asks Kereru bitterly. 'Look at that mother of theirs. What she did to Manu. And now her bad

Pakeha blood is coming out in Wikitoria. Every day, I see it more.'

Te Mara sighs. 'Kereru, what is done, is done. Angry words will never bring Manu back to us.'

'And Wiki? All along, I told you you spoilt her, that one. But did you listen to a word I said?'

As Kereru stalks out of the room, Te Mara finds he is crying. If only her father, Manu, were here to deal with Wikitoria. If only he had never . . . Te Mara has prayed incessantly to the Maori gods, even to Te Ariki, god of the Pakeha. But still he cannot accept his fate. No man should be required by the gods to suffer the loss of his only son.

♘

This Wednesday, Wrench is the host. He seems rather agitated, thinks Wilson, covertly studying him. Come to think of it, Wrench has been behaving oddly for quite some time now. Today, his bottom lip shoots disconcertingly forward and back, and several times he seems about to speak, then checks himself. And his mind is not on his game. Te Mara and Wilson have a disappointingly easy victory.

Wrench seems keen to detain them. 'Don't know if I ever showed you a photograph of the old family place?' he says, opening the tiara casket.

'Indeed impressive,' says Te Mara.

Wilson stares at the huge, turreted, many-chimneyed building with its mullioned windows, enormous wooden front door flanked by statues of what seem to be dragons, the stone steps below . . . 'Striking,' he says. 'Bit of a change from here. You must miss it.'

Wrench sighs. 'Fate of the younger son.'

Wilson searches for an appropriate reply. 'Roots, I expect. Bit like my own family.'

Te Mara looks up. 'Turangawaewae,' he says. 'Our Maori word for the same idea.'

Wilson has heard this before, particularly in relation to Te

Mara's grandfather's land. On no account must he let the chief get onto *that* subject again. 'Means "a standing place", I believe,' he says quickly.

Te Mara nods. 'The place where I put my feet. The place where I belong.'

Wrench's eyes gleam. 'I say. Bally amazin'. Don't happen to know the Chinese for it, do you?'

♜

Wilson is delighted with Edward-Wilson's Sixth Form school report. *A good solid member of the First Eleven . . . reliable fast bowler . . . steady at the wicket.* His marks are well up to scratch, too: B+ to B- average, with a couple of Cs and an A- in Latin, as Wilson has casually mentioned to Wrench at least four or five times during their last chess match. And Old Thundercloud, his housemaster, has written in the *General Remarks* column: *Castle is shaping up nicely. Next year, Varsity beckons?*

'Right,' says Wilson, 'Varsity it is. The Old Man's alma mater, Christ's.'

'Cambridge!' says Rosalba. 'What on earth's wrong with Victoria? I should have thought Wellington was quite far enough away.'

'I don't think you realise the advantages of an Oxbridge education.'

'Being at Vic doesn't seem to have hindered Charles. Or you, come to that.'

'I'm not budging on this one, Rosa. Edward-Wilson's getting his chance. I may have missed out, but I'm damned if he's going to.'

'If he studies at Cambridge,' asks Rosalba, 'will he still want to come back here to the practice afterwards?'

'Why ever not? The Old Man did.'

It seems to Edward-Wilson that these decisions flow over and around him with a momentum of their own; that he is a mere object in the path of some torrent, soon to be dislodged and swept off by it. '*Time, like an ever-rolling stream, bears all its sons away*,' sing the boys in chapel.

After years of being bullied and taunted, always on the outside – of watching the popular boys and puzzling as to what they did, and how, exactly, they knew the right word, the clever riposte that took them into the charmed circle – just as he has, by chance or accident, become a recognised member of the outer periphery, he is to be snatched from his fellows to begin all over again. 'I'm not sure I really want . . .' he ventures.

'Nonsense,' says his father. 'Not a chap alive who wouldn't give his eye-teeth for the chance to study at Oxbridge.'

So far these holidays Edward-Wilson has not seen Eru. Now, as he and his father are walking through Castleton, he spots his friend going into the baker's. 'There's Eru.'

Wilson snorts. 'Buying pies, no doubt.'

Edward-Wilson is puzzled. Why is his father criticising Eru? 'Maybe he's getting their bread.'

'I doubt it. It's a well-known fact Maoris exist on pies.'

Edward-Wilson knows this is false. When has he ever seen Eru eating pies? Only with me, he thinks. The image of those pies swims into his head. Shaped like little bathtubs, their brown-gold pastry lids with two softly steaming slits covering the luscious interior . . .

Watching Eru disappear into the bakery, Edward-Wilson tells himself he must speak up, be bold and defend his friend. 'That's not fair and not true either, Father,' says his confident inner voice. But his lips stay closed.

♛

Eru has spotted Edward-Wilson, seen the glance of recognition on his friend's face. 'Hey,' he has been about to shout, before realising that the Castles have turned away. Maybe, he tells himself, Ed didn't see me.

He is unusually downcast as he sits down to his midday meal and waits for Koro to finish saying grace.

'Cat got your tongue?' says Auntie Kereru.

Eru shakes his head.

'He's got the pip,' says Wiki. 'His big boarding-school friend's not speaking to him any more.'

Koro looks up. 'You fallen out with young Castle, Eruera?'

'No, Koro. He . . . didn't see me, is all.'

'He saw you all right,' crows Wiki. 'Turned his head right away from any dirty Maori.'

'Go on speaking like that,' says Kuia, 'and you'll leave this table.'

'Busy with his family, if he's just come home,' says Auntie Kereru. 'Why don't you go over and see him this afternoon?'

'I'll go tomorrow,' lies Eru. He eats on in silence, then turns to his grandfather. 'Koro?'

'Aie.'

'I was wondering if . . . if I could get a bike?'

'You've got Kingi. Better than any bike.'

♘

Mrs Emily Younghusband is planning a trip. To Rome. And will she seek out Hadrian's Arch, Trajan's Column or Nero's Domus Aurea? No. All Euclid's attempts to interest her in classical antiquity have failed. Slave to superstition, she intends to embark upon a pilgrimage around the Imperial City, beginning at the Steps of Pontius Pilate. Up that staircase, *on her knees*, she intends to crawl and crack her arthritic way, peering through the glass inserts at cochineal stains purporting to be the blood of Christ. Then – having, no doubt, been carried from the Steps, thinks Euclid – she will hobble on to pay homage to the blood of St Genarius. 'A most amazing phenomenon,' she announces, during luncheon. 'Quite astounding.' She pauses for dramatic effect. 'On his feast day, St Genarius's blood expands.'

Euclid snorts.

'I assure you it's true. Father Xavier saw it himself.'
'Scientifically impossible.'
'But, dear,' points out Lavinia, 'religion is not scientific.'
Euclid glares at them both. Now the blasted old trout is duping his own wife into betraying him. 'Since blood cannot expand by itself,' he says stiffly, 'either the substance is not blood or the phenomenon is due to some form of . . . mass hysteria.'

♜

Sorenson has dumped the oilskins and waders beside the fishing basket on the back seat of the Ford, and roped the food hamper to the running board.
On the way to the lake, Father stops at the Royal Arms. Edward-Wilson climbs out and, as Father slides across the seat, is astonished to hear him say, 'Why not have a go?'
The Ford is idling. Father has set the advance-retard lever in position and put on the hand-brake. Edward-Wilson clambers back in, selects one of the three floor pedals and gently presses it with his foot. The motor lurches backwards, judders and dies.
'Wrong pedal,' says Father, suddenly appearing. 'The middle one's the reverse. As I see you've discovered.' He laughs in a comradely manner as he reaches in and lays the brown-paper parcel of beer on top of the oilskins. 'Easy to do, but better than forgetting to put her in neutral while you're cranking, and running yourself over.'
'Has anyone ever run themselves over?'
'Surprising number of people. Right, let's start lessons straight away. Turn the ignition key, then out you get and give me a hand to crank her. But make sure you cup your hand, like this. Don't want your thumb busted on your first go.'

Clinging to the wheel, Edward-Wilson releases the handbrake, moves the pedal into first gear and they crawl onto Lake Road where the new tarmacadam gives way to unsealed loose metal.
'If you start skidding,' advises his father, 'whatever you do,

don't brake. Go with it. Steer into it. But for Heaven's sake don't brake or you'll send us into a real spin.'

Edward-Wilson, intent on coping with steering, accelerating and avoiding – though, as yet, they have passed no other car – attempts to commit this to memory.

'I must say,' remarks Wilson, 'you're doing deuced well for a first-timer.'

This is how I can bring it up, thinks Edward-Wilson. Ask about the possibility of a car of my own. Father's bound to say not till after Cambridge because of the expense. And then I can say going to Vic would be cheaper. And, as he is congratulating himself on this strategy, a swamp-hen plunges out from the long grass at the verge, right in front of the car. One minute the road is clear, the next the pukeko is half-running, half-waddling towards them. Edward-Wilson hauls the wheel to the right and drags on the hand-brake.

'Don't brake,' shouts his father. 'Steer into it, for God's sake.'

Forcing himself to release the brake, Edward-Wilson turns the wheel in what seems the suicidal direction of the skid. The Ford slips and slides, leaving a crazy wake through the shingle, as Edward-Wilson struggles to hold it to the road.

'Steer *into* it!' cries Wilson again.

Gradually the back begins to slew around and the car straightens.

'Better stop, I think,' says his father.

Considerably shaken, Edward-Wilson puts the car in neutral and tentatively moves the handbrake fully back. 'Do you think we killed the pukeko?'

'The damned pukeko almost killed us.' Wilson steps down onto the roadside grass, pulls out a handkerchief and mops his brow. 'I tell you, for a minute there, I thought we were goners.'

Edward-Wilson slides out behind him and opens his mouth to apologise but, before he can speak, his father claps him on the back. 'Great job you did pulling us out of it. Amazingly cool head you showed.'

Feeling his face suffuse, Edward-Wilson looks modestly at the ground.

'Lot of experienced drivers couldn't have managed that. You're a natural, you know.'

The faintly conspiratorial air that has sprung up between them continues all day. By late afternoon, Edward-Wilson's casting skills have improved, five sizeable trout lie in the fish-hamper, and he has shared his first bottle of beer with his father.

As they set off for home, Wilson at the wheel, Edward-Wilson ventures, 'At school, one or two of the chaps call me Ted.' He waits for the response.

'Ted,' says Wilson, as if balancing it for weight and gravitas. 'Good, manly name. Decent sort of ring to it.'

They are nearing town before Edward-Wilson finds the courage to broach his topic. 'About going to Cambridge . . .' he begins.

Wilson interrupts him. 'You make the most of it, my boy. It was only a pipe-dream for me but, by Jove, you're not going to miss your chance.'

'Won't it . . . cost a lot?'

'I'll let you into a little secret not even your mother knows. But Mum has to be the word.' He sniggers at his own wit. 'Just between us, all right.'

'I won't tell.'

'Promise, now?'

'I promise.'

'Well, I've made several rather good . . . investments . . . recently and I've tucked the money away into a Cambridge fund. So no problem there.'

'A lot of the Claybourne chaps are going to Wellington. To Vic.'

'And it's a sound enough place. But nothing – simply nothing – beats an Oxbridge education.'

Edward-Wilson makes one final stand. 'But what about Huia and Ku? I mean their coming-out ball and . . . any other things they might need?'

'You're a fine lad,' says his father. 'Thinking about your

sisters like that. But, don't you worry, I'll find a way to cover what they need.'

Dusk is approaching. Wilson switches on the headlights which throw two great owl's eyes onto the road ahead. 'And after your time at Christ's, the firm will be yours.' Is it a trick of the dark or has his voice thickened? He clears his throat, then, 'I'm counting on you, Ted,' he says in a voice gruff with emotion. 'Firm's been in the family for three generations. You'll be the fourth-generation Castle to run it.'

♙

'Some people have all the luck,' sniffs Flossie, slopping the wet mop along the planks of the verandah.

Huia holds out the plate of biscuits she is carrying. 'Go on, have one. But don't tell Atkinson or Mama, or I'll get into trouble.'

'You ain't a bad 'un,' says Flossie, taking two. 'Wore your hanky the other night. Looks good tucked in the pocket of me best black. You're all right, you are. I'll wear me locket to show you tomorrow.'

'What kind of flowers?' asks Ethel.

'Carnations. And white roses, for Mama.'

Today is Baby John Marchmont's anniversary. Wilson, Rosalba and Ku have gone in the rain to St Edmund's to place flowers on his grave.

'Why didn't you go?'

'I don't like the cemetery. Walking over all the . . . the . . . dead people under the grass.'

'But they're not there. Only their bodies. And they're dead so they don't know you're standing on them.'

Huia shivers. 'They might.'

♘

'Your move.'

Catching the exasperation in Castle's voice, Euclid jumps. 'Sorry.' Opposite him, Te Mara and Castle sit waiting. Euclid scans the board for their previous move. Is it the knight or the rook that has altered position?

'Mind not on the game today?'

'Lavinia's mater's goin' Home, y'know. In August. On the *Themistocles*. If she gets there.'

'Of course she'll get there. Excellent ship. Completely solid, totally seaworthy.'

'Not Home. I meant, if she gets to Wellington. And not just her. She's got a bally heavy cabin trunk.'

'The train,' says Te Mara. 'A great adventure, especially at the Summit. And a very fine ham sandwich with a cup of tea. All free from the Company.'

'She's eighty-two. She can't manage the train. And, anyway, Lavinia insists we all go to Wellington to see her off.'

'Very proper,' says Te Mara.

'Yes, yes,' says Euclid testily, 'all very well, but that makes nine fares. Not to mention the porter at the other end.'

Poor devil, thinks Wilson, frayed at the cuffs *and* the bank balance, and suddenly he hears himself saying, 'Perhaps I can ferry her down for you?'

'There's the trunk.'

'On the running board.'

Euclid gives a wolfish half-smile. 'I say. Might you? That'd be very decent.'

'Self-interest,' says Castle. 'You're partnering me next time.'

Interesting, thinks Te Mara. This afternoon has seen *two* games of cornering and clever strategy.

'How very, very kind of Mr Castle,' says Lavinia.

'I told him we're obliged.'

'What about the children?'

'Orpheus will squeeze in the motor and the others can go by train. And when they reach the Summit, they'll have a very fine ham sandwich and a cup of tea. Gratis.'

Mrs Younghusband stands glowering in the doorway. 'Mr Wrench, I demand the return of my property.'

Euclid looks up from his paper. 'I haven't the least idea what you mean.'

She holds out her hand. 'Now, if you please. Hand it back and we shall say no more about it.'

'But I . . .'

'May I remind you that theft is a criminal offence?'

Euclid turns to Lavinia. 'Demmed if I have a notion what the old . . .' he catches her eye '. . . the old lady's so agitated about.'

'Don't think for a moment I don't know what you intend to do with it.'

Above his collar, Euclid's neck begins to redden.

'Mother,' says Lavinia, 'what exactly . . .'

'My locket. It's vanished.'

'But why would *Euclid* want your locket?'

'That locket is solid gold.'

'Yes, Mother, I know, but . . .'

Mrs Younghusband stares contemptuously at her son-in-law. 'And *he*, of course, intends to melt it down for one of his ridiculous experiments.'

'But Euclid would never . . .'

'I shall be in my room packing. I expect my locket back, with an accompanying apology, before the end of the evening.'

The door slams behind her, as Euclid, shaking with fury, regains the power of speech. 'Accusin' me, like some common thief. Bally cheek. She's off her rocker!'

'Euclid, please . . .'

'Wretched woman. Mind's goin', I shouldn't wonder.' He stops. 'I say, didn't I see that priest fellow hangin' round the place earlier? Devil only knows what he was doin' here.'

'He just came to say a little private Mass for Mother . . .'

'Rapacious scoundrels, the lot of 'em. I know what the old trout's done with her locket. Given it to that Papist bounder.'

♜

As he chugs up the Wrenches' drive, Wilson Castle, anticipating a horde of boys encircling his motor, is surprised that no-one is about. Then he remembers: the boys and their sister have already left for Wellington on the train.

He raps on the front door and the ghoulish brother-in-law appears. To Wilson's horror, he appears to have been weeping. 'You'll be here for Mother,' he gobbles.

Wilson, who has no idea what the chap is trying to convey, says in his best legal tones, 'Yes, indeed.'

'She's not quite ready,' gargles Bertie.

'My word, really?' says Wilson.

The fellow sets off somewhere into the recesses of the house, but just as Wilson is congratulating himself on having got rid of him, the youngest Wrench steps from the shadows behind the stuffed dog. He stares at Wilson from disconcerting black eyes. For a boy, he has a very . . . brazen . . . manner.

Lavinia Wrench appears in the hallway. 'This is so kind of you, Mr Castle.' Her voice wavers. 'Mother won't be long.'

'Is there anything I can do to lend a hand?' asks Wilson. 'We should be setting off pretty sharpish.'

'We've had,' she says, 'a rather unfortunate . . . crisis. Mother's mislaid her locket. The children and I have scoured the house but . . . Poor Mother, it was a wedding gift from my dear father, you see.'

Wilson is beginning to regret his generosity. Why the devil did he ever think anything connected with Wrench could run smoothly? 'The fact is . . .' he begins, consulting his watch.

Lavinia Wrench gestures at the huge cabin trunk in the lobby. 'And then there's her box. It does seem rather large.'

Mrs Younghusband materialises beside them. 'Necessities,' she says. 'Clothing, my prayer book and concordance, holy water and an Infant of Prague.'

'An . . . infant?' says Castle.

'To ensure fine weather on the crossing. Father Patrick decapitated him at a special private Mass yesterday evening.'

'Claptrap!' roars Wrench, striding into the lobby. 'Papist poppycock.'

His wife clutches at his sleeve. 'Dear, it's Mother's last day.'

Bertie Younghusband is feeling very low. This business of saying goodbye to Ma is taking its toll. Clutching one end of the trunk, he staggers outside.

Wilson Castle indicates the running board. 'Should sit nicely on here.'

Together they heave and lift, but each time, the trunk slips off.

'Far too wide,' says Castle, in dismay.

'We could remove the blasted Infant,' suggests Euclid.

'But, dear,' says Lavinia, 'the *trunk* will still be the same size.'

'Try it on its side,' gobbles Bertie.

The others ignore him.

'What about tryin' it on its side?' says Euclid.

'Good idea,' says Castle.

But, even on its side, the trunk will not fit.

'I wonder . . .' ventures Lavinia, 'whether that little rack, at the back . . .'

'Just possible,' says Castle. 'Provided it doesn't slide off.'

'Perhaps,' says Lavinia tentatively, 'if one put a blanket . . .'

'Just what I was about to suggest m'self,' says Euclid. 'Fetch one, Lavinia.'

Lavinia returns with Argus's old red rug, Castle drapes it on top of the rack and, with great difficulty, he, Euclid and Bertie balance the trunk on it and secure it with a length of rope.

'Well,' says Castle, in a falsely cheerful tone, 'at least the confounded thing's on. We'd better be pushing off.'

'I'll tell Ma,' gobbles Bertie to Lavinia, marching off in as military a manner as he can muster.

Euclid strides firmly to the passenger side of the Ford.

'Mrs Younghusband,' says Wilson, 'will be more comfortable in the front.'

'Simply a matter of room,' says Euclid, shooting forth a long leg.

'Nevertheless . . .' says Wilson.

And Euclid is forced to hunch himself up, double over and insert his rangy frame into the back seat.

'But where,' asks Mrs Younghusband, 'are the windows? It's raining. Needling down quite hard.'

'We have no need of windows,' says Wilson, a trifle frostily. 'We are all well wrapped up.'

Mrs Younghusband clings to her rosary. 'I shall ask St Christopher to grant us a safe journey.'

Wilson moves the car into first gear. 'In all the many times I've crossed the Ranges, I assure you . . .'

Bertie reappears on the verandah. Buttoned into his old Army greatcoat, he clutches an overnight valise.

'Wait,' shouts Wrench. 'The brother-in-law.'

'No, no!' says Wilson. 'He can't possibly fit . . .'

'Uncle Bertie's crying,' says Orpheus, gazing back. 'Remember what you said, Pater? Only slaves and girls weep.'

The *Themistocles* glides backwards, away from the dock and into the harbour. The streamers linking the passengers to the wharf grow taut: a Maori group breaks into *Haere Ra*. '*Now is the Hour,*' sings the crowd, '*when we must say goodbye.*' The nose of the liner swings out towards the Heads and the streamers snap and flutter, trailing against the ship's side, tossing on the waves, littering the quay with broken scraps of paper.

The figures on deck have shrunk so much it is no longer possible to make out Lavinia's mother. A heavy sense of anticlimax falls over those left behind.

'Well,' says Wilson, tactfully ignoring Lavinia's tears, 'time to be off, I'd say.' And at that moment he notices a familiar figure in the Maori group nearby. 'Good Lord! It's Te Mara.'

Beastly bad luck, thinks Euclid. Castle is bound to offer the chief a ride home. And then who will occupy the coveted position next to the driver? Te Mara scores in seniority of age, but can a Maori – even one of chiefly status – rank higher than the second son of an English peer?

Te Mara detaches himself from the group, strides over to them and, seizing Lavinia's hands, presses his nose to hers and commiserates on the sorrows of bidding goodbye to a parent. And the deuce of it, Euclid tells himself, is that Lavinia actually clings to those large brown hands until Castle intervenes with the offer of a handkerchief.

Clutching his flax kit, Te Mara steps forward and with his other hand jerks open the front door of the Ford. Euclid feels a stab of rage at such outright cheek. Then, turning to Lavinia, the old man invites her to climb up and make herself comfortable. For all the world as if it were *his* motor. And Lavinia, after some hesitation and stepping back for the chief to take precedence, actually accepts. Without so much as offering to yield the seat to her own husband.

'And my great friend and chessmate, Mr the Honourable Wrench, and I will sit together in the rear and discuss important matters,' says Te Mara, graciously standing aside for Euclid to climb in.

After Lower Hutt, Te Mara falls asleep. As the car crawls up the Rimutakas, he tips sideways, toppling onto Orpheus who, in a domino effect, collapses on his father, who remains squashed against the side of the Ford for the rest of the journey.

♘

Bertie glues up a cigarette and slides it into his tracheotomy vent. Terrible how lonely it is without Ma. He finds he is even looking forward to the Chinkie's laundry collection. Yesterday, watching Lavvy milk the cows in the dairy, he had offered to give it a go. But, as soon as the stupid beast felt the touch of foreign fingers, it snorted and reared in such a terrifying manner that Bertie was forced to retreat to a corner of the dairy. And the hay had irritated his throat so much it had brought on a painful coughing fit.

Sorting chemicals in the wool-shed, Euclid reflects that it is quiet without the mother-in-law. Tediously quiet. At mealtimes, he finds himself waiting for an invigorating argument about the nonsense peddled by priests. He recalls, with relish, the particularly gratifiying altercation during which he had forced her to concede the foolhardiness of St Ursula in embarking with a thousand virgins to convert the Huns. Yes, he misses his daily battles with the old trout. And she is, after all, the only person in Castleton who has ever displayed any interest in his life's work.

♖

Bent over her roses snipping a few blooms for the drawing-room silver rose-bowl, Rosalba is suddenly conscious of being watched. Taking her secateurs from her trug, she forces herself to turn round. No sign of anyone. 'Yes?' says Rosalba, hearing her voice emerge shrill and frightened. Puffs of grey-blue smoke are hazing from behind the macrocarpas on the boundary line. 'Who's there?' Waving the secateurs, she advances to the trees. 'You're trespassing,' she cries. 'This is private land.'

'That old soldier from next door wiv the hole in his neck was hanging round again today,' offers Flossie, bringing in the soup. 'Creepy, I calls 'im.'

'Quite,' says Wilson. 'But we must always remember, Florence, that Major Younghusband was injured in the service of Queen and Country.'

No call for Mr Castle to know the 'old soldier' slips her the odd shilling, thinks Flossie. Smiling at her own cleverness, she clangs the ladle onto the silver tray. 'Kinder if they'd of finished him off, really.'

♘

Pointless to select Chocolate Mints, thinks Ethel. They are all the same: no excitement of dipping into the box, wondering what colour and flavour the inside of your chosen chocolate might yield. No, there are really only two contenders. Winning Post has a horse's head on its box, which is not as attractive as its rival, but, inside, it has the ultimate prize – a lucky chocolate on which is stuck a tiny horseshoe. Queen Anne's, though, are in a beautiful long white box bearing a picture of the monarch herself, looking just like the Queen of Hearts in the card pack. Beneath her stiff nun's headdress, Queen Anne's dyspeptic face stares disapprovingly at all browsers: she appears to have consumed too much of her own product. But there is something so elegant about the length of the box and she is, after all, royal. Yes, decides Ethel, it must be Queen Anne's.

'Chosen, have you?' asks Mr Maples, coming out from the back of his shop.

'Well, they're both nice, but Queen Anne's is better. The box is so pretty.'

'Good thinking,' says Mr Maples. 'Finer quality all round than Winning Post. Bit gimmicky with all those bits stuck on after. If a chocolate's good, it doesn't need any extra tarting about with, I always say.'

Ethel nods, pleased to have made the right decision.

'Got your list, young lady?'

Ethel extracts it from her string bag and hands it to him.

'Lovely weather,' says Mr Maples, coming round from behind the counter and standing close to her.

Ethel edges sideways. 'Beautiful.'

'Spring is upon us,' says Mr Maples ponderously. 'Lambs arriving already and daffodils, too.'

♟ ♙

The soft freshness of spring is everywhere. Sitting on the ground by the Castles' gatepost, Wikitoria breathes it in.

Ted bumps his bike over the metal bars of the cattle-stop and dismounts. 'What are *you* doing here?'

'It's a free country. I can sit where I like.'

'My dad'll run you over when he drives in.'

'He'd better not or he'll go to gaol. That's where they put criminals.'

'Well, you'd know,' he snorts, remounting his bike.

Leaping to her feet, Wiki grabs the handlebars, blocking his way.

Ted shakes the front of the bike to try to dislodge her, but she clings even tighter, bending her body towards him over the curving metal. 'You're stuck up, you know that? I wouldn't go out with you even if you asked me.'

'No chance of that.'

Without warning, she leans over still further and kisses him on the mouth.

'Don't bang the door like that, Edward-Wilson,' says Rosalba.

Ted glowers.

'I imagine you haven't forgotten you promised to make up a four at tennis?'

'I'm not playing,' he says irritably. 'They'll have to find someone else.'

'I hope you're not turning into one of those boring young men who lets people down.'

'Gwennie must know someone else who can come instead of me. What if I had bubonic plague or something?'

'Bubonic plague? Don't be ridiculous. You've said you'll go, so you must.'

Women! thinks Ted. Always interfering with everything in my life. 'I'm going for a ride,' he mutters.

'Be sure you're back in time,' calls his mother.

Snatching a bridle from the hook in the wool-shed, Ted strides into the horse paddock.

As he nudges Kruger out of the gate, Huia appears on the verandah. 'Gate,' he shouts. He knows she will not leave it open nor – as Ku would – pretend she hasn't heard.

By the time Ted turns for home, it is evening: the cabbage trees are sinister giants advancing on their rough, ringed chooks' legs across the shadowy paddocks. In the gloom by the dam, a darker shape is moving. Ted reins in Kruger. Lying on the ground, half-hidden in the long grass, are two figures he can barely discern, except to see that one is on top of the other.

Noiselessly, Ted dismounts, loops the reins to the fence and steals forward. It is Wiki. He is certain of that. Even in the dusk, he can see her springy hair spreading on the ground. But who can the fellow be? All Ted can see of him is his back. He is lying face down on top of the girl, his arms wound round her and his face obscured in her . . . in her breasts, thinks Ted.

He creeps closer. So absorbed are they in each other that they have no thought for anything else. And why should they expect anyone to be out here in the dark, spying on them? Noise drifts towards him. At first he thinks it is some night animal, then he understands. It is the girl. She is uttering feeble little grieving noises, small sighs and soughs. The man has begun to gasp, faster and faster, as his body rises up and down on top of hers. The woman's sighs turn to moans; the man pants heavily. Ted cannot tear himself away from their animal cries. He is swallowed up in their panting and moaning. Warring emotions engulf him: shame at himself for spying on them and furious, bitter jealousy. Only this afternoon, Wiki was kissing *him*.

Sorenson has slaughtered a lamb. Blood staining its woolly shoulders, it dangles in the meat-cage ready to be skinned in the early evening when the flies are not so thick. Turning away from what is hanging inside, Ted passes the wire window, swatting at the raucous clamour of blowflies. To his surprise, Eru is standing on the back verandah. These days, he comes to visit only when he is invited.

Ted struggles to find something to say. 'Er . . . Good to . . . see you.'

Eru seems awkward, too. 'You're off soon?'

'Right.'

'Long way.'

Ted nods.

'When're you home again?'
'Depends. If I pass my exams, three, four years, I'd say.'
Eru looks at Ted, then, without warning, his face crumples and tears run down his cheeks. He makes no effort to control or conceal them.
Ted regards him with embarrassment. A grown man bawling. Father is always pointing out that this is one of the problems with Maoris. They have no notion of how to keep a decent British stiff upper lip. 'I know you'll miss me,' he says, 'but I'll be back.'
'It's not us I'm thinking of,' says Eru, 'it's you. We've got one another, but you'll be on your own. I was thinking how much you're going to miss us.'
He presses his nose to Ted's in a hongi and Ted, to his horror, finds his own eyes filling with tears.

In the kitchen, a new sacking apron tied at her waist, Ethel hears the persistent knocking that signals the arrival of the post boy. By the time she has washed the dough off her hands, Uncle Bertie has already gone to the door. She can hear him gobbling.
The post boy is standing in the lobby, his Adam's apple working below the chinstrap of his hat. Her uncle waves at the post boy, then in her direction. 'What is it, Uncle Bertie?'
He gobbles again.
'Yes?' she says to the boy, who has backed off several paces.
'Delivery for a Miss Wrench.'
'Are you sure?' Ethel has never before had a parcel. Not even a letter.
'That's what it says here.'
Staring at her own name on it, Ethel takes the package.
Her uncle heads towards his room.
'He all right then?' asks the boy.
Ethel remembers Pater's repeated instructions. 'He's got a war injury.'

Briefly, the post boy looks impressed. He gazes after the disappearing Bertie. 'Oh, I nearly forgot. There's two letters as well.'

They are for Pater; one from *The Times*, the other from *The Journal of the Polynesian Society*. Ethel places them in the letter-rack, then, heart bumping, she takes another look at her parcel. What can it be? And who has sent it? The postmark is local: she does not recognise the careful schoolroom handwriting on the brown-paper-wrapped rectangular box – *Miss Ethel Wrench, Katharevousa House, No. 1 R.D., Castleton.*

When it is shaken, the box rattles slightly.

'There's some mistake,' she says.

'You mean you aren't Miss Ethel Wrench?' says the post boy.

'Yes, I am. It's just that, I mean . . .'

'Then it must be for you,' says the boy. Aware no tip will be forthcoming, he mock-salutes her clumpy boots and sack apron, remounts his bicycle and is off.

'Why, Ethel,' beams her mother, coming in from the dairy, 'you have a parcel.'

Within seconds, it seems, the room is full of brothers, all clamouring to see inside the wrapping. Ethel clutches it to her chest. 'I'll open it later.'

'No, now,' insists Orpheus. He turns to his father who has just appeared. 'Make her open it, Pater.'

'She wants to wait,' says Lavinia.

'Nonsense,' says Euclid who, like his sons, burns to know what is in the mystery package.

Reluctantly, Ethel strips off the outer brown layer, revealing an inner wrapping of soft white tissue paper.

'Hurry up,' cries Orpheus, craning over her shoulder.

Ethel folds back the inner covering. There, exposed, are the haughty features of Queen Anne.

'Chocolates,' shouts Orpheus.

Ethel can feel herself blushing.

'But, dear,' says her mother, 'wherever did they come from? Who sent them?'

Ethel's blush deepens.

Euclid rubs his bony hands together. He is partial to chocolate, a luxury rarely available to him. 'Come now, Ethel, young Cupid has you as his Psyche. Somewhere, somehow, you must have felt the tinglin' of his arrow.'

Lavinia frowns at her husband. 'Time for luncheon,' she says.

'So, Ethel,' says Euclid jovially, as they seat themselves, 'reveal the identity of the mysterious donor. Not a Greek, I trust?' He beams around the table. 'Timeo Danaos et dona ferentes. I . . .'

'. . . *fear the Greeks, even when bearing gifts,*' cries Hector.

'Excellent,' says Euclid. 'Hector has earnt first choice from the box.'

'She won't let you have a single one,' says Orpheus. He thrusts a hand across the table. 'Let me hold them. Only for a minute.'

Ethel shakes her head.

'You're mean as Midas. I only want to see the queen on the lid.'

'The fairest way,' says Euclid, 'would be to draw lots and select one each in turn. Startin' with Hector.'

Lavinia stands up. 'The chocolates,' she says, 'are Ethel's. So it is for Ethel to decide who will eat them and when.'

'Naturally.' Euclid turns hastily to his daughter. 'And to whom do we owe the pleasure of their presence?'

Ethel gulps. She lowers her head and stares at the tablecloth. 'I think,' she says, 'they may have been sent by Mr Maples.'

Euclid chokes on his mashed swede and carrot. 'Don't be so idiotic, Ethel. Why would the grocer be sendin' *you* chocolates? It's not as if we're account customers.'

♜

'The only possible way to give everyone a chance to say goodbye to Edward-Wilson,' says Rosalba, 'is to hold a garden party.'

'But Rosa,' says Wilson, 'the expense . . . The marquee alone . . .'

'Only a small marquee. For the food and drink.'

'We'd have to keep the numbers under control.'

'That's no problem. I always feel it's better to keep things exclusive. It makes the invitations so much more highly prized.'

'Hmm,' says Rosalba, working away at her guest list, 'the Wrenches.'

'They're neighbours. We're downright obliged to invite them.'

'There are eight of them. Nine, if you include that appalling brother of hers.'

'We can't leave them out.'

'They might not even realise it was on.'

'With a deuced great marquee taking up half the horse paddock? Be realistic, Rose. You can't snub them like that.'

'Well, just the parents, then.'

'Couldn't we invite Ethel?'

'I hardly think so, Huia.'

'She's my friend, and she *is* the only girl.'

'I'm aware of that, thank you. As I'm also aware she'd be likely to come in a sugar bag.'

'She's always very polite.'

Wilson looks up from his paper. 'Deuced kind of Huia. I like to see that in a young woman. That's another one settled, Rosalba. Wrench, his wife and their daughter. Who's next?'

'Your Maori friend and his wife. No point in asking *them*. They didn't come to our Christmas carol party.'

'Te Mara was taken ill.'

'We can't count on that twice running.'

Wilson decides to take a stand. 'Hang it, Rosalba, Te Mara's a chief, not one of your common pa Maoris. He's my chess partner. He visits this house on a regular basis. I insist he's invited.'

Nothing annoys Rosalba more than Wilson's 'court voice'. But she has set her heart on an evening dance in the marquee, with musicians on a dais flanked by floral displays in classical urns, all of which is going to cost a considerable amount. 'Whatever you think best, Wilson,' she murmurs, inscribing the names of Te Mara and his wife in violet ink at the bottom of her list.

♛

It has never occurred to either Rosalba or Wilson that Te Mara and Tiatia have no wish to attend their garden party.

'A Pakeha party? Never.' Tiatia tosses the silver-embossed invitation to the floor.

'It's a very honourable card requesting the pleasure,' remonstrates Te Mara. 'You said so yourself. So why not spend a happy afternoon walking in the Castles' garden?'

'Drinking vile-tasting tea, being patronised by a group of squatters whose parents have been barely a generation in Aotearoa? No, thank you very much, Mr Liberal-Maori Chief.'

Te Mara sees from her expression that a terrific sulking session is about to ensue. This, he knows all too well, can last for days. He thinks quickly. 'You surprise me,' he says. 'You, a chief's daughter, a chief's granddaughter, and you want to behave like one of Heke's mob.' He sees he has struck his target. 'Here you have the simple – the gracious – solution, but this you do not even want to contemplate.'

'What solution?'

'The solution of acceptance.'

'I told you, I am not going.'

'First, we accept. With thanks. Then, alas, just when we were so looking forward to this promenade in the Castles' garden, we are unfortunately called to a tangi. A relative, in Pahiatua.'

'You have no relatives in Pahiatua. I have no relatives in Pahiatua.'

'Exactly. The last-minute obligation of a mythical tangi.'

Tiatia, though impressed, shakes her head. 'What a foolish idea, tempting the gods like that. And, besides, then we would have to be prisoners in the pa for the next four days. How could we go into town, go anywhere those Pakeha might see us?'

Te Mara feels his patience slipping. 'Better,' he cries, 'you should never have married a chief if you refuse to be bound by chiefly obligations.'

Secretly, Tiatia likes to see him assert himself, but pride compels her to put up further resistance. 'Who can have chiefly obligations to the Pakeha? Tell me that, eh?'

'Right,' roars Te Mara, 'stay here alone and I will go to the party.'

Tiatia winds herself round him. 'No, no. I will do as you ask. The Pahiatua solution.'

Te Mara pushes her onto the bed and lies beside her. 'You know the Pakeha expression?'

Fixing her dark eyes on him, she slides her hand inside the waistband of his trousers. 'Which Pakeha expression? I know many.'

'*Noblesse oblige.*' And then, because he likes the sound of it, he repeats it. 'Noblesse oblige.' He presses his nose to hers. 'And now, Tiatia, you will please oblige *me*.'

A black-edged letter has been delivered by special messenger to Katharevousa House. *Tragically,* says the captain's letter, *Mrs Younghusband has passed away. Fortified by the rites of the Holy Mother Church, she was buried at sea.* No doubt, thinks Euclid sourly, with her rosary locked by rigor mortis in her clawed hands. Lavinia has cried herself to sleep. Even Euclid feels a pang of pity as he pictures the shrouded figure plummeting through fathoms of water. Could the *Themistocles* have been above the Marianas Trench? He sees the winding sheet unravelling as it falls down and down, pictures the feeding frenzy of sharks ripping at the wrinkled flesh, tearing it ravenously from the bones. Edging closer to the now-sleeping Lavinia's ample body, he wraps himself around the reassuring plenitude of her hefty buttocks and thighs.

♜

'I need you to stay on today, Florence,' says Mrs Castle.

'I can't, Mum. Not today. Got to meet me mam in town.'

'I'm sure she'll wait for you.'

'She's got to come in all the way from Drovers' Hill, Mum, and she's got terrible bad knees,' lies Flossie. 'She can't stand that long.'

'There's no shortage of places to sit in town. Where did you say you're meeting her?'

Flossie struggles to think of a landmark in Castleton. 'The Cenotaph.'

'Well, then,' says Mrs Castle, 'there's no problem. She can wait on one of the memorial benches.'

'She'll be cross with us.'

'I'm sure your mother understands that your employer's needs come first.'

Flossie scowls at Mrs Castle, but remains silent. Her friend will be expecting her at the usual time. Maybe he won't wait. Then Flossie will miss out on the extra tip he slips her after their stroll. They never walk out in town, though. No fear. Too many Percy Prys. Flossie always makes sure their meeting place is safely out-of-the-way, usually on the turn-off past the Masterton road, where almost nobody goes.

'Me mam's got a bad heart. She's not supposed to worry.'

'I shan't require you for long and the sooner you start, the quicker you'll be finished.' Mrs Castle stands up.

Flossie doesn't feel comfortable with the look on her face.

'And there's one other matter, Florence.'

'Yes, Mum?'

Mrs Castle stares at her sternly. 'Atkinson tells me that certain . . . items . . . have gone missing from the larder. Do you know anything about them?'

Flossie colours. 'I never took nothing, Mrs Castle. Just stuff was going in the pig-bin anyway. Seemed like a pity to waste it. There's nine of us. Me mam don't find it that easy.'

♙

Ted is putting on Kruger's horse-blanket when he senses someone behind him. Turning, he sees it is Ethel Wrench.

'Huia's out,' he says ungraciously.

She shuffles her feet. 'I didn't come to see Huia.'

Silence.

What the devil does she want? wonders Ted.

'Huia said you're going soon.'

'In three weeks.' He picks up the bucket.

Ethel watches as he fills it at the tap. 'Lucky you. I'd love to go back to England.'

Ted empties the water into the horse trough. 'Oh.'

'I don't really remember anything about it, of course.'

'I suppose not.'

Ethel reaches into the string bag she is holding and pulls out a tissue-paper-wrapped package. 'I brought you this.'

Frozen with embarrassment, Ted stares at her.

'It's not very much, but it might come in useful. Pater says Cambridge is bitter in winter.'

Taking the package, Ted sees it is, in fact, two parcels, the smaller secured to the larger with purple wool. 'Thanks,' he mutters. Today, he thinks, her hair seems to be sticking out even more than usual.

At almost the same moment she runs her hands over it, trying to flatten it down. 'My hair's all everywhere. I just washed it.'

Has she read his thoughts? Ted searches for something polite to say. 'I washed mine this morning, too.'

'Oh.'

The parcel is weighting Ted's hands. Why, he asks himself, doesn't Ethel just go? She seems to be waiting for something.

There is another long pause. Then, 'I hope you like it,' she ventures.

'I'm sure I shall.'

'If you don't, you don't have to wear it.'

Wear it. Ted shudders. What ghastly item of Wrench clothing can the tissue be concealing?

Ethel is still standing expectantly.

Is the dratted girl ever going to move? he wonders. Then, he realises. She wants him to undo the parcel. He sighs.

'You're not worried about going, are you?'

'Not a bit.' He pauses. 'I'll . . . open it, if you like.' He unties the double-bow of purple wool and unwraps the smaller parcel. Inside lie two chocolates.

'Queen Anne's.' She looks at him anxiously. 'You do like chocolate, don't you?'

'Yes, of course. I . . .' Does she expect him to take them to Cambridge?

'That one's a lime centre and the square one's caramel.'

'Very nice.' He has an idea. 'Why don't we have one each?'

'I couldn't possibly. They're for you.' She watches as he undoes the larger parcel.

Ted tries to control his expression. What can it be? And why has Ethel Wrench, of all people, decided to give him a farewell present?

It is some kind of knitting. Lifting it out, Ted sees it is a green and red striped scarf. In one corner, in white wool chain-stitch, are Ted's initials – EW.

'It's a muffler.'

'Yes.'

'I knitted it myself. It should be light blue, I know, but Mater only had red and green.'

'It's . . . very nice. It'll be useful in England, I'm sure.'

Ethel takes a confidential breath. 'I made it for myself, really. And then, when Huia said you were going, I thought . . . I thought it'd be nice to . . . I didn't have time to knit another, you see, and then I suddenly realised. You and I have exactly the same initials.'

Ted is mortified. He must get rid of her. He shoves the chocolates at her. 'Go on, take one. I insist.'

'Well, if . . . Which one would you prefer? I like both.'

Ted seizes the nearer chocolate and crams it into his mouth.

♘

Bertie Younghusband has taken his mother's death very hard. Life in his sister's household is becoming intolerable, but if he leaves Castleton where will he go? His pension will not permit him to run to the purchase of any sort of outfit, even here in New Zealand. By Jove, it'd be capital to have his own place. None of this yapping in dead languages, or glaring disapproval whenever he indulges in a harmless cheroot. With a home of his own, he might even find a decent girl. Damned tight of the neighbours not to include him in the garden party invitation. Total snub, really. And just the sort of event where he might have found Miss Right.

Bertie can feel himself becoming restless. From time to time he gets an attack like this, a sort of compulsion that forces him out into the open air. He knows from experience he needs to walk off his agitated state and stride out for a cracking good hike. It used to worry Ma, all this marching about the countryside. Sometimes, he'd be off for so long he'd be hard pressed to recollect where he'd been . . .

♟ ♙

Wafting its comforting smell of grass and sheep-dung, the wind blows Ted's hair as he walks beside the dam. He can hear distant shots: Sorenson is potting at the rooks in the walnut tree. From the tops of the poplars and the macrocarpas, other rooks screech raucously at one another.

Ted tries to fix in his mind the familiar images of home: the fence palings at the roadside are crooked so that the wires of the fence run randomly uphill or down.

'You going soon?'

He jumps at the sound of the disembodied voice from the manuka bushes. 'Who's that?' But, even before he hears her giggle, he knows. 'Stop following me everywhere, can't you?'

'I was not following you,' protests Wiki. 'I was here first.'

'It's not your land.'

'It's not yours, either.'

'It's my father's, so it *is* mine.'

She emerges from the scrub. 'It used to be my great-great-grandfather's. So it's mine, too.'

Ted sits down on the bank with his back to her.

Wiki sits down beside him. 'What you got against me, eh?' She fishes in the kit beside her on the ground, brings out a white clay pipe and thrusts it at him. 'In case you ever need a smoke or something. While you're away.'

Ted stares at her. Her tangled hair covers her face so he cannot judge her expression, but her voice is different. Softer. Not the rasping tone of the wild, harsh Wikitoria he knows.

'Why don't you like me?' she says.

'I didn't say I didn't like you.'

'You don't though, do you? You haven't asked me to your garden party.'

Ted flushes. 'Mama sent the invitations, not me.' He picks up the clay pipe and turns it in his hands. 'Thanks. It's nice.'

'Is it because I'm a Maori?'

Ted stares at her. 'Don't be dumb. Eru's my best friend.'

'He won't be, after you get back from that English university. And you haven't invited him, either. I thought it was supposed to be a party for you.'

Ted prods at the grass. 'Look, if you and Eru want to come, you can. In the evening. For the dancing.' Another long silence. A pulse beats in Ted's throat. 'Well, thanks for the pipe,' he says.

Wiki says nothing.

'It's nice. I like it. I never had a pipe before. Sorry I haven't got anything to give you.'

Wiki looks at him.

'Unless, I mean, if you like . . . I . . . I could give you a kiss.'

Slowly Wiki leans towards him.Ted's heart is thudding. He reaches out an arm and puts it round her shoulder. His throat is dry: he swallows, then pulls her against him.

She is soft. Everywhere. Her hair floats against his cheek. Ted puts out his free hand and strokes her face. Her skin is warm and smooth under his fingers. Putting both arms around her, he crushes her against him and kisses her lips, over and over.

Wiki smiles. 'That's a lot of presents.'

Ted can feel the hammering between his thighs. Pushing her down on her back, he lies on top of her, thrusting his tongue greedily inside her mouth. 'Wiki,' he murmurs, 'Wiki.'

He slides his hands under her jersey and spreads them out to encompass her breasts. Her nipples rub against the palms of his hands. 'Oh God,' he groans.

'Better stop, eh?' whispers Wiki. 'Or we might never.'

But Ted is incapable of stopping. Now his hands are tearing at her skirt while his mouth sucks frantically on her nipple. He can feel the wiriness of her hair and the outline of the hidden slit beneath it. He slides his fingers inside her. He is aware of wetness everywhere: inside Wiki, oozing from the end of his cock. All he wants, all he can think of, is burying himself as hard and as far as he can inside her.

He struggles and fumbles with his trousers, dropping them down to his ankles. Wiki lies, her hair flowing across the grass, her legs apart, waiting for him. 'We shouldn't.'

Ted flings himself on top of her. Holding it in his right hand, he guides his cock through the springy hair, between the soft wet lips, and begins to push and thrust.

'No,' sobs Wiki. 'Ohhh.' Her nails are digging into his shoulders, her body tossing and turning beneath him.

Ted is conscious of a tremendous throbbing, a resistance, then a sudden giving-way as he pushes himself deep, deep inside her.

Inhaling the lanolin stickiness of the sheep staring witlessly at him from their paddock, Bertie paces the fence-line. He kicks at a dried cowpat, scattering bits of dung with his shoe. As he digs in his pocket for his tobacco and papers, he realises his hands are shaking. The strain, he tells himself, of having to constantly face up to his sister's nightmare family. How much longer can he stand it without Ma? Now, his attacks seem to be coming in the daytime, not just at night. How will he manage if they get worse? What if someone has spotted him on one of his agitated walks? Marked him out and followed him?

Clenching and unclenching his fists, he manages to get the tremor in his fingers under control, lowers himself to the ground and lays his tobacco tin in his lap. In the next paddock, Chrysomallus lowers his devilish head and watches him from yellow vertical-pupilled eyes. Bertie is struck by the size of the ram's equipment. Damned nearly as big as a cow's udder. 'Fine pair of nuggets you've got,' he gobbles. A couple of sheep approach warily, then trot away, dags shaking, the twin woolly cushions of their backsides wobbling. At a safe distance they stop and settle down to grazing. Stupid things, thinks Bertie, as his fingers automatically flatten out his papers and pluck tobacco shreds from their block in the tin.

Time to roll up. He glances down. My God, there's blood all over his paper and shreds. Bertie looks at his right hand and the scratch marks gouged into it, which are leaking crimson into his lap. How the blazes did they get there? His hands have begun shaking again. Get a grip, he tells himself. Must've done it on the barbed-wire fence. Damned dangerous, those vicious stranded knots.

With difficulty, he binds his handkerchief round the scratches, discards the stained paper and starts again. This time he manages to roll up the tube, wet the paper edge and gum it back on itself. Propped against the tree-trunk, he loosens his scarf, slips it down to his collar-bone and roots in his pocket for a light. I'm a war hero, he tells himself, decorated for service to my queen and country.

The handkerchief has fallen off his hand. Bertie hesitates, looking again at the scoring on his skin. With his free hand, he strokes his naked vent, then plunges the cigarette into the middle of the ridging round the hole and lights up. But, today, not even the soothing inhalation of nicotine can calm him. His agitation mounts; he feels himself quivering and sweating. Scrambling to his feet, he tells himself there is nothing for it but to march it off again.

At the top end of Main Street, Bertie sinks down onto a garden wall and awards himself another cigarette. He gulps in the restoring smoky infusion, feeling it tingling against his palate, glowing down into his lungs. But something is wrong. His chest is burning. Red-hot. Bertie struggles to gasp in breath. The fire in his upper body intensifies. Raising a hand to his neck, he touches his tracheotomy hole. Empty.

♖

Oh God, thinks Ted, feeling himself stiffen as he recalls, for the hundredth time, lying on top of Wiki: kissing her . . . forcing himself inside her . . . What if she . . . if she gets . . . pregnant? What was it Mulholland had told him about chaps using sausage skins? Sausage skins! He goes limp with revulsion at the thought.

He remembers the sudden yielding, the blood afterwards. What had she said? '*Never did it before. Never wanted to.*' Could she get pregnant from just that one time? Will he have to marry her? How will he ever face her again?

He buries his head in his pillow and rubs his aroused body against the sheets. God, how he wants to feel her underneath him again.

But what if somebody has seen them? If Wiki tells someone? Eru? Or worse, her koro? And could Father or Mama possibly know, just from looking at him, that he . . . that he . . . ? He feels it must, somehow, be visible to everyone. Thank God, he'll soon be gone. Right away from here.

'There's a very rough-looking boy at the door,' says Ku, interrupting her mother at her writing bureau. 'Atkinson's told him to go away, but he says he's come all the way from Drovers' Hill and he has to see you or Papa.'

'How tiresome. Who is he?'

'I don't know. He wouldn't say.'

'It must be Flossie's brother,' says Huia, coming in. 'He's got exactly the same colour hair.'

'Well, perhaps he can shed some light on why she hasn't bothered to come in to work today. Totally thoughtless and inconsiderate when she knows we have the garden party.'

'Atkinson thinks,' says Ku, 'she's run off with a beau. She'd just had her wages.'

'Fortunate,' says Rosalba drily, 'that she's paid in arrears.'

'What if she *has* eloped?' Sixteen-year-old Ku is seized by the romance of this possibility.

'Please do try,' says her mother, 'to be a little less vulgar.'

Flossie's brother is as tongue-tied as Flossie is bold.

'Is Florence ill?' asks Rosalba.

'No, Missus. Mam wondered if she'd been staying over with you last night. With your garden party coming up and all.'

'We haven't seen her since lunchtime yesterday,' says Rosalba. 'It was her half day.'

'Our Mam's that worried. It's not like our Floss not to come home at night.'

'It seems to me,' says Rosalba, 'the best thing is for Mr Castle to have a word with your father.'

'Our da's been dead nine years, Missus. Got crushed when the cart fell on him.'

'Florence has got herself into trouble,' says Rosalba, over breakfast next morning. 'You know what these working-class girls are like.'

To her surprise, Wilson is angry. 'Steady on, Rosalba. You've not a shred of proof of that.' He picks up his hat and strides out.

Fortunate, thinks Rosalba, that Wilson left early. The florist's estimate has arrived in the morning post: despite his ridiculous attitude about Florence, she will have to make peace with him. Wretched girl, leaving just when she was needed. But perhaps telephoning Wilson at the office and asking solicitously about Florence will soften his annoyance.

The party line is busy. For over an hour Rosalba tries, without success, to get a line.

Hearing the trill that signals the phone is free, she rushes to snatch up the receiver, only to hear that Thelma Fraser has got there first. And this, she knows from experience, means at least another twenty minutes' wait. Rosalba slides her index finger down on the phone lugs, trapping them in the half position and ensuring she doesn't make any sound as she positions the receiver against her ear.

'. . . something definitely going on,' she hears Thelma say.

'No. Honestly?'

Rosalba presses the cold circle of the earpiece closer to her head, taking care not to breathe into the mouthpiece.

'. . . she does queen it a bit, I grant you.'

'I mean, when all's said and done it's not as if they're *Wellington* society.'

'He's from an old family, but she was a Sherrington-Smith. Not anyone *I've* ever heard of.'

With a jolt, Rosalba realises they are now talking about her. How utterly disloyal. Thelma is her best friend. In her agitation, she releases her finger, which has become almost numb from holding the lugs in position.

'Hello,' says Thelma, 'hello? Are you still there?'

'Yes.'

'Did you just bump the phone?'

'No, I thought it was you.'

'Clodagh,' says Thelma in her most imperious manner, 'if you don't get off this line right now, I'm going to report you.'

The line is free. Rosalba revolves the metal handle at the side of the wooden box.

'Exchange.'

'Mrs Castle here, Clodagh. My husband's office, please.'

She hears the phone ring in Wilson's chambers. 'It's Mrs Castle, Miss Venson.'

'Rosalba?' Wilson's voice is faint. 'What is it?'

'I've been . . . worrying . . . about Florence. Did you report her missing?'

'Yes, at lunchtime. And . . .'

The operator's voice cuts in. 'Clear the line, please! Clear the line!'

'I shan't be a minute, Clodagh,' says Rosalba in a commanding tone.

'Sorry, Mrs Castle, I can't give you even half a minute. It's an emergency.'

♘

Summoned to the cottage hospital, Lavinia waits on a hard wooden bench. The nurse indicates a shrouded cubby-hole. 'Doctor is ready for you now.'

Lavinia thrusts herself between the curtains. 'I must see Bertie. Right away.'

'Do please sit down, Mrs Younghusband.' The doctor rubs at what seems to be ash on his white coat.

'No. I . . .'

'I'm terribly sorry. We did all we could, but I'm afraid . . . under the circumstances . . .' His voice trails off.

Lavinia stares at him. 'There must be some mistake. I'm not Bertie's wife. I'm his sister. He doesn't *have* a wife.'

'I do apologise, Mrs . . . er . . .'

'Wrench. Lavinia Wrench. But where *is* Bertie? He'll be expecting me.'

The doctor fiddles with his stethoscope. 'Well, no, Mrs Trench, I don't think he . . .' He stands up. 'We had no possible chance of saving him, you see. He was D.O.A.'

'D.O.A.?'

'Dead . . . deceased . . . on arrival. That is to say, Major Younghusband had . . . he had passed on before he got to us.'

'*Dead?* Bertie? But that can't be right. He was perfectly well this morning.'

The doctor looks away. 'I'm so sorry, Mrs . . . You see, he

was . . . found . . . earlier today, on a garden wall.' He pauses. 'Smoking . . .'

'But he always smokes.'

'I don't mean Major Younghusband was . . . er . . . smoking a cigarette. I mean *he* was smoking. That is to say – smoke was pouring from . . . from his . . . er . . .'

'But he does that often. It's his party piece. He can whistle, as well.'

'Yes, I'm sure. Splendid,' says the doctor. 'But you see, this time he had some kind of . . . accident. It was a . . . a . . . spontaneous combustion, you might say. Happens all the time in America, I gather.'

'America? Bertie's never been to America.'

'You must remind yourself, Mrs Trench, that the major – your brother – passed on in the way he would have wished. Enjoying life, right to the . . . the end . . .'

Lavinia gazes at him. 'You mean Bertie's *dead*?'

'I'm afraid so. I'm sorry.'

She fights back her tears. 'Did he . . . suffer?'

'Absolutely not,' says the doctor. 'I was here when they brought him in.' He hesitates for a moment. 'It may bring you some small comfort to know he was wreathed in perfect smoke rings.'

♖

'Dash it, Rosalba, of course we ought to cancel the thing. Poor chap's barely cold.'

'I suppose,' says Rosalba, 'if the Wrenches are in mourning, at least that makes three fewer on the guest list.'

Wilson slips off his black armband and loosens his collar. 'Pretty grim event, I must say. Barely enough of us to fill two pews.'

'I said it was a mistake to go.'

'I'm very glad I did. Apart from the family, only Te Mara, the doctor and I turned up. Oh, and the chemist.'

'The chemist?'

'Wrench seems to be quite thick with him. Can't think why.' He glances round the kitchen. 'How're the party preparations going?'

'Please don't trouble yourself about *me*. After all, what have I got to do all day but supervise caterers and the marquee company and the band and . . .'

'The band? Rosa, we agreed a band was out of the question.'

'I didn't agree. You said . . .'

'I'm quite aware of what I said. You'll simply have to cancel them.'

'I can't cancel them. Not this late on.'

'Then I shall cancel them. Right away.'

'Wilson! I cannot believe how . . . how petty . . . how penny-pinching . . .'

'We don't have the funds for a band.'

'The invitations specifically say, "*Dancing till 11-00*". You can't let people down now. I'll be a laughing stock.'

'Arkie Montgomery's brother can play the fiddle. I'll sort it out myself.'

Rosalba gives him a murderous look. 'The shearer's half-witted brother. I hope you'll be satisfied, Wilson, when you've single-handedly ruined your daughters' social prospects and your son's last public appearance.'

'Don't be melodramatic. Give me the telephone number. I'll do it now.'

'On the telephone? The whole of Castleton will know about it by this evening.'

'Then I'll go and see the band-leader. And call in at Arkie's brother's on the way back.'

'Mater,' says Ethel, 'do you think . . . I mean, now that Uncle . . . it's not as if he'd know. Or mind . . . I . . .'

Her mother looks at her from swollen red eyes.

'I've never been to a garden party, Mater. And I don't suppose anyone will ever ask me again. Do you think it would be all right for me . . . to . . . ? '

'Pater would never permit it.'

But, when it's dark, thinks Ethel, it couldn't hurt to slip over to the boundary fence and just look.

♖

In a floating pale-blue tea-gown and matching broad-brimmed hat, Rosalba glides among her guests.

'My dear, your peonies,' says Thelma Fraser. 'They're gigantic.'

'Sorenson's secret ingredient.'

'I wish we had a Sorenson.'

'These club sandwiches are simply . . .'

Another guest plucks at her sleeve. 'Rosalba, how *do* you manage it?'

Rosalba looks up as a late arrival strides towards the marquee. Good Lord, it's Wrench. The wretched man has come after all.

'A fiddler,' says Thelma. 'How . . . quaint.'

'The latest thing in Wellington,' says Rosalba. 'Wilson's brother, Charles, says everyone wants a lone violinist. Terribly Viennese. Charles is a silk, you know.'

'You said. Oh . . .' Thelma looks towards the house. 'I didn't know you'd invited the whole town.'

Rosalba, following her gaze, sees Wiki and Eru cautiously approaching the lawn in front of the marquee. 'The cheek! We invited the grandfather, of course. You know Wilson and his views. But he . . .' She breaks off. 'Well, really. Gatecrashing a private function. It's too much.'

'That's the trouble with all this equality business,' says Thelma. 'The next thing you know, you have Maoris thinking they can go anywhere they like.'

Huia and Gwennie Fraser are standing by the tea-table, eating ices.

'You must give me Ted's address in Cambridge,' says Gwennie. 'I'll write.'

'Yes, well . . .' says Huia, who knows how much Ted dislikes Gwennie.

'Lucky him. I wish I was going overseas.'

'So do I.'

'Maybe you'll all go over to vis . . .' She breaks off. 'Look who's just arrived. You didn't tell me *they* were invited. And look at what she's wearing. That must have been her confirmation frock.'

'Excuse me,' says Huia. 'I'd better go and make sure they're all right.'

'Well,' says Gwennie, 'rather you than me.'

'Hello,' says Huia, advancing across the lawn towards Eru and Wiki.

'Ed said we could come,' says Wiki belligerently.

Eru holds out a hand to Huia. 'Hello. Look, we aren't going to stay or anything. Only say goodbye to Ed, that's all.'

Huia shakes his hand. 'Of course you must stay.' She looks around for Ted. 'Come into the marquee and have an ice.' At all costs, she must stop Mama from spotting Wiki and Eru.

But, as they turn towards the tent, she sees her mother sailing towards them.

'Huia!' Rosalba cocks an imperious finger. 'A moment, please.'

'The ices are over there,' says Huia quickly. 'Help yourself. ' Apprehensively, she makes her way towards her mother, but is halted by the ringing of a teaspoon being chinked onto a glass.

'Quiet, please,' booms her father's voice. 'Silence, everyone. Let's have a bit of hush.'

Most of the male guests are farmers who have gravitated to the edge of the marquee, where they are huddled together discussing the shocking fall in the price of the wool-clip. At the other end of the tent, the women are comparing knitting patterns or exchanging comments on the food, the weather, their children and the various ensembles of the other guests. They shush one another noisily.

'Ted,' calls Wilson, and various hands push a reluctant Ted towards the dais. 'Up here, old chap.'

Poor Ted, thinks Huia, who knows exactly how humiliated he will be by this public show.

'And Mother. Come on, Rosa, up you come.'

Saved! thinks Huia. As soon as I can, I'll get Eru and Wiki out of the marquee. She sneaks a glance at Eru. She has never seen him in a suit before. How handsome he looks.

Everyone is turned expectantly towards the dais. Ted, aware that his face is now crimson, glances over at the tea-table where he sees Eru and Wiki. At the sight of Wiki, he reddens even further. Is she . . . Has she . . . told Eru? Feeling a familiar tingling in his nose, he pinches the bridge tightly. Please, God, not now. Not in front of all these people.

'. . . off to Cambridge, this brain-box son of ours . . .'

'Alma mater,' shouts Wrench, waving his glass of punch.

'And now,' continues Wilson, 'a toast. Please raise your glasses. To Ted.'

'Ted,' echoes the assembled company.

'Edward-Wilson,' murmurs Rosalba, dabbing at her eyes.

'God speed, old man, and safe return.'

'Safe return,' shout the guests.

Huia, who has wormed her way through the crowd, takes Wiki's arm.

'Never had an ice before,' says Wiki. 'They're very nice.'

'Take another. Go on. And you, too, Eru.' Huia snatches up two cold dishes of lemon ice and leads them outside. 'It's so hot in here. Let's go back to the house.'

'Shouldn't we go and speak to Ted first?'

'Too many people round him right now.' Huia can feel Eru's eyes on her.

'You look very pretty,' he says.

Huia plucks at her pale-green sleeve. 'Do you like it?'

'It suits you.'

'Why don't we sit on the verandah and eat our ices. Oh, here's Ku.'

'You'll never guess,' says Ku, 'who's hanging round the boundary fence. Ethel and the Orful Wrench.'

'Are they coming over?'

'They're not allowed. They're in mourning.'

'Their father's here.'

'Maybe,' says Ku, 'we should warn them.'

'You get them an ice each, Ku.' Huia takes Wiki's arm. 'We'll go and tell them.' She pauses. 'And if you see Mama, say you've no idea where I am.'

As they slip towards the darker part of the garden by the boundary fence, she feels another hand slide into hers and squeeze it gently. Eru's.

Ted, standing below the dais, has had his hand grasped by what seems like the entire populace of Castleton. Ku materialises beside him. 'Huia says, as soon as you can, come over to the boundary fence. Wiki and Eru want to say goodbye. And Ethel and the Orful Wrench are there, too. And Huia says, whatever you do, don't breathe a word to Mama.'

Wiki. Ethel Wrench. All of Castleton pumping his hand in farewell. Thank God, thinks Ted, I'm off next week.

♙

Curled in his bunk on the *Zealandic*, Ted listens to the moaning and retching of his three fellow passengers. Fighting nausea as yet another wave hurls the ship down, down, down, then suddenly up again, Ted asks himself why on earth it is called the Pacific Ocean. Nothing remotely calm and soothing about the voyage so far. Since they passed through the Heads and out into the open sea, they have been battered and tossed by gales.

His stomach lurches again. Ted groans and closes his eyes. Half-remembered images of his departure slide in and out of his consciousness: the girls weeping, Mama wiping her eyes with a violet-scented handkerchief, Papa's tight grip on his shoulder, the final trudge up the gangway, the quay receding as the ship broke free and steamed away.

Under his bunk is stowed a hamper in which rest Afghan biscuits, caramel slices and two large fruit cakes. At the thought of them, Ted's gorge rises.

Somewhere in his trunk is Ethel Wrench's scarf. What had Huia said? '*You can't leave it behind. What if she's over here and sees it?*' So in it had gone, Wiki's pipe tucked inside it.

Wiki. Ted groans again. Can a girl get pregnant from just the one time? He tries to recall the reproduction cycle of the rabbit from his biology lessons at Claybourne. And if she is . . . Will everyone in Castleton know that he, Ted Castle, is the father? He will send a postcard, he decides, from the ship's next port of call. To Eru and Wiki. Give them his regards, thank them both for coming to the party to say goodbye . . . But, he thinks in dismay, all these years I've been going to the pa and I've no idea of their address.

♛

Picking up Mama's letter first, Ted holds the thick envelope to his nose to catch any faint residue of violets. Her perfect flowing script occupies the exact centre of the right-hand side of the envelope. Homesickness briefly engulfs him as he peers at the postmark. But, he thinks, would I really want to be back home again? Occasionally, yes, but, in the main, no. A thousand times, no. It's not as if he doesn't miss them all, especially Huia, but life here is so . . . so exhilarating, and Castleton, with all its petty concerns, seems no longer real, like some kind of dream.

Ted consults his watch, a farewell present from Father. He slips the unopened letters into his pocket, shrugs into his gown and sets off for the Trumpington Road. If he leaves it any later the queue will stretch back almost to Christ's.

A don in the waiting line nods briefly to him. 'Morning, Castle.' The spicy smell of Chelsea buns floats from the doorway, conjuring up warm, brown sticky wodges embedded with currants. The queue shuffles slowly forward: now Ted is beside the bakery window with its display of Dundee cakes, Madeira cakes and Victoria sponges so breathlessly light they almost float above their plates. In front of them swarm delicate butterfly cakes, their sponge wings protruding from backs of clotted cream.

'Mind if I join you, Castle?'

It is Manners, finding a way to circumvent the queue.

'Feel free.'

'You decided what you're having? Mine has to be a Chelsea bun.'

'Mine, too, I expect,' says Ted, 'although that Dundee cake looks pretty good.'

'More weight in a Chelsea bun,' says Manners. 'Lasts longer in the stomach.'

'You a tennis player?' asks Manners. 'Late in the season, I know, but still dry enough for a knock-around.'

'Good idea.'

'Thought you might like to join me on Sunday. I'm motoring over to the parents in Suffolk for lunch. Bit rural, but I expect you're used to that. More sheep than people in your neck of the woods, I'm told.'

'More cows, too.'

'Any large cities? Like London?'

Ted laughs. 'I used to think so, but now I've seen London, I'd say even Wellington's more like a Wild West town.'

'How many people in the country?'

'Just over a million.'

'A million!' Manners feigns exaggerated horror. 'You must all be related.'

'Not quite. But it does sometimes feel like that.'

♜

Again, Ku has not appeared at breakfast. Huia raps gently on her locked door. 'It's me. Huia.'

'Go away.'

'Let me in for a minute. Please.'

'No.'

'What's the matter?'

'Nothing. Leave me alone.'

'Mama's getting very cross. You'll have to come out sometime.'

'I can't.'

'If you stay in there much longer, Papa'll get Sorenson to break the lock and then you'll have to come out.'

The door opens a crack.

Huia is taken aback by her sister's appearance. Ku's blonde hair, lank and greasy, is flattened to her scalp. 'What on earth's the matter?' She shuts the door. 'What's happened?'

'I wish I was dead,' sobs Ku, shivering in her stained nightgown.

The room smells funny, thinks Huia. Sharp and sour. She reaches for the window latch, but Ku grabs her arm. 'No. Don't open it. Someone might look in.'

'No-one ever comes round this side of the house. You know that. Let me open it for a minute.' She pushes up the sash the few meagre inches that Ku will allow. 'Shall I run you a bath?'

'No, someone'll see me.'

'I'll keep cave.'

This seems to satisfy Ku. She nods, but makes no move. Then, suddenly, she bends forward, clasps her stomach, blows out her cheeks and clutches her mouth. Still hunched over, her hand blocking her lips, she stumbles to the door, fumbles with the key, peers out into the passage and is gone at a run towards the bathroom.

Huia snatches a clean nightgown from Ku's drawer, grabs her hairbrush, and shuts and locks the bedroom door.

Ku is bent over the washbasin, retching and coughing. The nasty odour of sick hangs in the air. Exactly, realises Huia, like the smell in her bedroom. She puts the plug in the bathtub and turns on the tap. 'Right. It's deep enough. You can get in now.'

Once she is in the bath, Ku appears calmer. Busying herself

with tidying the medicine chest, Huia ponders what to do next. 'I brought you a clean nightie,' she says.

'No. I'd better get dressed. Can you keep cave again?'

Huia is uneasy about the bedroom, which smells awful. 'We ought to try to tidy up a bit before Atkinson comes to do your room.'

'Why?'

'It's . . . we just should, that's all. Mama's in a terrible mood. She and Papa have been arguing again. I know it was months ago, but she's *still* going on about Ted's party.'

'Oh, the party,' says Ku, in an odd voice.

'She's convinced we should have had a band. I keep telling her it was lovely, especially the dancing, but she says it was so penny-pinching she's socially ruined. You know how she is.' She smiles at Ku. 'You seem much better.'

'I won't be tomorrow.'

'Of course you will.'

Ku slumps in her chair. 'No, I won't. I'll never be all right again.' She turns to look at her sister, half-defiant, half-despairing. 'You may as well know. You'll have to soon enough. I'm expecting.'

'*Expecting*?' says Huia. 'You can't be. You're sixteen. You've never had a boyfriend. To get pregnant, you have to have . . . you have to – you know . . . go with a boy.'

Ku begins to sob even harder, great shudders heaving through her whole body. 'But I have . . .' she chokes. 'And it was horrible. So nasty, I can't bear it. And now . . .'

Huia changes tack. 'Why don't you tell me who he is? This boyfriend.'

'Boyfriend! He's not my boyfriend. I hate him. I can't stand him. I never want to see him again.'

'But if you don't love him, how did you . . . when did you . . . ?'

'At the party,' cries Ku.

Huia stares at her. 'The party?'

'While everyone was dancing. You remember Mama told Wiki and Eru to leave, but Papa said of course they were welcome?' She breaks off in tears again. 'And then, when Mama had gone, you came out and you went off somewhere with Eru . . .'

Huia blushes guiltily.

'And Wiki kept asking where Ted was. And then Eru came back and . . .'

Huia's heart lurches. 'It was Eru?'

'No, of course not.'

Huia's heart slips back into place in her chest. 'Who, then?'

Ku looks up. Her face is streaked, swollen and wretched with grief. And, realises Huia, with something else. Shame. 'You don't have to tell me if you don't want to,' she says.

'I do want to.'

'So, who is he? The father? If you really are expecting, that is.'

'I am. I know I am.' Ku struggles to carry on. 'It was . . .' She brings out the words with difficulty. 'It was the Orful Wrench.'

'Orful?' Huia is so astounded she almost laughs. 'Well, if you love him,' she says, 'and you are expecting, he'll just have to marry you, that's all.'

'I don't love him. I told you, I can't stand him.'

'But . . .'

'He shouldn't have been there. He wasn't even invited.'

'I know.'

'You and Eru went off and Ethel was peeping into the marquee, so I was left with Wiki and Orful. And Wiki said I was a stuck-up little Pakeha and . . . and . . . I wanted to get away from her. And Orful said, "Why don't we ditch her and you come and show me your pater's motor." He said he'd never seen it close up.

'So I took him to the wool-shed and then he said, he asked, could he just sit inside in the back seat? And he opened the door and then he asked me to . . . to come in and sit beside him. He said he could see the moon through the wool-shed window and he wanted to show it to me.

'And then, then . . . he put his arm round me and started stroking my hair and telling me I was pretty, and then he asked me if I'd ever been kissed. I told him not to be so stupid and then . . . he grabbed me and kissed me all over my face. My eyes and my nose and then my mouth. Quite hard. And when I tried to pull away and get out, he wouldn't let me go. He said if I shouted or called out, he'd tell everyone I'd invited him into the car. And then – it was just horrible, Huia.' Her face contorts. 'It hurt. It was so disgusting. Worse than you can ever imagine. I can never, never go out again. I can't bear to see anyone.'

Huia is careful to keep her voice neutral. 'I don't think you can get a baby from doing it just the once.'

'But I have, I have.' Tears run down her face. 'I've got to get rid of it. There *are* people. Flossie used to talk about them.'

'You can't. You mustn't. Don't you remember what Flossie told us about Nora Rennie? She went to see a woman in Featherston and the next week she was rushed to Wellington Hospital and all her toes went black and fell off and she died in agony. And anyway, even if you did find someone, you haven't got any money.'

A fresh outburst of sobbing. 'But what am I going to *do*? Papa and Mama will kill me.'

'Kill Orpheus, more like.'

'I'm going to have to be sick again,' says Ku. 'Please, Huia, please, will you tell Mama?'

Squaring her shoulders, Huia forces herself to walk into the morning room. 'Ku's up now, Mama.'

Rosalba is bent over her petit-point. 'I should hope so.'

'Mama,' says Huia, her tongue sticking to her dry palate, 'there's something . . . something . . . important . . . I have to tell you.'

Rosalba lays aside her needlework ring. 'Yes?'

'Mama, please don't be angry. I . . .'

'If you've broken something valuable . . .'

'No, it isn't that.' She gulps in a large breath of air. 'It's Ku, Mama. She's expecting.'

Rosalba stares at her. 'If this is your idea of a joke, Huia . . .'

'No, Mama. It's true.'

'Do I understand you? Are you seriously suggesting that Kotuku is in the family way?'

Huia avoids her mother's eye. 'Yes, Mama.'

'And who, pray, is the father?'

Huia swallows.

'Answer me, please? As far as I am aware, Kotuku doesn't even have an admirer, much less a beau. So . . . who is the father?'

'Orpheus Wrench, Mama.'

Rosalba recoils, recovers herself. 'Look at me, please. Answer me again. Who is the father?'

Huia feels tears welling. 'Orpheus Wrench. At least that's what Ku . . .'

'And you believe her?'

'Yes, Mama.'

'I see. And you knew about this . . . this liaison . . . yet you failed to do anything to stop it? It didn't occur to you to mention it to me. Or to your father?' Her voice is rising, and Huia braces herself for what is surely coming next. Rosalba shakes her head. 'I simply cannot understand why, in a just Universe, you should have been spared and my poor perfect little Charles Willoughby taken.'

Wattles edge the roadside in a line of yellow sunbursts, the sky is infinitely blue, and ochre powder swirls round the girls' ankles as their feet disturb the dust of the road. The sheep in the grazing paddock turn disdainful faces towards them, watching them climb the stile. Ku folds herself onto the close-chewed grass with its scattered brown pellets; Huia settles down on a dry tussock, pulling out a grass-stalk and sucking on its furled pale end. Seen from here, their house looks like something in a painting. If only they had painted parents. Huia pictures them, brushed in at the edge of their front garden, happily fixed in their frame, permanently content.

Ku's voice sharpens. 'So, what am I going to do?'

'Mama will think of something. You're her favourite, you know that. And it's not your fault. It's that horrible . . .'

'Don't,' says Ku. 'I can't bear to think of him.' She stretches out on her back, staring at the sky. Huia, watching her, sees her eyes close. She looks at her sister's slender, sailor-suited figure. Impossible to believe she has a baby growing inside her.

The walk back feels longer than usual. As they approach the house, their steps slow. 'Better go into the drawing room and face it,' says Huia nervously.

'Maybe they won't be there,' says Ku.

But Papa and Mama are both there, stiff on the Chippendale chairs, waiting. Papa stands up. 'I've sent Atkinson and Sorenson off early,' he says coldly. 'Sit down.'

Ku reaches for Huia's hand. Papa stations himself in front of the empty fireplace with its pleated white fan in the grate. He lifts his coat-tails and surveys his daughters as if they are total strangers. Finally, he speaks. 'Your mother has told me. I cannot believe that any daughter of mine could be so underhand . . . could lower herself . . . let down her family's good name . . . Between you, you have broken your mother's heart.'

Mama kneads her hands. Ignoring Ku, she turns her fury on her elder daughter. 'I can scarcely endure looking at you,' she hisses. 'Conniving at your sister's ruin behind my back.'

'But, Mama,' cries Ku, 'that's not fair! Huia . . .'

'Be quiet!' snaps Rosalba. '*You*'ve caused quite enough trouble already.'

Ku, gets up and, sobbing, stumbles from the room. Huia, rising to follow her, is checked by her father. 'I want a serious talk with you, Huia.'

She sits down again.

'Whatever you may believe, this is going to reflect on all of us. The gossip and finger-pointing are not going to stop at Kotuku. The whole family will be implicated. Are you aware of that?'

'But Papa . . .'

'Don't interrupt. If this is to be hushed up, we must keep cool heads. The first thing is to be quite certain no-one else gets an inkling that something is amiss. Tomorrow, I shall take you and your sister to the station and put you on the Wellington train.'

'Wellington?'

'I've spoken to your Uncle Charles. Fortunately, Aunt Evadne is away. I have not told your uncle of Kotuku's circumstances, merely that you girls want to make a shopping trip. He is happy for you to visit for a week.' He regards her frostily. 'I forbid either of you to mention anything of this to another soul. Is that understood?'

'Yes, Papa.'

'And while you are away, we shall arrange a quiet wedding.'

Huia is aghast. 'A wedding? But, Papa, she can't marry the Orful Wrench. She doesn't want to.'

'She should have thought of that before she cheapened herself and disgraced her entire family.'

♛

'Eruera wishes me ask you to convey to Ted his good wishes,' says Te Mara, laying out his chessmen on Castle's board. 'Is he enjoying his new life in England?'

'Yes, he's fine, thanks,' says Castle abruptly, ignoring Wrench.

Te Mara is conscious of the coolness between Wrench and Castle. Formerly, their chess matches have been entertaining affairs with both men engaging in light-hearted banter, while Te Mara has been the one striving for victory for himself or his partner. Now the two of them are battling on the chessboard like deadly foes.

Since the announcement of the coming marriage of Castle's pretty little daughter and Wrench's youngest son, the atmosphere between them has been frostier than the Rimutakas in winter. And the longer this hatred lasts, thinks Te Mara, the more difficult it will be to bring about a thaw. Te Mara is aware that the forthcoming marriage will be of the Pakeha shotgun variety. Tiatia has explained this, but still he cannot understand what all the fuss is about. Two healthy young people, living next door to each other, seeing each other every day, the beckoning grass, the ripe summer weather, the come-hither glances, the rushing blood of youth: it seems to Te Mara entirely natural that things should have taken their course. Yes, the girl is hapu. But why should that be such a problem? Surely it proves that she is fertile, that she will have no difficulty producing many children. What does a month or two here or there matter as long as the baby is healthy?

♖

Smiling, Rosalba walks down the aisle of St Edmund the Martyr. How different this is from the wedding she has always imagined for Ku. It could have been, should have been, an elegant marquee affair, six bridesmaids attending on the bride, the dean officiating, the cream of society gracing the manicured lawn.

In the absence of Edward-Wilson, Rosalba is being escorted to her pew by Wilson's brother, Charles. He pats the hand she has laid on his arm. 'Chin up, old girl,' he murmurs as they pass by the assembled guests.

Rosalba notes that her sister-in-law, Evadne, has worn an unnecessarily large picture hat and veil. She considers her own new violet silk costume and its toning mauve toque with the pheasant-feather trim. Yes, she has achieved just the right balance between festivity and sobriety. She gives a slight nod and the pheasant feather dips gracefully.

Behind her sister-in-law sit two Sherrington cousins, the Frasers, the Lomaxes, the Bickfords, the Middletons, and a wealthy elderly aunt of Wilson's who has always been very fond of Ku. They are all dressed as befits the description given by Rosalba in her many conversations after the issuing of the invitations. 'A simple, country, family marriage. After all, it's less than a year since poor Orpheus lost both his grandmother and his very dear maternal uncle. Not really appropriate to insist on a lot of show under the circumstances. So unfair to his mother. Still in mourning, really. The English upper classes attach *so* much importance to good form. Most unfortunate timing for the poor children, though. No, not grand at all. Kotuku's own insistence . . . and, after all, it is her Big Day, not ours. She wants it without unnecessary show. Just like Kotuku. So modern. Yes, simply the one bridesmaid. She and her sister are very close. Well, no . . . Ethel is such a lot taller and one doesn't want the dear little bride . . . eclipsed . . . at her own wedding.'

Thelma Fraser had been rather too probing. 'Strange she should have set her cap at young Wrench. Bit of a surprise for you and Wilson, I'd have thought.'

'Surprise?' Rosalba had raised her eyebrows to her hairline, let a tiny laugh escape her. 'Not a bit, I assure you. A little bird told us some time ago, but we were sworn to absolute secrecy. And Orpheus is such a promising young man. Wilson has arranged for him to be articled to his brother in Wellington. Charles is tremendously impressed with him. Says he has a wonderful future.'

'I'm not sure,' Thelma had said, 'that I'd want Gwennie marrying into that family.'

'Oh, but you don't know them as we do. So cultured, so well-connected, so thoroughly English. And then with Orpheus going off to Wellington and Ku left behind pining . . . well, they pleaded and pleaded with us . . . what could we do but give them our blessing? And she is marrying into one of England's noblest . . .'

Rosalba and her escort have reached the end of the aisle. As Charles hands her into her seat, she glances with hatred at the Wrenches opposite. Wrench Senior is, at least, wearing tails, albeit they are shining with the greenish bloom of age and ironing, but Lavinia . . . 'Have you seen the bridegroom's mother's get-up?' she hisses to Charles.

Lavinia Wrench is clad in a black and white tea-gown with a clumsily inserted panel of black satin, and a perfectly ordinary straw hat topped with a black satin bow.

'Too embarrassing,' mutters Rosalba.

Charles leans closer. 'I shouldn't think twice about it,' he whispers. 'Quite proper she should be in mourning.'

Not for the first time, Rosalba wonders why on earth she ever turned aside Charles's overtures in favour of his older brother's. Now that Wilson has gained weight and his hair is thinning, there is little to choose between them. And life in Wellington has so many advantages.

No sooner are Rosalba and Charles seated than there is a clomping and clattering and the heavy tread of boots on the wooden floor. Briefly Rosalba closes her eyes and sees, on opening them, the bridegroom's three middle brothers hovering awkwardly between the rows of pews.

Their mother leans forward. 'In here, boys,' she says, a shade too loudly.

One youth squeezes himself in beside her and the whole line edges up to make room for the others. Surely, thinks Rosalba, it is obvious they are not all going to fit in?

The other two boys stand shuffling helplessly.

Rosalba averts her eyes.

Again, Charles comes to the rescue. He rises from his place, firmly takes the arm of the nearer Wrench and plants him in the pew behind his parents. 'Here, I think.' Then he guides the other brother in beside him and returns to his sister-in-law's side. And all done so discreetly, thinks Rosalba.

Again there is a clumping and banging. This time it is the young Wrench from his parents' pew who is rising to rejoin his brothers.

Rosalba swivels her head. The three boys have a carbolic gleam. Their identical ginger heads have had their springy curls wetted down. Their ties sport meagre knots, and the tallest one's has the underside hanging below the front. All of them have outgrown their shirt-sleeves so that their hands, protruding pink from their cuffs, dangle double-size between their knees as they shift uncomfortably on the unyielding wood.

Lavinia leans sideways across the aisle and stage-whispers to Charles, 'Twins. They can't bear to be parted.'

Charles is imperturbable. 'Quite understandable.'

Fortunate, in a way, Rosalba tells herself, that the Wrenches have not all been able to fit into one pew, since there are no other guests on their side to fill the rows behind them. Providential, too, that Orpheus's uncle's grisly demise has spared them the embarrassment of his presence.

Perseus, standing at the steps beside his youngest brother, is clad in what must be his father's better set of tails. The jacket brushes the underside of his buttocks and strains across his shoulders, restricting the freedom of his arm movements. His pearl-grey waistcoat has been lent by Wilson and, though Rosalba knows that the shoulders have had to have silk panels inserted, it is impossible for the casual observer to discern this. His hair is slicked down with water and bay rum. Rosalba can catch a faint whiff of it. As best man, Perseus will just pass.

But his sister! Red-haired Ethel is wearing a pink frock. Its V-neck satin bodice has been cut high and sits awkwardly across her chest, and the dropped waistline and gathered satin skirt with its tulle overskirt make her narrow hips look immense. On her head is a navy cloche hat – surely one of her late grandmother's cast-offs, thinks Rosalba – to the side of which is pinned an enormous, home-made pink satin rose. Poor Ku, with such a guy for a sister-in-law.

If Ethel had been a bridesmaid, Rosalba tells herself, Wilson certainly would have been required to pay out for her dress and would have made the most enormous fuss. Just as he did over Rosalba's own costume and toque and Orpheus's morning suit, top hat and shoes. Not to mention the hundred pounds a year he has had to settle on Ku.

Rosalba sighs aloud. She feels her hand grasped. 'You all right?' mouths Charles.

Rosalba flashes him a smile.

Abruptly the organist ceases his rendition of 'Jesu, Joy of Man's Desiring', sounds a single chord, then breaks into the Wedding March. The congregation rises, Ethel Wrench knocking a hymn book to the floor. The best man feels in his pocket, then confers with his brother, and Orpheus, for the first time, turns his dark head. Such a sulky expression scarcely befits a bridegroom. I only hope, Rosalba thinks, that Perseus has remembered the ring. Also paid for by Wilson.

Clinging to her father's rigid arm, Ku wanly proceeds up the aisle. What a marvellous bride she might have made for the right man, reflects her mother. She is looking palely beautiful in a short cream crêpe-de-Chine gown with two floating side-panels, a cream silk cap headdress caught low over her brow with a silk ribbon and a short, though billowing, veil. Her stomach is cunningly concealed behind an enormous trailing bouquet of lilies and musk roses. Both she and her loyal bridesmaid – who looks, thinks Rosalba, exactly like a huge pale-blue meringue – are shod in matching cream French-kid shoes. Another battle Rosalba had to fight with Wilson. When she considers the open-handedness of Charles, standing here beside her . . .

'Dearly beloved . . .' The vicar's voice cuts through Rosalba's thoughts. 'We are gathered together today in the sight of God . . .'

Ku hands her bouquet to her sister and steps forward.

And what chance now, her mother asks herself, of another marriage, a proper wedding, to offset the humiliation of this one? It is unlikely any man will ever offer for poor plain Huia.

♛

My Dear Edward-Wilson,

I hope this finds you well and studying hard to make the most of your opportunities. Here, I am pleased to say, we are all in good health and spirits. Cousin Roderick has spent three nights with us. His medical studies are progressing satisfactorily and he is enjoying life in Otago. He was en route to a friend in Fielding, Cyril Blampton. Roderick thinks you were at Claybourne together. He sends you his best wishes.

Bobby Fraser crashed his father's Ford into a tree last Thursday and sustained a concussion. The car was badly damaged, so he is lucky not to have been more seriously hurt. Your father believes that, were it not for the solidity of the Ford, Bobby would have been killed or paralysed for life. I think it has rather put Papa off the idea of allowing you a car in Cambridge, though Euclid assures him the Cambridge landscape is very flat and I dare say he knows.

In the past few weeks, Euclid has doubled that frightful collection of rubbish behind his wool-shed. It is becoming an eyesore and, sooner or later, someone from the Borough Council is going to have to do something about it. Poor Lavinia. It must be quite a trial. Though, of course, the Wrenches are a very noble *family and one of England's oldest, and, as your father is always saying, Euclid himself is a genius.*

Your little sister is married. The wedding was a very quiet one and took place last Saturday. Just family and a few close friends as they are so young. But so in love, it is quite the most romantic thing. Papa was against it at the start, but when he saw how devoted they are, he finally consented. Kotuku made a beautiful bride. She wore a cream crêpe-de-Chine frock and matching cap with short tulle veil and cream French-kid shoes and gloves. Huia was her bridesmaid and wore ice-blue satin. Also French-kid shoes and gloves.

The weather continues hot. We are considering installing a fan in the breakfast room as it becomes like a furnace in there by evening. Although it is early December, we have had very little rain and the paddocks are already much too dry. We hope the forecast wet weather will arrive next week.

Well, this must be all for now as Atkinson is waiting for me to go through tomorrow's menus with her. She is getting very forgetful and slow, but reliable help has become so hard to find and, after the business of Florence running off, I am reluctant to start training yet another servant for the benefit of someone else.

Euclid says Cambridge student life is very jolly. Wrap up well, work hard and be a credit to your family,

Your loving
Mama.

With increasing bafflement, Ted re-reads Mama's letter. Ku married! But to whom? Mama has omitted to name the bridegroom. He tries to recall any particular boy in whom Ku has shown an interest. Many boys have shown an interest in his sister but, to the best of his knowledge, none of them has ever excited any reciprocal spark in Ku.

Dearest Huia,

I have had the strangest letter from Mama. She mentions, in passing, that Ku is married. *But not* who to! *It isn't true, is it? Has there really been a wedding? I had no idea Ku even had a beau. And, if there has been a marriage, why haven't I had an invitation? I am her brother, after all . . .*

Ted snatches up his coat and scarf and stalks out of the college to FitzBillies. He examines today's window display. Here, on their white doilies, rings of chocolate log lie next to custard slices oozing yellow under their pastry covers. On the next silver plate are piled puffed-up Eccles cakes, shiny-backed chocolate éclairs and macaroon pyramids. And the cakes!

Ted breathes in the dense, warm, sweet smell of baking. He may not have been invited to his own sister's wedding, but he can, at least, enjoy a wedding breakfast.

The assistant waves her tongs.

'A macaroon, a chocolate éclair and a slice of fruit cake, please,' says Ted. 'No, that piece, there. With the glacé cherries.'

♘

'We must face the truth, Lavinia,' says Euclid, peering at the Willow Pattern plate on which are arranged the reconstructed biscuits for today's afternoon tea. 'There's a crack in this china, y'know.'

'Only a hairline fracture,' says Lavinia. 'Nothing serious, dear.'

'Great oaks from little acorns grow. We can't afford to ignore the obvious.'

Lavinia looks at him blankly.

'We must resign ourselves to the fact that Ethel is never going to marry.'

'Oh?' Lavinia's tone freezes.

'Ethel is simply not a Circe.'

'You were expecting that Ethel might ensnare shipwrecked sailors here in Castleton?'

'Don't be bally ridiculous, Lavinia. Castleton is virtually land-locked.'

Lavinia's lips have disappeared altogether. She stands up. 'May I remind you,' she says icily, as she sweeps from the room, 'that through no fault of her own, Ethel has no dowry.'

Rubbing his square-cut nails against his palms, Euclid struggles for composure. But even Zeus, Commander of the Heavens, he reminds himself, was obliged, from time to time, to suffer humiliation at the hands of an angry wife.

♛

Dearest Huia,

I still can't believe the news about Ku. The Orful Wrench! What on earth has possessed her? I have just had a horrible thought. Do you realise this marriage of Ku's makes us related *to the Wrenches? I wonder what Mama thinks of that? Though I suppose she loves the idea that his grandfather was an earl.*

Have you seen Wiki lately? And Eru of course? I wonder how they are. Let me know in your next letter.

♜

Dear Ted,

I am so sorry. Mrs BanTam is dead. I found her in the run this morning, her poor little claws all stiff and curled.

Ethel was very upset about Mrs BanTam, too, and while Sorenson was mending the fences, she and I buried her under the pepper tree at the side of the vegetable garden. I have scratched a mark on the tree trunk so you will know where her grave is when you get home.

Ku's baby is due very soon. The minute it is born, I'll write and tell you what it is.

Ethel says she can't wait to get away from Castleton herself, but, of course, she has no way of doing anything. She is very interesting and has some unusual ideas. I am glad she is my sister-in-law, even though her brothers are all a bit, well . . . odd. She hopes you are finding her scarf useful.

Eru wants to get a transfer to Wellington, to work in Lands and Survey or the Justice Department, but his grandfather will not hear of it. You are so lucky to be in England, though we all miss you very much.

Your loving
Huia.

P.S. Gwennie wants your address as she wants to write to you. She pestered me so much I had to give it to her. Sorry.

A cart rattles along the Wrenches' rutted driveway. Across its tailboard, invisible from the house, are lettered the words: Maples General Stores. It pulls up and a stout man in his early forties climbs down and tethers the horse.

Euclid, who has left his study to take tea, peers from the window. 'Who is it?'

Fear seizes Lavinia. 'I . . . I'm not sure. Shall I go?' she asks as the front doorbell is pulled.

'I'll go m'self. What on earth can the fellow want?'

'It might be better if I . . .'

But it is too late. Euclid is already striding towards the lobby.

Lavinia hears voices, then the sound of the study door opening and shutting.

Ethel has gone out with Huia Castle again. It is good for Ethel to have a friend, thinks Lavinia, especially as she has no sisters. Huia is such a nice girl and now, after all, they are sisters-in-law. Lavinia sighs. Euclid has not been the same since the wedding. He refuses to visit his son and daughter-in-law in

Wellington and, for a time, forbade her, Orpheus's own mother, even to write to the young couple.

Her reverie is interrupted by a roar of fury. From the study bursts the unmistakable sound of Euclid in a tantrum. Scuttling back to the kitchen, Lavinia busies herself with setting out the plates and cutlery for the evening meal – far too early, really, but it will take her mind off what may be happening elsewhere.

'Bloody bounder,' roars Euclid. 'Get out or I'll horsewhip you.'

Maples, pink and agitated, clutching his hat against his chest, flusters his way to the door. Catching sight of Argus, he recoils, steps back and bumps heavily into Euclid who, grabbing him by the shoulders, propels him forward again.

'I'm sure there's no need to take such offence, Mr Wrench,' stammers Maples. 'I give you my word, my intentions are entirely honourable.'

'Out,' bellows Euclid.

Lavinia can hear that he is quite beside himself with rage.

Maples makes an attempt to restore his dignity. 'If I'd of known you'd take it this way, Mr Wrench, I'd of wrote. I'm a respectable man of business. A lot of young ladies might think me something of a catch, I assure you.'

Euclid's billiard-ball eyes glare from their pockets. 'Do you know who I am, Sir?'

Maples does not answer.

'I said, do you know who I am?'

'Well, obviously, Mr Wrench.'

'I,' says Euclid, magnificent in his anger, 'am the second son of an earl. From one of the oldest families of England.'

'Well, I'm sure I . . .'

'The Wrenches of Gawminsgodden.' He fixes a terrible gaze on the grocer. 'And you, Maples, are . . . ?'

'From Hokitika, originally. But I've got Featherston connections on my mother's side.'

Lavinia sets out three reconstructed cocoa fancies on a plate and pours boiling water on the tea-leaves in Mother's

Rockingham teapot, all that remains of the set. Euclid cannot take tea from anything other than fine china. She knows it is better, at the moment, to say nothing.

'Confounded cheek.'

Lavinia pours a tawny stream of tea into his Spode cup.

'Not too strong. Bally bounder. How dare he?' He takes a sip. 'Too hot.'

Silence. Lavinia waits.

Euclid slams his fist on the table. Lavinia hastily moves the teapot to the coal-range.

'I can see how upset you are, dear,' she says, 'but, of course, if Ethel *were* to marry Maples, it would certainly solve the problem of the grocery bill.'

Euclid rises, draws himself up to his full height. 'Groceries! Provender! I should barter my only daughter to a tradesman in exchange for *commodities*?'

'Of course not, dear,' says Lavinia, 'but at least he isn't a Papist.'

♖

Ku has had a daughter, Unity, weighing an unfortunate eight pounds, ten ounces. Rosalba has already privately dubbed her the Orful Infant. Ku is so unrepentant, she thinks. A more sensitive daughter would have stayed away from Castleton for a decent interval, but Ku has brazenly returned a fortnight after the birth, and Rosalba has been obliged to accompany her in perambulating the family's mark of shame through Castleton's Friday-night shoppers. Though outwardly calm and dignified, Rosalba tells herself she will never forgive Ku for the humiliation of this huge 'premature' baby. As she smiles and nods her way along the footpath, a thought occurs to her. What if Baby Unity should take after Lavinia Wrench and metamorphose into a large, doughy child with a face like a raisin?

'Rather a pretty frock,' she says to Huia as the three of them window-shop outside Glaser's Emporium.

'Awfully drab blue,' says Ku.

Rosalba ignores her. 'What do you say, Huia?'

Huia rocks the iron pram. 'Neckline's flattering.'

'Not for anyone carrying extra weight,' says Rosalba, dissecting her younger daughter's figure with a scalpel glance. 'Very unforgiving. I hope you're going to try to get back in shape, Kotuku. A man doesn't appreciate a woman who lets herself go.'

'Mama!' says Huia.

'You're very loyal to your sister, Huia, and I dare say that's the modern excuse, but I had my figure back within two weeks of each of *my* confinements, I'm happy to say.'

Ku has fallen from favour. Rosalba has decided that a plain daughter at home has her uses.

'Go on,' says Huia, alone with Ku in her bedroom, 'tell me. What's it like?'

'Being married?'

'Yes. And . . . you know . . .'

'Having a baby,' says Ku, 'is agony. Unspeakable. I'm never, ever going through it again.'

'But if you and Orpheus . . . I mean you're bound to have another if you're . . . doing it.'

'There are things,' says Ku, 'that a man can use to stop a woman getting pregnant.'

'But what's – you know – really like?'

'Disgusting,' says Ku. 'So messy. And I hate Orful. But living in Wellington is utter bliss. I'm never in my life coming back to a dump like Castleton.'

'Oh,' says Huia, turning away so that Ku cannot see how hurt she feels.

♛

I hope you and the girls are all well. The weather is warming up and yesterday a group of us went punting on the Cam. A couple of the chaps brought their sisters along and I have been invited to a tea-dance by one of the girls . . . I hope it comes off, but one can never tell.

Odd thing about the English. They certainly aren't like us. I now have a tutor and he invited me to 'drop in sometime for a sherry', if I was passing, so I thought I'd better take him up on it, just to be civil. But when I knocked on his door and was finally admitted, he seemed stunned to see me. I don't know whether I interrupted him at a crucial moment or something. He seemed to think I wanted help with my work. No sherry on offer at all.

How is everyone over there? I often think of you all. What news of Eru – and Wiki? What are they up to now, I wonder?

My studies are continuing well . . .

♔

'Unity's a lamb,' says Ethel. 'I wonder what she'll grow into. She looks so young and so old at the same time.'

'Babies often look old,' says Huia. 'I think it's because they're bald.'

'It's funny about being born and dying,' says Ethel. 'You have to keep on getting older, no matter what you do. And whatever you do, you end up having to die. Whenever I walk across the churchyard, I can't help thinking about those bodies under the ground who were all people once.'

'Ethel! That's horrible.'

'But it's what makes things interesting. You think you're looking at one thing, then underneath there's something quite different.'

'What about ghosts?'

'I don't believe in ghosts. It's only the bones that are left, nothing else.' She looks around them. 'I expect every place has some old bones buried somewhere.'

'Don't say that. I hate the idea that we're sitting on top of . . . on top of . . .'

'Not here,' says Ethel hastily. 'Here there'd only be moa bones. Or maybe nothing at all.' She makes a determined effort to change the subject. 'Is . . . does Ted . . . like Cambridge?'

♛

. . . I went to the pictures with a few of the chaps yesterday, then to the pub afterwards. I must say, I am getting to like it here and finding the work really interesting.

I looked up the photograph of Grandfather's graduation year. He looks a lot like Father. Did you know he was a rowing Blue? I'll never be able to live up to that, though I've done a bit of punting on the Cam.

Do you think you might see your way to stumping up something for a set of wheels, Father? Nothing grand, but it would be a help to be a bit more mobile. I have a decent bike, but it does get a bit cold and wet and, of course, I can't expect a girl to want to go out for the evening on a bicycle bar!

♜

Huia has just gone into her bedroom when she hears a noise outside. Glancing at the window, she screams. A face is pressed against the glass, watching her.

Instantly, the face disappears, but Huia has recognised it. Wiki.

'Why was she peeping in like that? She's done it to Mama, too.'

'I know.' Eru sighs. 'Your father told Koro and he asked Auntie to have a word with her.'

'But what does she want?'

'I don't know,' says Eru slowly, 'but, I think . . . You know our Mum was Pakeha?'

'I'd forgotten that. I suppose I always think of you as Maori, not Pakeha, really. Because of your grandfather and . . .'

'Well, I think Wiki wonders what it'd be like if she lived the Pakeha side of her life, not the one at the pa. I don't think she wants to frighten you. I think she's just curious. About how it would be if our mum had taken us with her and not left us with Koro and Kuia and Auntie.'

Dearest Huia,

It is snowing a bit here, but I have a fire in my room and have been toasting muffins.

This place is certainly different from Castleton. And I must say that, even though our new 'relative', Mr Wrench, is a complete misfit at home, over here he would fit in perfectly. You wouldn't believe how many chaps like him there are, spouting in Greek and Latin at the drop of a hat. A lot of them are dons, of course, but there are loads of other fellows so completely wrapped up in their subjects they're incapable of talking about anything else. Some chap next to me in the refectory the other night droned on for the entire meal about molluscs. If Mr Wrench had been there, I can tell you, I'd have welcomed his batty ramblings by comparison.

I've arranged to meet Daphne later. Daph's not 'up', but her brother, Gil Manners, is on my staircase. I've had lunch at his parents' place in Suffolk a couple of times.

'I think,' says Rosalba, handing Wilson *The Dominion*, 'I should order this for Ku to use when she's here with us.'

'But we already have a perambulator.'

'The children's old one. I'd've thought you'd want to see your granddaughter in something modern.'

'Rosalba, we're in a slump. The roads are full of men without jobs working for nearly nothing. Money's short everywhere. Half my bills aren't being paid because people have nothing to pay them with. I'm having trouble keeping Ted at Cambridge, not to mention paying out for Ku. We simply cannot afford anything that's not essential.'

'Of course it's essential that Unity shouldn't be seen out in her mother's old perambulator. What are people going to think?'

'If they think anything at all, undoubtedly it will be that –

like everyone else right now – we have the good sense to make a few economies. I forbid you to buy it, is that understood?'

'There are times, Wilson,' says Rosalba, 'when I despair of your provincial attitudes.'

♙

'I've made up my mind,' says Huia.

'But what will your mother say?'

'I don't know but I'm sick of looking so . . . old-fashioned, and once it's done, it'll be too late for her to say I can't.'

Ethel glances at her. Lately, Huia has been . . . different. Still friendly, but somehow defiant. It must be because, being the only one at home, she is the sole target of Mrs Castle's displeasure.

'So, will you?'

'Come with you? Yes, as long as you're sure. I'm not getting mine done, though. Pater would kill me. And anyway, I haven't got any money.'

♕

Last weekend, a party of us went to Gil and Daph's parents' country house in Suffolk. Rather grand with a butler and housekeeper and, after dinner, the ladies 'retired', leaving the gentlemen to their port and cigars. Gil's father is something in the City and a very decent type. He told me that, as a young man, his own father spent several years on a sheep-station in Australia. He seemed to think Australia and NZ were almost next door, which, if you are miles away over here, I suppose, in a way, they are . . .

♘

Ethel slowly unties the scarf Huia has lent her. For the first time in her life she is conscious of her own ears. The air in the dairy feels cold on her neck.

'Ethel!' shrieks her mother. 'What's happened to you?'

The chill seems to have descended to Ethel's stomach. 'The

barber. In Castleton. I think . . . Huia and the barber thought . . . it suits me. It's called an Eton crop.'

If all five of her brothers were at table, thinks Ethel, she might have hidden herself among them, but now the twins have gone down to Takaka to farm and only Perse and Lysander are at home, Pater's eye is certain to fall on her. She stares at her plate, waiting for him to come in.

'It doesn't stick out,' whispers Perse. 'Not the way it did when there was more of it.'

'Bit like a boy, though,' hisses Lysander. 'Look out, here he comes.'

Euclid, striding into the dining room with Lavinia fluttering behind him, stops in the doorway, gapes at Ethel, closes his eyes, shakes his head, then gawps at her again. 'Ethel?'

'Yes, Pater.'

'What the deuce is the meanin' of this . . . this mutilation?' His voice is rising.

'I . . . I had my hair cut, Pater.'

Euclid's eyes bulge. 'With Mater's permission?'

'No, Pater.'

'Or mine?'

Ethel is silent.

'*Or mine*?'

'No, Pater.'

'So you took it upon y'self to gallivant into Castleton and allow some razor-wieldin' fool to denude you of a woman's crownin' glory?'

'It's the latest style. All the girls are having it done.'

'The latest style,' roars Euclid. 'And if *all these girls* decided to have their bally heads cut off . . .'

'It does look . . . tidy, Euclid,' puts in Lavinia. 'And you *are* always complaining about how . . . wild her hair is – was . . .'

Euclid rounds on her. 'Statin' a fact, Lavinia, is *not* complainin'. And I most certainly never intended she should disfigure herself by havin' her head shaved like some bally convict . . .'

'Oh, Euclid, of course, she doesn't look like a convict.'

Euclid thumps the table with his fist. '. . . or madwoman out of Bedlam.'

Tears blur in Ethel's eyes.

'And where did you find the funds to pay this quack?'

'I didn't have to pay, Pater. I didn't even mean to get my hair cut at all. But Huia had hers done and it looked so nice, and the barber said . . . he'd do it for nothing if he could have my hair.'

'Am I to understand a daughter of mine bartered her hair? With a *barber*?'

'Not barter. More of an . . . exchange. And he didn't take all of it. I've still got some left. He gave it to me in a parcel.'

'Thought you might re-attach it at home, perhaps?'

Something inside Ethel begins to unfold. She blinks away her tears, slowly stands up and, to her own surprise, glowers back. 'I'm twenty-one, Pater. I can do as I like. I'm of age.'

'You're under my roof. You'll do as I tell you.'

'No, Pater. It was *my* hair and *I* decided to have it cut. And it's done now, so there's nothing you or anyone can do about it.' She stands up. 'Excuse me, Mater. I'm not hungry.' In the doorway she pauses and looks directly at her father. 'At least, now, you can't say I look like the Medusa.'

'Pater's sorry, you know, Ethel. It was just the shock when he wasn't expecting it. But it's hard for him to . . . to apologise.'

'He doesn't need to apologise.'

'I think . . . he'd appreciate a lock, if you have one. For a keepsake.'

'I'm sorry, Mater, but if he wants one, he'll have to ask me himself.'

♖

Wilson reads aloud:

I have been assigned a new tutor and I can't believe my luck. It is Dr Breville *who was a student of the great Plucknett. I'm sure you know P. is one of the finest legal historians of all time. Dr Breville has chosen our subjects for individual study and has assigned me the Mortmain Statutes.*

'Mortmain?' interrupts Rosalba. 'What on earth's that?'

'Well, literally, it means "dead hand" but what Ted's referring to is a sort of early trust law. Ownership of land by the Church.'

'I don't see what the Church has to do with dead hands. It sounds more like something criminal.'

Wilson laughs. 'It just means ownership in perpetuity. Because the Church never died, it was seen as an immortal institution and could cling to all its property with a dead hand that was out of the control of the state's taxation system. A sort of early form of tax evasion, if you like. We've never actually had it here. Maori land's covered by the Treaty.' He returns to the letter:

I thought they would be very dry and boring, but I am finding the research really interesting and was congratulated by Dr Breville on my first presentation to our tutorial group.

'I must say it doesn't sound terribly exciting,' says Rosalba.

My next paper is to be on Edward I's Mortmain Statute of 1279, so I shall be spending a lot of time in the library.

'I don't see why he has to study things that are going to be of no earthly use to him.'

'Legal history's the cornerstone of the law,' says Wilson. 'Now, where was I? Ah . . .

Dr Breville says Plucknett knew F.W. Maitland, so you see how historic this place is, though lectures vary a lot depending on who is delivering them. You would enjoy the legal arguments, I know. Do ask Uncle Charles if he's heard of Dr Breville. Of course, he will know of Plucknett.

My love to Mama and the girls.

‘He’s really settled in well this second year,’ says Wilson. ‘Wish I’d had his chances.’

Rosalba smiles at him. ‘I’ve just had a perfectly marvellous idea. Why don’t we all take a trip to England at Christmas to visit Edward-Wilson?’

‘Don’t be idiotic, Rose. I told you, it’s hard enough at the moment for me even to find the funds to keep Ted there.’

♛

‘You’re late,’ says Eru. ‘I thought you weren’t coming.’

Huia sits down beside him. ‘It was Mama. She had a thousand reasons for needing me at home. Just let me get my breath. I’ve run most of the way.’

‘Maybe we should find somewhere closer to meet?’

‘Too dangerous. Someone would be bound to see us.’

‘That’s the whole trouble with Castleton,’ says Eru angrily. ‘You can’t do anything without everyone knowing.’

‘We seem to be managing all right.’

‘But we aren’t really, are we?’

‘Have you spoken to your grandfather again?’

Eru shrugs. ‘He won’t hear of it. Auntie’s fine, but Kuia and Koro don’t understand why I need to get away.’

‘But you’ve been offered a transfer to Wellington, and the way things are now . . . I mean, there are so many people out of work . . .’

‘That’s not how Koro sees it. “*One day, when I have passed on, you will be chief here. Why do you need to go off? It was good enough for me, for my father before me . . .*” You know the kind of thing.’

‘So what will you do?’

‘I’m going. It’s not as if it’s so far off. Not like Ted in England.’

‘He loves it over there. He’s doing really well with his law studies and he’s got a girlfriend, now. Daphne, she’s called.’

‘He won’t come home.’

'I don't think so, either. But Papa can't really afford to keep him there much longer. Or that's what Mama says.'

'Perhaps that's just a way of getting him to come back.' Eru runs his hand across Huia's head. 'I like it now I'm used to it.'

Huia smiles at him. 'It took a while, though, didn't it?'

'Maybe I'm more like Koro than I think.'

♛

Ted links his arm through Daphne's.

'Look at those great black birds screeching over there,' she says, snuggling against him. 'So noisy.'

'Rooks,' says Ted. 'Ripping up a sparrow's nest by the look of it.'

'Poor sparrow.' She glances at him. 'You're so clever. I can never tell one bird from another.'

Ted tries to look unmoved by the compliment. 'We have them at home. They're always attacking the walnut crop.'

'But we don't have a walnut tree.'

'Probably why they're going for the sparrow's eggs. They're terrible thieves. Intelligent, too.'

They walk on in a silence broken only by hoarse cawing. Ted can feel the warmth of Daphne's body beside him. What a terrific girl she is. All that dark curly hair and creamy skin – and such a soft, sweet nature like . . . like a chocolate éclair. Shall he say that to her? Better not. Not yet, anyway.

'Daddy wondered if you're going to go back.'

'To New Zealand? I couldn't possibly. Not now. Not since I've . . .' He hesitates. 'It's strange, really. Before I left, I didn't want to come here at all. I was all for going to Varsity over there. But now, I . . .'

Ted considers how petty and restricted life at Castleton seems. How free things are here. How unfettered. The exhilaration of studying, being singled out for – well, praise, really – by his tutor. And all his new friends. How well he fits in here. And then, there's Daph . . . What a cut above all the other girls he's ever known.

'But what about your family? And your father? Won't he want you to go back to the practice?'

'I'll go back for a visit, of course,' says Ted, 'but, since I've been here, I . . .'

Daphne smiles up at him. 'You're so adorable, Teddy.'

She likes me, thinks Ted, gathering up his books. He lets himself remember the feel of Daph's body against his, the way she looked at him when he told her about the rooks – plundering pests that they are, but how impressed she was by his knowledge . . . Suddenly, he has an image of his father sitting at the Pembroke table with Mr Wrench and Eru's grandfather. And hears again the old chief's voice, 'I have your rook, Castle.' And Wrench saying, with his odd braying laugh, 'A castle from a Castle. Very fittin'.' Rook. Castle. Why has it never occurred to him before? If ever I get a coat of arms, like Daph's father's, he tells himself, I'll have a large black bird atop a white castle. Very fitting.

He has arrived at the college library.

'How do, Castle?' says Ferguson, the tall, ginger Scot who shares tutorials with him. 'Coming to the pub tonight? Bunch of the chaps are heading off after Hall.'

'I'll be there.'

♖

Wilson skirts the gravestones in Thorndon cemetery. Passing several angels, an urn and a monumental stone anchor, he arrives at his destination: '*Sarah, beloved wife*' and her eight children, all buried in the same month of 1919. Spanish 'flu, no doubt, thinks Wilson, covertly scanning the undergrowth. No, not here today, and he could have sworn . . . Wait, over there . . . Wilson's heart beats faster as the familiar figure slips discreetly in his direction.

The moon is whitening the tombstones. Still pressed against the slight young body, Wilson feels in his pocket, takes out a note and slides it into the open palm. Two knowing brown eyes turn towards him. For a moment, in the reflected light, it seems as if . . .

'You want to see us again?'

'I'll be back in three weeks. Wednesday. Remember.'

'I'll be here, too.' A giggle. 'Unless something better comes along.'

The wind is howling, rattling at the Ford and almost blowing it off the road. As the car climbs up towards the summit, Wilson thinks with loathing of yesterday's encounter. Why the devil does he do it? Next time, he must go to a hotel, rent a room. But then, what if he is recognised? What if someone has already seen him? I'll fight it, he tells himself. I won't chance my luck like that again. Seeing them more than once is always dangerous. And, this time, he felt . . . What was it exactly he had felt? A kind of love. A rush of recognition? How could he ever have thought there was any resemblance . . .? 'No,' he shouts into the wind. He has Rosalba, the family, the firm. He is one of the most respected men in Castleton. He must not jeopardise all this for a sordid fumble with a trollop.

It is only eleven in the morning, but, from the west, darkness is bearing down as if it were night. The eerie golden light makes black silhouettes of the macrocarpas. Euclid hears a distant burst of thunder. He reaches for another metal dowel and places it delicately against the pyramid of its fellows.

Last night, unable to sleep, he had sought out Plotinus. And then the hand of Destiny had led him back to his bookshelf where, abstractedly pulling down Lully's *Clavicula*, he had chanced upon his missing element.

Vinegar, salt, wine, sulphur, sal ammoniac, he has used abundantly in a multiplicity of proportions, with utter lack of success. But now, suddenly, he has found his Little Key. Nitric acid. *Nitric acid*, a dissolver of base metals. Euclid has noted today's date in his journal: the third of January, nineteen hundred and thirty-one, a day that will change the world for ever. Even the configuration of numbers is propitious. Three, one, one, nine, three, one.

This morning, he visited the chemist. His new flask of nitric acid is waiting with his other ingredients in the shed. By this time tomorrow he will be vindicated: the Wrench name will be enshrined in history.

The sky is dense with black clouds, the air thick and sultry. In the distance, a growl echoes across the plains and the ground trembles below the pyramid of brass and iron rods. The heavens glow around him; there is another crash as the thunder cracks and rolls and the storm raves across the sky in a fury of sound and light. Euclid smiles. Zeus, the Thunderer, is juggling his lightning forks, tossing them left, right, up, down, in his own wild magic-lantern show.

For almost an hour, the storm rages. Then, it begins to abate. Fat single raindrops chill on Euclid's head, lengthen into rapid spurting shafts, and expand into a drenching downpour that soaks the dusty ground.

As rapidly as it came, the downpour stops. Light struggles through the clouds to form rainbows arching from east to west: the puddles begin to steam. And, as the sun bursts forth again, it reveals in the newly fresh air the body of Euclid Wrench flung across his cast-iron pyramid, his blackened right hand fused to his flask of nitric acid.

WRENCH. The Hon. Edgar Peregrine (Euclid Pythagoras) M.A. Cantab. (Hons).

Suddenly, at his residence, Katharevousa House, Castleton, on January 3rd 1931. Younger son of the late Horace, 14th Earl of Gawminsgodden, Gawminsgodden Manor, Shropshire, and his wife,

Mabel, brother to Archibald and Horatia (deceased). Husband of Lavinia, father to Perseus, Hector, Hercules, Lysander, Ethel and Orpheus Ulysses, grandfather to Unity, man of letters, scholar and chymist.

Mors illi ultra non dominabitur.

Poor Lavinia has been greatly exercised by the matters of both the funeral and the public notice. In Euclid's top right-hand study drawer, she and Perse, rummaging nervously, each fearing the shade of Euclid might at any moment materialise and order them out of his private domain, have discovered their patriarch's last will and testament and a small bundle marked: *In the Event of my Death*.

Lavinia has not dared open it. It has fallen to Perseus and Ethel to reveal the contents: a neatly written manuscript with instructions that it be sent to *The Journal of the Polynesian Society* for posthumous publication; a further manuscript, dense and full of unintelligible formulae and numbers, also for publication, but destined for the Royal Society of Chemists in London; and two notices of death, one in Latin for *The Times* and the English one for *The Castleton Courier* (to be copied, also, to *The Dominion* in Wellington); but nowhere a mention of money. And how, Lavinia asks herself, is one to keep faith with dear Euclid – here she begins to weep again – without money?

And what of the funeral? Death is a costly business. She cannot permit the economy of burying him on the property, but how is she to afford the obsequies appropriate to the scion of one of England's oldest and noblest families? If she were to appeal to Euclid's brother, Archibald, in far-off England, and even were he to agree, how long might Euclid's body have to lie awaiting the funds to commit it to the earth?

Ethel ushers in Te Mara and his grandson, Eruera. Te Mara presses his nose first against Lavinia's, then Ethel's, and, weeping, insists that Wrench must lie in state on the marae outside the meeting house in honour of their long and honoured friendship, and that the tangi, the funeral, must be held at the pa.

Unsure how Euclid would have viewed a Maori funeral, grieving and flustered by the necessity of decision, Lavinia has clung to Perseus, who – having the barest of recollections of Grandpater's ancestral home, but a much stronger grasp of the cost of a funeral – has reminded her of the pater's monograph, *The Maori – Sons of China?* What could be more fitting for a scholar than an anthropological burial?

And somehow, despite the furious protestations of Orpheus, arriving, too late, from Wellington, Euclid's remains have been transported to Te Mara's settlement, and here she is, Lavinia Wrench, née Younghusband, formerly of Northamptonshire, England – sitting on the ground in New Zealand beside Te Mara's wife, Tiatia, hearing herself lowing with grief, like Europa when her last bobby calf was taken away. And fearing, furthermore, that she has done wrong to her late husband. For the death notice, so carefully crafted by Euclid with spaces at appropriate places for the insertion only of dates and times, has been amended. And it is she, Lavinia, who has made the changes:

> *The remains will lie in state at the Tungawharoa Marae before interment by his relict and children at the Cemetery of St Edmund the Martyr on 6th January at 2.30 p.m.*

Lavinia contemplates the generosity of Wilson Castle who has offered, insisted really, that he be allowed the privilege of dealing with the insertion of the notices in *The Times* and *The Dominion*. What kindness people have shown, thinks Lavinia, since . . . since Ethel went out to see why Pater had not come in to luncheon, and found . . . An old Maori woman behind her lets forth a howl of grief and Lavinia gives way to another torrent of moaning, rocking back and forth and allowing the other women to comfort her.

Ethel looks at Pater, lying in his open coffin, wearing his morning suit with its green sheen of mould. She has heard Te Mara saying that, while Pater is on the marae, he must never be left alone, as his bodiless spirit is still here among them. Is his spirit frowning at her cropped hair? Is he still angry with her? To appease him, she mentally conjugates *perfrigefacere,* one of the harder verbs. *Perfrigefaceo, I make to shudder*. She looks again at Pater, stern in his sarcophagus. *Perfrigefacis, you make to shudder*. She slides her hand into her pocket and, steeling herself, approaches the coffin where, unnoticed by Mater or her brothers, her eyes averted from Pater's face, she slips a lock of her red hair under the left lapel of his frock-coat, the nearest she can reach to his heart.

The living Wrenches stand awkwardly grouped around the coffin of their late patriarch. At one side of the grassy marae in front of the meeting house, come to pay their last respects and looking even more awkward than the bereaved, wait Wilson, Rosalba and Huia Castle, the chemist, and a reporter from *The Castleton Courier*. Te Mara, in his best black suit, stands on the meeting-house verandah just in front of the doorway, leaning on an ornately carved walking stick.

'Te Mara looks very distinguished, I must say,' murmurs Wilson to Rosalba.

'Why is he using a stick? He can walk perfectly well,' whispers Rosalba.

The chemist leans across conspiratorially, fixing his eyes just a little too long on Rosalba's bosom, encased in expensive dark-grey silk. 'Ceremonial. Takes the place of a spear.'

Rosalba returns a frosty stare. 'I wish we hadn't come,' she mutters to Wilson. 'One might have thought that a member of the English aristocracy would at least have wanted a Christian burial.'

'It *will* be a Christian burial,' whispers Wilson. He glances at the coffin. 'Good Lord,' he hisses to the chemist, 'the casket's open. I can see Wrench's face.'

'Coffin's always open at a Maori tangi,' whispers the chemist. 'Tradition. Warn your wife. She'll be expected to touch the body in farewell, too. We all will.'

The tangi is over. Ethel watches as her father's five sons and Mr Castle shoulder the now-closed casket and bear it to the waiting hearse for conveyance to the cemetery of St Edmund the Martyr.

Rosalba appears with Ku beside her. Ku is wearing a stylish black costume and a small veiled black hat tilted to one side of her upswept hair. Her pencil-thin eyebrows have been skilfully darkened, her cheeks are rouged, and her scarlet lips are set in a pout.

'We're looking for Huia,' says Ku. 'Have you seen her?'

Ethel knows exactly where Huia is and who is with her, but she shakes her head. I shan't breathe a word, she thinks. I shall be as mute as Philomel. At the thought of poor Philomel, Ethel waggles her tongue and sticks it out to make sure it is still there.

Rosalba and Ku walk on. 'Did you *see* what Ethel was doing?' snorts Rosalba. 'Hanging her tongue half out of her mouth like that. Two days with the Maoris and already the stupid girl is aping everything they do. Next thing we know, she'll be marrying one.'

♛

Te Mara, walking heavily along Castle's path, finds he is cocking an ear in the direction of Wrench's house. Even the screeching of Galli-Curci would lift his heart, but the early evening air is silent.

Castle opens the door. 'Evening,' he says, without enthusiasm. 'Brought your chessmen?'

Te Mara nods.

'Thought you did a very fine send-off,' says Castle awkwardly. 'Just what Wrench would have wanted.'

'A noble gentleman.'

'Tea?'

'A kind offer, but no, thank you.'

Te Mara has aged, thinks Wilson. He looks tired. Despondent, even. Aloud he says with forced heartiness, 'Well, better get on and set up the board, I suppose. May the best man win.'

'I fear,' says Te Mara, 'that the best man is with the Martyr St Edmund.'

♟

Wiki lolls against a tree, scornfully watching the other girls. Kereru, coming out in her house-dress and apron, seizes a passing small boy. 'Wiremu, tell Wiki her auntie wants her, please.'

She watches Wiki saunter towards her.

'You and I need to have a serious talk, Wikitoria.'

'I'm busy.'

'It'll have to wait,' says her aunt. 'Sit down here. I got something to say you need to be sitting down to hear.'

'I hope it's not going to take long.'

'It'll take the time it takes.'

Wiki flounces to the old sofa and slams herself into one corner of it.

'I think you know what Koro and Kuia and I feel about how you've been behaving lately.'

Wiki raises her eyebrows and shrugs.

'The way you're going on, anyone would think you were some silly baby, not a fully grown woman. It's about time you started to make something of your life. Look at Eru.'

'Oh, look at Eru,' mimics Wiki. 'He's your favourite all right. Mr Good Boy, Can't Do Any Wrong.'

'Well, I don't see *you* trying to be a help and a credit to Koro and Kuia. No-one would guess you're a chief's granddaughter.'

'I didn't ask to be a chief's granddaughter. I didn't ask to be born. Maybe Koro should have let me go off with my Pakeha mum and not kept me here.'

Kereru flushes a dull red. 'Maybe it's time,' she says, 'you knew a bit more about your mum.'

'I know about her already.'

'Stop interrupting, Wikitoria.'

Wiki sighs loudly.

'Your dad was my only brother.'

Wiki opens her mouth, then shuts it again.

'Before the war, he went down to Wellington to work and he met Vera, your mum. One thing led to another and next thing you were on the way, so they married.'

'I know all that.'

'And then, things got a bit . . . difficult . . . between them, and your mother was unhappy. So she went back to her own Pakeha family.'

'To show me off?'

Kereru hesitates. 'No. She went by herself. She left you with Manu, your dad, and he brought you here for Kuia and me to look after. Then, a month or so later, Vera went back to your dad. Said she missed him and they ought to try again. Eru was born about a year after.' Kereru pauses. 'And . . . then . . . she and your dad had a disagreement.'

'What about?'

For some time, Kereru doesn't reply. Then she says, slowly, 'Over some . . . friends . . . he'd made. And, by this time, the war had started and your dad felt he ought to go and fight for his country, but Vera didn't want him to go.'

Wiki is sitting completely still.

'So when he came home one day and told her he'd enlisted, they had a terrible row. Your mum said . . . she wouldn't . . . she couldn't look after the two of you on her own, without a husband. So your dad brought her here to the pa, to us. And he went off.'

Kereru has tears in her eyes. 'And eight months later, Koro got the telegram. Your dad had been killed – in action.'

'Saving his friend's life. Koro's told us.'

Kereru wipes her eyes on her apron. 'And Vera . . . packed up her things, told Koro she was going to change her name, build herself a new life with her own people, and she was leaving you two with us. For good.'

Wiki is staring into space, but Kereru can almost hear her listening.

'Vera said . . . she said . . .'

'*You* weren't there. How do *you* know what my mum said?'

Kereru's voice sharpens. 'I most certainly *was* there. I remember your kuia weeping.' She fights her own tears. 'Vera said . . . she didn't want you two kuri-dogs to ruin her life.' Now, Kereru is crying. '"Stay here," Kuia told her. "Stay here with your babies. You have lost someone you love. We have all lost someone we love." And Vera looked at Kuia and said, "If you mean Manu, I don't love him any more. How could I?"'

Wiki stares stonily at her aunt. 'You're lying,' she says through stiff lips. 'You're making it up.'

Kereru shakes her head.

''Course my mum loved my dad.' Wiki's voice rises. 'He was a war hero. He got the Military Medal. Koro said. Everyone knows that.'

'Listen to me, Wikitoria. There's no Military Medal in that waka huia box.'

'There is.'

'If you don't believe me, go and look.'

'It's tapu.'

'It's *empty*. There never has been a medal in there.'

'Where is it then?'

'It's nowhere. Your dad never won any medal, ever.'

'You mean . . . Koro lied to us?'

'Not lied, exactly. Just tried to make it easier for you. To spare you a bit, eh.'

'Then Koro's a liar. And a cheat.'

Furiously, Kereru heaves her great bulk to her feet. 'Don't ever let me hear you speak of your koro in that way. He did what he did to protect you, not to harm you. Grow a bit of sense, girl.'

'I hate you,' cries Wiki. 'I hate you. I'm going to find my mother. And when I do, she'll tell me you're just a . . . a . . . no-good kuri-dog yourself.'

♛

This afternoon I had a tutorial and Dr Breville, our tutor, was handing back our papers when, in front of Ferguson, he said to me, 'First-class legal mind in that head of yours, Castle.' I was pretty chuffed, I can tell you. I've asked Daphne out tonight to celebrate . . .

The pawn shop in the alley behind Christ's College has a pair of field glasses in the window. Just the thing for bird-watching with Daph. For more than a fortnight Ted has told himself not to be idiotic. What would Father say about such extravagant, such unnecessary, expenditure? But Father isn't here. He is 12,000 miles away. And this is not Castleton. There is no-one here to note and report Ted's every doing. I can act as I please, he tells himself. Exhilaration propels him through the shop doorway. He points at the field glasses. I'm free, he thinks exultantly.

♛

Eru is on the path by the river bank when he sees Auntie Kereru waddling towards him on her swollen feet, flailing her arms to attract his attention.

'What is it, Auntie?'

'Thank goodness you're back!'

'It's not Koro or . . .'

She shakes her head. 'It's that sister of yours. She's vanished. No-one's seen her all day.'

'Maybe she's in town.'

'It's getting dark.'

'Don't worry, Auntie. She often comes back in the evening, eh?'

'Something's wrong, Eruera.' Auntie puts a hand over her heart. 'I can feel it. Here. You said yourself yesterday how quiet she's been lately.' She hesitates. 'Did Wikitoria say anything to you about . . . a . . . a little . . . chat we had a while back?'

Eru looks at Auntie. Would his unknown mother have been slender? Blonde? Smartly dressed? But Auntie, he reflects, *is* his mother. It is Auntie who has brought him up. Comfortable, solid, immovable Auntie has always been part of his life.

'Wiki's tough,' he says. 'Don't you worry, Auntie, she'll turn up.'

But Wikitoria does not turn up.

'Try your Nga Puhi cousins,' says Tiatia to Te Mara. 'She could have gone up North.'

'I tried them already.'

'She must be somewhere.'

'You tell me where. I've sent messages to every relative I've got, every relative you've got, all over Aotearoa, but nothing. No-one's seen her, no-one's heard from her.' Te Mara lowers his head into his hands. 'I even got young Tamahere to go and search the wharves in Wellington.' Tears fall between his fingers. 'Now these Pakeha have taken everything – my koro's land, my only son, my little kohine.'

♛

Dear Father,

I am writing with wonderful news which I hope will please you.

As I told you, I did creditably in all my exams, but most particularly in History of Laws, and my tutor, Dr Breville, whom I have mentioned before, says I have 'the makings of a fine academic lawyer'.

I have now met the great Plucknett. He came up from London to lecture on Maitland, and Dr Breville arranged for me to meet him. I was so overawed I didn't know what to say, but he mentioned that Dr Breville thought very highly of my research on the Mortmain Statutes and asked whether I had considered staying on and working up my studies into something publishable. He, too, is working on the Statutes and said he would be interested to monitor my future progress.

Dr Breville feels it would be a waste for me to return to New Zealand at this stage. Here, I have all the facilities I need to pursue my ideas.

I am of the opinion that the Mortmain Statutes should be repealed and Dr Breville wants me to make this the basis of a thesis for my doctorate. He is going to try to organise a Scholarship for me so that I can complete a Ph.D., though I shall still need some financial support from you.

Daphne's people have invited me for Christmas, but I'll be thinking of you all over there in the summer heat.

♖

Wilson runs his fingers across the smooth, comforting surface of his white bishop.

'Your mind is preoccupied?'

'I'm off my game today.'

'Aie.'

'Thing is, it's Ted.'

'Ah.'

'Doesn't want to come back here into the firm. Wants to stay on and study over there. Deuced awkward. There just aren't the . . . funds . . . to keep him at Cambridge any longer.'

'A problem.'

'That's right. And he won't listen to a word against his plans . . .'

Te Mara sighs. 'I, myself, have just such a difficulty.'

'With Eru?'

Te Mara nods. 'All he wants is Wellington, Wellington.'

'In my day,' says Wilson, 'I did as my father told me. Never would have dreamt of standing up to the old man and demanding this and that. Grateful for anything he put my way.'

'And I, too, obeyed the wishes of my father, of my grandfather.' Te Mara shakes his head. 'What is it I – we – have done wrong in their upbringing?'

'Deuced if I know.'

As Wilson is leaving, Te Mara touches his arm. 'A delicate matter. I need to speak to you.'

'If you mean the land for the Maori school, I'm still looking into it,' says Wilson quickly.

'No. More serious even than that. Wikitoria has disappeared.'

'I say, I am sorry to hear that. Any idea where she's gone?'

'She is nowhere. I have even been myself to Wellington and Rotorua but there is no trace of her.'

'Oh.' Wilson sucks in his breath. Not again, he thinks. Aloud, he says, 'I hate to say this, but I think you should report it to the police.' He hesitates. 'Just as a precaution.'

'I do not want to involve the Pakeha police. Wikitoria is not a criminal.'

'No, of course not,' agrees Wilson, 'but . . .' Catching sight of Te Mara's expression, he checks himself. No point in reminding the old man of the fate of the poor little Bertram girl.

♛

Dear Father,

I was dismayed to receive your letter. Studying academic law is definitely not a waste of time and of no use to me in the future. To cite just one example, what I am researching has many applications to Maori land matters.

However, I have realised, as Dr Breville says, that I am an academic rather than a practising lawyer. I need to be in a varsity atmosphere. This is really my last chance to take the

Scholarship they are holding open for me, but I can't accept it unless I have some additional funds from you. Being offered a research position like this is a great honour, as I'm sure Uncle Charles will tell you.

Please reconsider. And reply to this as quickly as you can. I await your change of heart. This is the only chance I have. I must *take it.*

CASTLE CHRISTS COLLEGE CAMBRIDGE ENGLAND STOP IMPERATIVE YOU RETURN IMMEDIATELY AFTER YOUR FINALS STOP YOUR PASSAGE BOOKED ON SPIRIT OF THE SOUTH STOP LETTER FOLLOWS STOP FATHER

'Look, Castle, why don't I write to your father?' says Dr Breville. 'Set it down for him, explain . . .'

'He's already booked my passage, Sir.'

Dr Breville steeples his fingers. 'The point is, Castle, if you're planning a career in academic law, you certainly can't contemplate living in New Zealand for the rest of your life. I've nothing against the Colonies and they've produced some fine lawyers in their time, but I'm afraid, for *you,* it's Oxbridge or nothing. So it's up to you to make the most of what you're being offered here. Res ipsa loquitur, eh? The thing speaks for itself.'

Ted nods miserably. 'Yes, Sir. I know, but . . .'

'I advise you to stay here and carry on with your research. In four years, your father will have forgotten he ever ordered you home.'

Ted thinks of the hushed calm of the library, the smell and feel of the huge law volumes, the excitement of chasing a lead among the thousands of legal sentences, the following of a strand of thought stretching back into history, the Magna Carta, the Mortmain Statutes . . .

'It's a question of funds, Sir. They've dried up completely. And I think, perhaps, it'd be better if I went back and talked to Father, face to face. Get him to reconsider.'

'Your uncle's a silk, isn't he? Can't he put in a word for you?'

'I'll sort things out with Father and be back within six months.'

Dr Breville nods. 'But you understand *my* position, Castle. You're a good chap and I'll do my best to hold the research place open for you, but I can't give you more than, say, eight, maybe nine, months at the outside.'

'But, Teddy, we're practically engaged.'

'I know, Daph. Just give me a bit of time to get Father on side, and sort things out with them. They're so far away.'

'Mums says they're probably frightfully upset that you've got a serious English girlfriend.'

'If you'd met my mother,' says Ted, 'you'd know nothing would please her more. Will you wait for me, Daphne?'

Three

'of full age, and within the four seas and out of prison'

♚

The carved figures in the meeting-house glare at Kereru, contempt in their paua-shell eyes: the air around her hums with the condemnation of her ancestors. How terribly she is punished for her angry words to Wikitoria. Ever since Wiki left, Kereru has not slept through a single night or spent a single day without praying she might be permitted to undo the past and take back what she has said. But all her gods are deaf – the Maori gods do not hear her, and Te Ariki of the Pakeha hangs on his cross reproaching her.

Twice, she has taken a length of rope and gone to the tree by the river, but how can she end her own suffering by adding to that of her parents? No, this is the retribution the gods have exacted from her. She must live, dishonoured by the knowledge of her own cruel words, flung out in anger.

Her flesh hangs on her body, her hair is turning grey, her spirit, once so alive, has sickened and shrunk. She has driven away the child she loved.

♖

'Seen you in your car on Lambton Quay yesterday.'

Wilson leans back against *Sarah, beloved wife*. Oh, Christ, he thinks.

'Going to give us a ride home, then?'

'No.'

Briefly, the brown eyes lock with his. 'Don't seem right, really. You with a car, and all, and us with nothing.'

♔

Life is very different without Pater, thinks Ethel, as she walks down Main Street. Now, Mater seems to rely on Perse to tell her what she can and cannot do. At his suggestion, she has had the telephone installed and is planning a visit to Wellington to see Orpheus, Ku and Unity. Uncle Archibald's lawyers have provided Mater with an annual stipend and, since Mater is generous, for the first time in her life Ethel has a little money of her own.

Guiltily, expecting that at any moment Pater will materialise and chastise her, she hovers outside Glaser's shop-window, and then, breathing deeply, pushes open the glass door.

The saleswoman approaches.

'I thought,' begins Ethel as she is steered towards a rail of frocks, 'perhaps . . .'

'Teal-blue,' says the saleswoman, replacing on the rail the brown costume Ethel has picked out, 'is the new colour for spring.' She holds the dress against Ethel's faded print skirt and blouse. 'Why doesn't Madam try it on?'

'I . . .'

Ethel finds herself in a small curtained cubicle, climbing out of her own clothes, sliding into the softness of the fine woollen material. She does up the buttons on the placket and steps out into the shop.

'Perfect,' says the assistant. 'Look.' She ushers Ethel to the full-length mirror. Staring from the glass is a creature transformed. Can this really be her?

'Could have been made especially for Madam.'

'How . . . how much is it? The price, I mean.'

'One moment, please, Madam,' says the woman and disappears.

Ethel shifts uneasily. Should she pull on her own clothes and leave now, while the assistant is away? How can she be contemplating spending money on herself like this?

'Here,' says the woman, returning, 'try this one. Always classic, emerald green.'

This dress is even prettier than the first one.

'It's the cost. I mean, I wondered how much . . . ?'

'Very reasonable. Nothing like you'd pay in Wellingon. And for the two, I'm sure I could make some reduction.'

'I couldn't possibly take both.'

Clutching the string of the box, Ethel sets off home. Yes, as the saleswoman has pointed out, teal-blue is such a serviceable colour. And how kind she was to reduce the price so much. Ethel glances at her reflection in the photographer's window. She hears again the saleswoman's voice, 'With those green eyes, it's a positive sin for Madam not to take the emerald, too.'

She will just have to avoid passing Pater's study.

♖

'I wonder,' says Wilson to Te Mara, 'if you'd be kind enough to pass this on to Kereru? Just Sergeant Reilly's note of what the police have done so far. Wikitoria's still listed as a Missing Person, so they're obliged to keep working on her case.' He hesitates. 'I give you my word, Te Mara, they're doing everything they can.'

♔

'Is it very old?' Huia turns the tiara box round between her hands.

'Quite old, I think. It was Great-Grandmater's.'

'Are the stones real?'

'I shouldn't imagine so. And Mater has no idea. Of course, Pater said they were, but . . .' She shrugs. 'Poor Pater. He was always pretending.'

Huia looks at her in surprise.

'I suppose that's how he kept himself going. He said his mater kept her tiara in it, but . . .'

'Did you ever see the tiara?'

'No. It's supposed to have gone to my uncle's wife, but maybe it never existed. Pater used the box for his papers and now Mater's given it to me.'

'It's very . . . unusual . . .'

Ethel laughs. 'You're so tactful, Huia. Hideous, you mean.'

'Well, it is a bit . . . loud, I suppose.'

'It's so loud,' says Ethel, 'it's positively screaming.'

♖

That thunderstorm last night certainly churned up the roads, thinks Wilson, sliding across the front seat and climbing out of the Ford. The sides of the motor are splattered with mud right up to the door handles and the mudguards are caked and dripping with pale-brown slurry. Sluicing through puddles, he lets himself into his office.

Miss Venson is already at her desk.

'Morning,' says Wilson. 'Quite a storm, wasn't it?'

'In all my time in Castleton,' says Miss Venson, 'I've never seen the like of it.'

'Sorenson calculates three, maybe even four, inches of rain.'

'Goodness,' says Miss Venson. 'Nice for the farmers, I suppose, but Arthur and I found it very unnerving. All those lightning flashes. We kept thinking about that unfortunate neighbour of yours, didn't we, Arthur?'

At the sound of its name, the dachshund in the basket under her desk looks up.

'. . . you know, that poor Mr Wrench.'

'Yes, well . . .' says Wilson briskly. 'Sun's out now, so we'd better be getting on.'

♔

'Depressing,' says Rosalba, 'how much standards have slipped. Last time I was in Masterton the shops were so much smarter.'

'Those handkerchiefs are pretty,' says Huia. 'Pure linen and only a shilling a box.'

'Two washes and they'd be in rags.'

'Shall we look at the hats, Mama?'

'See how they're piled up any old how.' She turns. 'Oh, there's Dulcie.'

'And Betty's with her. And the baby. Do let's all have a cup of tea, Mama.'

'That was fun,' says Huia, as they drive home in the trap.

Her mother sighs. 'I find Dulcie so trying.'

'Why?'

'Terribly selfish. She barely asked me a thing about myself or Ku and Unity.'

'But you've always said you liked Dulcie. And Baby Veronica's a dear little thing.'

'That child,' says Rosalba, half-shocked, half-exultant, 'has Maori blood.'

'Don't be ridiculous, Mama.'

'I'll thank you not to call your own mother ridiculous. Let me tell you, when you get to my age, you realise how much these things matter.'

'How on earth could Veronica have mixed blood? Betty and her husband are as Pakeha as we are.'

'So you say,' says Rosalba, 'but blood will out. How much does anybody in Castleton actually *know* about Betty's husband? Who has any idea what skeletons may be hiding in his family cupboard?'

'But Veronica's as blonde as Ku.'

'Since when,' hisses Rosalba with the air of a lawyer exposing a lying witness, 'has that been a long-term indicator of anything?' She flicks the reins. 'And, anyway, I have proof. While the three of you were in the Ladies, I checked.'

'Checked?'

'Come now, Huia, don't be faux-naïve. The eye test, of course.'

'Mama, you *didn't*.'

'I've always known something about that child wasn't quite as it should be, and one look at the whites of her eyes was enough. Little Veronica has a touch of the tar-brush.'

♖

'It's Sergeant Reilly, Mr Castle,' says Miss Venson.

'Give me a couple of minutes,' says Wilson. He waits till she is safely out of the room, then hastily stuffs some papers into a filing-cabinet drawer and locks it.

'Have a seat, Reilly.' Wilson indicates a chair. 'What can I do for you?'

'It's about that girl, Mr Castle. The chief's granddaughter.'

'You've found her?'

'Could be. We've found the body of a young woman. Age and height fit.'

'Oh, Lord. Where . . .?'

'Out by the lake. She'd been done in, I'm afraid. Skull smashed on one side. Just like that poor little Bertram girl.'

Wilson puts his head in his hands. 'Oh, my God.'

'Looks as if someone killed her first, then buried her out there, but we can't be sure yet. All that rain last week washed her up.'

'Can't someone identify her from the remains?'

'Not a chance, I'd say. And frankly, Mr Castle, it's a sight you'd rather her family didn't see.'

'So what makes you think it's Wikitoria?'

'Doc says she was expecting. Those Maori girls are all a bit forward that way.'

'I say, steady on,' says Wilson.

♛

'We must have her back,' says Tiatia. 'She should be here with her own people, not lying all alone in that police mortuary.'

Though Kereru knows that Wikitoria's body has been taken

to Wellington for further tests, she has not dared tell Te Mara or Tiatia.

'They don't know for sure it's her,' says Te Mara.

'Who else could it be, eh?' sobs Kereru. Why, she asks herself for the thousandth time, did I ever tell Wiki the waka huia was empty?

Te Mara thumps his stick on the bare floor. The kuri-dog growls. 'You heard what Castle said. Ninety per cent certain. You've been to school, Kereru. Ninety per cent is not one hundred.'

Tiatia looks at him. 'You forgotten what else he said? Better to be prepared. Better it doesn't come as a shock.'

♜

'No,' says Wilson, 'we simply cannot afford a welcome-home party for Ted and that's that.'

'Not a party, as such. More a tea-party. Only forty or so. Bridge fingers and sandwiches.'

Wilson slams his fist on the kitchen table. 'No! I said. Are you deaf?'

'There's no need to be vulgar.'

♕

Ted stares out at the once-familiar landcape. How tawdry the houses look. Even Wellington, which he had once thought such a metropolis, is just a little colonial centre clinging to the sides of the harbour hills. Not a single building anywhere can match the mellow gold-grey stone of the Cambridge colleges. He conjures up a vision of them: solid, unchanged for so many hundreds of years, emanating the reassuring comfort of ancient tradition . . . Here, everywhere Ted looks are ugly, squat boxes that pass for houses, empty unpaved streets – not a cobble in sight – fringed by cheap weather-board shops, the local horses hitched to the wooden upright posts supporting the unsightly green or red corrugated-iron roofs. Some of the houses are simply sheets of the same iron bolted together to form primitive dwellings. How can he ever bring Daphne here?

Where are the quaint bow-fronted shops, the museums, the libraries . . . the cycling young men, gowns flying? How many serious conversations over good wines is he likely to enjoy in this backwater of a country? And as for Castleton itself . . . No, he can never spend the rest of his life here. Maybe, he tells himself, it's a good thing I was forced to return. At least I know this I not where I belong.

How, he wonders, does Huia stand it, day in, day out?

Opposite, coming out from the miserable little library of which Castleton is so proud, is a girl. A very attractive girl. Her shingled copper bob catches the sun as she walks away. She is wearing a green frock and . . . 'Good Lord,' says Ted, aloud, 'it's Ethel Wrench.'

'This is her,' says Ted. 'Stunning, isn't she? You'll love her, Huia. She's the greatest girl ever. Such fun. And she can't wait to meet you.'

Huia examines the photograph. 'Is that their house?'

'Yes. Quite a place.'

'Her parents must be very . . . grand.'

'Not a bit,' says Ted, suppressing the memories of how Daphne's father had intimidated him, quizzing him endlessly on the subject of fox-hunting, of how her mother had patronised him . . .

He sighs. More than anything, he longs to be back in Cambridge, in his quiet masculine rooms, sitting in his upholstered armchair, his documents spread around him, his mind deep in the thirteenth century. And then, a quick foray off to FitzBillies for a sticky Chelsea bun. 'I have to get back, Huia. I *must*. I'm starting work with Father in the office, tomorrow. How am I going to stand it?'

Huia squeezes his arm reassuringly.'You'll be fine once you get used to it.' She hesitates. 'Actually, there's something rather horrible I ought to tell you. In case you bump into Eru. It's about Wiki . . .'

Dead? Stunned, Ted thinks back to Wiki leaning over his bicycle bar; lying underneath him, her dark hair spread out on the ground, and how he . . . And not just dead. Murdered. Wiki . . .

'. . . expecting,' says Huia. 'But don't, for Heaven's sake, let on to Papa that you know. I overheard him telling Mama.'

Pregnant, thinks Ted. And I . . . No, wait. Of course, I can't possibly be the father. Not of this baby, anyway.

His shock gives way to selfish relief.

'It's awful,' says Huia. 'They haven't been able to have a funeral. Her body's still in Wellington, you see. Being . . . examined.'

♖

Wilson sees an old Maori woman walking slowly along the road. He has almost driven past her when he realises it is Kereru. My God, he thinks, this business with Wiki has aged her. Nostalgia sweeps him. He remembers her standing with her brother, Manu. So fine-looking, both of them. Almost regal. And now . . . And the poor devils have still not had the girl's body released from Wellington for burial. A nightmare, the whole thing.

He brakes. 'May I . . . give you a lift?'

Kereru's face contorts. 'You!' she spits at Wilson.

He leans across and opens the door. 'Why don't you hop in?'

Kereru remains standing. 'All this is *your* fault . . . Everything. Right from the beginning. All yours!'

Wilson is silent.

Her voice rises. 'You think I don't see through you! You think I don't know what you are?'

Wilson's eyes flick towards his briefcase, lying on the floor beside him. Is it possible that, somehow, she has got wind of . . .

Kereru is shouting now. 'Just because you are a lawyer and a Pakeha and you go around this town being such a respectable man, do you think I am so stupid that you've fooled *me*?'

'Stop it, Kereru, please.' Wilson slides across the seat and gets out of the car. 'You don't know what you're saying.'

Kereru's hair is unkempt, her cardigan grubby and torn.

Wilson goes to place his arm across her shoulders.

'Don't you touch me!' She flings off his arm and turns to confront him. 'Shall I tell you what drove Wiki away? Why she went? Because I told her . . . the truth.'

Wilson feels his face change. '*What*? How could you?'

Kereru is silent.

'*Everything*? You told her everything?'

'No, not everything.' She pauses. 'We're not all as low as you.'

♜

'It's the Wrench girl from next door,' calls Atkinson.

Rosalba steps onto the verandah. 'Huia's out with Gwennie. I've no idea when she'll be back. They're *such* great friends, I imagine they'll be nattering together all day.'

Ethel flushes. 'It's not important. I . . .'

'Well, since you're here,' says Rosalba, 'you may as well come in and have a cup of tea.'

'Oh, no, really, I couldn't, thank you. Mater will be needing me in the dairy and . . .'

'I'm sure your mother can spare you long enough for a cup of tea.'

'We won't stand on ceremony,' says Rosalba, leading Ethel into the breakfast room. 'Just an informal pot in here.'

'But Mater . . .'

'Nonsense,' says Rosalba briskly. 'I'll make the tea myself right away. And while we're drinking it, you can tell me all about your poor uncle's tragic death. I've never heard the full story. Now, do you prefer China or India?'

Ethel stares at her.

Slowness in any form infuriates Rosalba. 'Well?' she demands.

Ethel struggles to pull herself together. She musters her resources. 'Broken Orange Pekoe, thank you,' she says.

♛

'Father,' says Ted, 'I need to talk to you. Right away.'

Wilson glances up irritably from the papers on his office desk. 'I'm up to my ears, Ted. Can't it wait?'

'No,' says Ted. 'It's about my future. I have to go back to Cambridge.'

His father sighs. 'Shut the door then, and give us some privacy.' He takes off his reading glasses. 'Look, I'm really sorry about this, old chap, but going back to Cambridge is out of the question.'

Ted stares at him. 'What?'

'Impossible, I'm afraid.'

'How can you say that? You know Dr Breville's offered me a scholarship? A research place? I'm to have access to Plucknett himself. One of the greatest legal minds there's ever been. I have to take this chance. There's a hundred others waiting to snap it up if I turn it down.'

'Ask this Plunket chap to hold your slot for you. If he thinks highly enough of you, he'll do it.'

'But I . . .'

'You see, just at the moment, things are tight. Very tight. Charles thinks it'll be a few years before we're back to where we were.'

'I don't see what Uncle Charles . . .'

'There simply aren't any funds to support you while you study, scholarship or not. That's the nub of it.' He pauses. 'To be frank, Ted, I've run out of money.'

♔

'How's Ted? He must be finding everything quite strange.'

For a moment, Huia is tempted to confide in Ethel, tell her how miserable Ted really is. She decides against it. After all, as

Eru said, Ted will probably be fine in another month or two. 'He's settling back in. Hoping his girlfriend will come over for a visit before too long. Daphne, she's called. And she's so pretty. He's got her photo on his tallboy. I'll show you next time you're over.' She hesitates. 'I was wondering if . . . I could . . . ask your advice about something. Something private.'

♜

Driving out to the pa to play chess with Te Mara, Wilson passes a bizarre figure clad in a flour sack tied at the top into two rabbit ears. The chap is striding along through the steady drizzle, oblivious to anything around him. It takes Wilson a second or two to realise it is the eldest Wrench. Weird outfit, the whole bunch of them. Why on earth did Ku have to get herself mixed up with that lot? He sighs. Next month, the yearly hundred pounds he agreed to settle on her falls due again, and where the devil is he supposed to find *that* in the middle of this slump?

♛

Since Ted Castle has been back, Ethel has seen him in the distance by the boundary fence and once, in Main Street, where she managed to turn into a shop before having to come face to face with him. How stupid she has been, all the time he has been away, even to think he might . . . And Daphne, his girlfriend – Ethel recalls the girl in the photo Huia showed her. The sleek dark bob, smooth unfreckled skin, doe-eyes, the pearls at her neck. Although, muses Ethel, her expression had been a little . . . well . . . vacuous. And her mouth set in an unyielding line. Stop! she tells herself. You've never even met the poor girl. You're jealous, that's all. And for no good reason. When has Ted Castle ever shown the slightest interest in *you*?

♛

The gods are testing Te Mara again. Tiatia has had pains in her chest. They have had to take her to the hospital.

'A heart attack,' said the Pakeha doctor.

Te Mara knows that her heart has been weakened by sorrow. Now, she must stay there. In bed, in the Pakeha hospital.

He hears Eru's tread on the boards of the verandah.

'Kia ora, e-Koro,' says Eru, pressing his forehead to the old man's.

'Ah, my Eruera,' sighs Te Mara. 'You cannot leave me now. You are all I have left. It is you who must comfort me in my old age.'

♖

The phone shrills out the Castles' ring.

'Blast,' says Wilson from behind his paper. 'Take it will you, Ted? You may as well get used to night-time calls. One of the realities of the job.'

Ted comes back in slowly. 'It was Sergeant Reilly. They've just had a wire from Wellington.'

Wilson lowers the paper. 'And . . . ?'

'They've identified that girl's body. The one they thought was Wiki.' He swallows. 'Reilly says it's . . . Flossie. Our maid, Flossie McPhee.'

The paper falls from Wilson's hands.

Ted lies sleepless in bed. Every time he closes his eyes, he conjures up another image of Flossie. Flossie holding his stolen bottle with its dregs of violet scent. Challenging him. He seems to hear her voice. '*Pinch me a feather off of that boa of hers, then . . .*'

Flossie whistling her strange little tune, offering him a battered cigarette. *Didn't know I had a beau, did you?*

Flossie, lifting up her skirt, seizing his hand and . . .

Ted flings back the covers and pads down the hallway to the kitchen. There is a thin line glowing under the study door.

He pushes it open.

At his desk, Wilson starts. 'Good Lord, you made me jump. What the Hell are you doing, creeping in like that, spying on me?' He lays an arm across the wig-box in front of him.

'I'm sorry. I thought you'd gone to bed and left the light on.'

'Why the devil aren't *you* in bed? It's nearly two.'

Ted registers the glass and the half-empty whisky bottle on the desk. 'I couldn't sleep.' He picks up the glass and pours himself a slug.

The lamp's light catches the liquid in the glass as he swills it round and round. Golden, strawberry-blonde. Like Flossie's hair.

'For God's sake,' says his father, 'don't just play with it. Drink the bloody stuff.'

As Ted lies, willing himself to sleep, he suddenly hears again Flossie's pert voice. '*Your dad gave us a tanner.*' '*Your old man's a good stick. Gave us a florin yesterday.*'

'But how,' asks Rosalba, 'do they know for sure it's Florence? You said the . . . she . . . was . . .'

'Clothing would've been too far gone, as well,' Wilson sighs. 'I don't know exactly. They found a bangle round her wrist-bone, apparently. And when they searched the area, they found a locket, Reilly said. Her mother recognised the locket as Flossie's. Reilly seems pretty sure it's her.' He shakes his head. 'Miserable business.'

Huia, still seated at the breakfast table, has turned pale. 'I . . . Papa, are you sure about the bangle . . . ?'

'Sorry, old girl, it is pretty distressing.'

Huia's voice is faint. 'It's just that I . . .' She turns to her mother. 'It was an old one, Mama. Quite worthless. I didn't want it any more, and Flossie . . . she . . .'

'Are you saying it was *your* bangle? That Florence stole it?'

'No, Mama. I gave it to her. I . . .'

'*Gave* it to her? And why, precisely, would you be giving jewellery to servant girls?'

'I . . . she . . .'

Wilson puts down his cup. 'And you'd know this bangle again, if you saw it, Huia?'

'Yes, Papa.'

'You're sure?'

Huia nods.

'I'll phone Reilly as soon as I'm in the office. They'll want you to go in and identify it.'

Huia clutches at the edge of the table. 'You mean, go and . . . *look* . . . at Flossie? Oh, no, Papa, please.'

Wilson answers the after-hours' knock on his office door. 'Good of you to come.'

'Dad said that girl's body isn't Wikitoria.'

'Yes, it's very good news. I'm delighted for you. While there's life . . .'

'That's not why you wanted me to come here.'

'No. We need to . . . to finish off our other conversation. It's important, Kereru.'

'The past is the past. Talking about it now can't change anything.'

'I know. But there are things I want – I need – to explain to you . . .'

'About Manu? About you?' Her voice rises. 'About Manu's death? About what you had to do with *that*?'

'On my honour, I never saw Manu that night.'

'Look me in the eyes and swear it.'

Wilson gazes directly at Kereru. 'I give you my word.'

'If you had left Manu alone . . . If you had never ruined him, forced him, done those filthy . . .'

'Maybe you won't believe me, but I've never in my life forced myself on anyone, Manu included. It was Manu who . . .' Wilson is silent for several minutes. With an effort, he goes on. 'In Wellington, there are places where . . . men can find other men like them. One night, in one of these bars, I saw Manu. I turned to leave and *he* came after *me*. I give you my word.'

'Then you should have left Castleton; gone off to live in Wellington. You and he, both.'

'Do you think it would have made one jot of difference to me or to Manu, if we had been in Wellington and not here, in Castleton?'

'Wellington's bigger.'

'You mean,' says Wilson harshly, 'that we would have had more places to hide? No, Kereru, you have no idea. Even Wellington would have been too small. Here or there, it would have been the same. The same furtive meetings, the pretence, the fear. The same fingers pointed if anyone suspected. For God's sake, if we'd been discovered, we'd have been jailed.'

'It's filthy, disgusting. You worry about being jailed. You should worry about being damned.'

'If I'm damned, it will be for worse things than loving Manu.'

She turns her head away. 'I'm sorry. I just don't understand how you can . . . do that . . . with another man.'

'You've been in love.'

She looks at him angrily. 'What you and Manu did, that's not love.'

'It's a kind of love.'

There is a silence, then Kereru says, 'Does your wife know?'

'Good God, no.' Wilson scrutinises her face. Does she mean to tell Rosalba? No, she seems resigned, defeated even.

'Why did you marry her?'

'The same reasons Manu married Vera. To be safe. To have a family. I was young. I was attracted to Rosalba. She was so spirited and full of life. And, back then, before the babies died, she was loving. I thought perhaps marriage would cure me. Make me normal.'

'And?'

Wilson shakes his head. 'The urge is still there. All the time. It's like having something stalking you and not knowing when it might strike. And, believe me, it would have been exactly like that for Manu.' He sees that she seems less hostile. 'Tell me,' he says cautiously, 'how did you know? Manu surely didn't . . .'

'I saw you. More than once.'

'God, were we so careless?'

'No. But you went several times to the Domain, and my boyfriend and I, it's where we went, too.'

Now, Wilson can't seem to stop himself talking. 'When Manu was in camp, we managed just a few meetings. In Wellington. When he had leave. The first time I saw him, he was black and blue.' He blinks. 'Someone – several of them – had found out, somehow, that he was . . . And had told the others. Manu was beaten half-unconscious, kicked, spat at. They did things to him in the camp, terrible things. His own Maori comrades.'

He hides his face in his hands.

Kereru sighs. 'Maybe,' she says slowly, 'I should tell you what happened on the night Manu died.'

Wilson looks up. 'Please.'

'It was just before the Pioneer Battalion was to sail. Manu asked for leave from the camp to say goodbye. To ask his father's blessing. The battalion was a Maori one, so the commander knew the importance of this and he granted it. But he said Manu must go and return on the same day. Many men asked for this: it was the same for them all.'

'Yes.'

'But when night came, Manu was not back at the camp. Instead, he was at the lake. Fishing.'

Wilson says nothing.

'Do you believe he was fishing ?'

'No.'

'That is what your Pakeha coroner said. *A fishing accident.*' Kereru begins to weep. '*A brave soldier, one who enlisted, who went to say farewell to his family, to ask his father's blessing . . .*'

'Did Te Mara bless him?'

'Yes. But do you think he would have given him that blessing, if he'd known what Manu planned?'

'I . . .'

'He had his father's blessing, his mother's kiss, his wife's, he embraced his tiny children, and then, he went to his sister, his only sister, and he said to her, "Kere, I will not come back. I know it. And Vera will not stay here at the pa, so give me your oath you will love and guard my children as your own and you will be sure they never know the truth."

'And then the brave soldier took his fishing rod *and, on his way back to camp, he stopped to fish at the lake*. That's what they said in court. Just as he had done with his Pakeha friend when they were children. Only, this time, *a rainstorm came and the water rose too quickly. He fell in and was drowned.* And for three days and nights the lake held onto his body, clutched it below the water and then released it. So it was only then that we knew he was dead.'

Wilson feels the tears on his own cheeks matching hers.

'And his father, when he saw his son's body – before, so handsome, now, so ugly, swollen . . .'

'Kereru, don't!'

'The father said, "My son died a hero. A war hero. He gave himself to his country." But the sister knew that, all along, he had planned . . . that he would never leave Aotearoa.'

'I know.'

'*You* know? How can you?'

'He wrote to me. A letter of farewell. He said he couldn't bear it any longer. He couldn't face the troop-ship, the tormenting. It was torture for him. He said he would rather do away with himself than carry on. He said he would wrap the line around his body so that no-one could ever be certain . . .'

♔

'Will you come with me, Ted? Please. I can't bear the idea of having to go and look at poor Flossie's bangle.' Huia involuntarily clasps her right hand over her left wrist.

Ted has a sudden flash of the meat-safe, a butchered lamb dangling from the gambrel, its blood clotting on the earth below . . . the blowflies screaming against the wire-mesh window. 'Sorry, Huia. Much too busy. Won't Mama go with you?' He sees her expression. 'Forget I suggested that. Gwennie, maybe?'

Huia shakes her head. 'You know what a snob Gwennie is. She'd never dream of going to identify a maid's things.'

'Why not try Ethel Wrench? You and she seem very thick.'

'In here, ladies,' says Sergeant Reilly. 'All we need is for you to take a good look, Miss Castle, and see if you recognise any of the articles on that table.'

Huia approaches the table, Ethel beside her. She points to the bangle. 'Yes,' she whispers. 'That's definitely it. The one I gave to Flossie.'

The sergeant indicates a battered shoe. Huia shakes her head.

'And that one, Miss?'

Ethel starts. Huia turns to look at her and sees she has gone white.

'Anything else familiar, Miss Castle?'

'Yes,' says Huia. 'that locket. It was Flossie's, too. She said . . . it was a present.'

'Did she say who from?'

'Only that it was her sweetheart who gave it to her.'

'Must've been quite a well-off sweetheart. That's solid gold. Worth a fair bit. Or so they said in Wellington.'

'What,' says Ethel in a small voice quite unlike her own, 'happens to the jewellery after . . .'

'After the inquest, Miss? It goes to the family. Expect they could do with it, too. She's a widow, Mrs McPhee, with a large brood to feed.'

'What was the matter? You looked as if you'd seen a ghost.'

'I had. I didn't want to say with that policeman there but I'd know that locket anywhere. It was Grandmater's.'

'Your *grandmother's*? But how did Flossie . . . ?'

'I . . . I don't know. I need to think . . .'

♛

'Letter for you,' says Huia, sifting through the post. 'With an English stamp.'

Ted seizes it. 'Daphne.' He turns to Huia. 'I haven't actually told her I'm not coming back yet. I'm going to have to find a way to get the funds. Borrow from Uncle Charles, or something. No point in upsetting her for nothing.'

He opens the letter.

Huia watches his expression change. 'What's the matter?'

Silently, Ted hands her a small clipping from a newspaper.

'Oh, Ted,' she cries. 'I'm so, so sorry.'

Mama sweeps in from the breakfast room. 'Sorry about what?'

Huia glances at Ted.

He nods.

'Ted's just got this, Mama. In the post.'

'Forthcoming Marriages,' reads Rosalba, aloud. 'The engagement is announced between Captain Hugh Jamieson Ramsbottom, elder son of Major and Mrs V.M. Ramsbottom, etc . . . etc. and Daphne Violet, only daughter of Sir Walter and Lady Manners of . . .' She stops reading. 'The way your father's been lately, I shouldn't think you've a hope of attending a wedding in *Wellington*, let alone in England.' She looks again at the clipping. 'Poor bride-to-be. Ramsbottom! Not a name *I'd* care to be burdened with.'

♛ ♛

Coming out of his father's office, Ted almost cannons into Eru.

'What about a beer?'

'Good idea,' says Eru. 'My office is like an oven.'

'Huia says you're working in Lands and Survey.'

'They've offered me a transfer to the Justice Department in Wellington, but, right now, I can't leave the old people. You've heard about all this business with Wiki?'

'Yes. I'm really sorry.' Ted hesitates. 'At least the bod . . . the girl . . . they found wasn't her.'

'No. But it was pretty bad while we were waiting to hear.'

'And no-one's got any idea where she might be?'

Eru shakes his head.

A chill settles over Ted. 'Does anyone know why Wiki went? I mean . . .'

'I keep thinking that maybe she got herself into trouble.'

An awkward silence falls.

Ted slaps a shilling on the bar. 'Same again, thanks.'

It is as if all their old camaraderie has fallen away, leaving two strangers conversing politely. Odd, Ted thinks, how stilted we are together now, when once there weren't enough hours in the day for everything we wanted to do together. 'We ought to go fishing sometime,' he says.

'Why not? Good idea.'

♜

Wilson re-reads the badly written, misspelt note. He feels no surprise at its contents. His life is unravelling, the carefully fashioned existence he has created for himself and his family disintegrating further each day.

He gets up, goes into the scullery, selects a key from the bunch on the hook and heads down the hall. Unlocking the gun cupboard, he takes a small brass key from its hiding-place, then relocks the cupboard.

Back in his study, he takes another little key from his pen-and-wiper tray. He slips this into the locked bottom drawer of his desk, turns it and pulls out the drawer to its furthest extent. For a moment, he stares in at the contents, then, taking his grandfather's wig-box, he slowly unlocks it with the brass key from the gun cupboard and from among the papers lifts out an old, well-thumbed letter wrapped carefully around a photograph. He gazes at Manu's handsome face, returns the half-smile in the image.

For some minutes, Wilson struggles to make up his mind,

then he presses the photograph briefly to his face, places it back in the box, locks it and slides the brass key into his pocket. He flips the little key in the drawer lock, retrieves it and drops it back into the pen-and-wiper tray.

The rest of the family is in bed. Wilson takes a match, strikes it and, touching the flame first to the blackmail note, then to Manu's farewell letter, reduces both to white ash.

♛

The moment he gets home, Ted knows his mother is in a mood. An invisible weight presses on everything: even the kitchen door needs extra force to open it.

Mama and Huia are shelling peas in the kitchen.

Ted assumes an air of heartiness. 'Evening, Mama. Evening, Huia. Pleasant day?'

'Ted,' begins Huia, 'did you . . .'

'Pleasant day?' says Mama. 'Why must everything be "pleasant" nowadays? There was a time when weather was pleasant, journeys were pleasant. One certainly didn't have "pleasant days".' Slashing a fingernail along the edge of a fat pod, she tears it in half and rakes out the row of tender little peas. 'Such a frightful debasement of language.' She tosses the empty pod in the basin. 'It's a disease of all you young people. Slang. Coarse American expressions straight out of detective stories.'

'But, Mama,' remonstrates Huia, 'you've never read an American detective story.'

'Certainly not.'

'So . . . how can you know?'

'Are you implying your own mother is ignorant?'

'Well, I,' says Ted, breaking in, 'had a terrible day. Father was in court all morning and half the afternoon, and Miss Venson seems to have lost the entire Fisher file, lock, stock . . .'

'*And cowboys*,' crows his mother. 'More Americans. Invading every part of the English language.' She stands up, several dozen peas dropping from her lap to the floor. 'With everybody's standards slipping,' she says, 'I shouldn't be surprised if the king, himself, were to start using slang in his next Christmas Broadcast.' She brushes off her skirt. 'Was your father still at the office when you left?'

'No. He came back from court, but he went out again almost straight away. To get some papers signed, I think.'

'Where?'

'He didn't say.'

'What time do you make it now?'

Ted pulls out his watch. 'Nearly half-past seven. I'm late, I know, but because Father wasn't around, I got the full blast of Fisher's fury when I couldn't locate his file. Old Venson's really . . .'

'Do pay attention to what I'm saying. Your sister thinks your father should have been home by now.'

'He's probably playing chess at the pa.'

At half-past nine, when Wilson's dinner has congealed in the oven, Ted telephones the office. No reply. 'I'll bike into town and take a look in the diary,' he says.

Father is not in the office, nor is his car parked anywhere nearby. Now Ted himself is becoming uneasy. He flicks through the diary on Miss Venson's desk. The court appointment: that was certainly kept, but there are no others written in.

It is ten-forty by the time Ted gets home. As he walks in, the telephone begins to shrill. Two short rings, then a long one. 'Ours,' he says. 'I'll get it.'

Rosalba looks up from her chair. 'I knew he'd telephone, sooner or later.' She turns to Huia. 'I told you he'd be stuck somewhere wrestling with a flat tyre.'

They can hear Ted's voice in the hall.

'I see. Yes . . . yes. No, not to my knowledge, but . . . I will . . . yes . . . very kind.'

There is a long silence.

Huia gets up and goes into the hall. In the darkness, she can see Ted with his face pressed to the panelling.

'What's the matter?'

He turns to her. 'How can you *stand* this place?' he says harshly. 'It's like being sucked down into a swamp!'

'What *are* you talking about?'

'Go back in to Mama. She's going to need you, too. That was Sergeant Reilly. There's been an accident on Drovers' Hill. Father's dead.'

♛

Wilson Castle's motor accident is on the front page of *The Dominion*, complete with a head-and-shoulders photograph and another of the wreck of the Ford in the ravine.

Te Mara looks at Wilson smiling from the newsprint, picks up his chess set, takes his carved bone pieces and lays them in his waka huia box. 'I have had enough of this world,' he says as he closes the lid. 'I have already lived too long.'

♕

Uncle Charles lifts his valise from the trap. 'You sure you'll be able to hold the fort, old chap?'

Ted secures Kitchener's reins to the hitching post and falls in beside his uncle as they make their way along the platform. 'I . . . yes, I think so.'

'I'm concerned about your mother. She's not taking this at all well. Good thing Huia's still at home.'

'Yes.' Ted hesitates, then plunges in. 'Uncle, there's something I need . . . something you ought . . .'

'Funds, is it? Don't worry about that.' His uncle pulls out a wad of notes. 'Brought this with me to tide you over till you sort out your father's affairs. The thing they never tell you is that death's a costly business.'

'That's awfully good of you. I'll pay . . .'

'Wouldn't hear of it. My contribution. Now, what time's the train due?'

Ted pulls out his watch. 'Another ten minutes.' He hesitates. 'Uncle, it's not the money I wanted to . . . It's about Father.'

Uncle Charles puts an arm across Ted's shoulder. 'Ghastly bad luck. A finer, more decent chap never lived. Don't you worry, Ted. You'll do him credit. And remember, if you need me, I'm just a toll call away.'

Ted cracks the whip across Kitchener's rump and the trap rattles and jolts uncomfortably. Surely not? Not Father. How can Ted be so disloyal as even to consider it? To harbour such terrible thoughts. And yet . . . Again, he hears Flossie's voice. '*Your dad gave us a tanner.*' '*Your old man's a good stick. Gave us a florin yesterday.*' '*Me beau.*' And what had she said to Huia about her mystery admirer? '*Mine to know and yours to guess.*'

Should Ted drive to the police station and tell Reilly all he knows? Which is what? That his father's accident was on Drovers' Hill, that Flossie lived on Drovers' Hill? That his father occasionally gave their maid small sums of money? That an older man may have been attracted to a saucy young redhead? That Myrna Bertram was also a 'carrot-top' and that her father was a client of his father?

And suppose Ted's awful suspicions are right. What earthly good will it do for Father to be branded a . . . to be named after his . . . his suicide? A dead man can't stand trial so there would have to be an inquiry, a humiliating, long-drawn-out business, during which his father's, mother's, uncle's and sisters' names – his own name – would be dragged through the mud and splattered across the front pages of every scurrilous rag in the country. It's not as if the dead can be brought back to life. And no-one but Ted will ever be any the wiser.

Kitchener slows, until he is ambling. But I'm an officer of the court, Ted tells himself. I've been admitted to the Bar. I've sworn to uphold the law. 'Oh, bloody hell,' he shouts. 'Why couldn't I have stayed in Cambridge and avoided all this?'

♛

'Someone's knocking, Kere,' shouts Te Mara.

Shuffling slowly, she grumbles her way down the passage. 'Yes?' he hears her say as she opens the back door, then there is silence. He checks the time. Seven o'clock. Early in the morning for a visitor. He follows her out to the verandah.

Kereru and Wikitoria are standing absolutely still, their noses pressed together. Te Mara watches them inhale each other's spirit. He closes his eyes, then opens them again to be sure he has not imagined it. No, it is his Wikitoria. She has come back from the dead. He shuts his eyes again and breathes in the familiarity of his granddaughter.

There is a scrabbling on the floor beside him. Te Mara looks down and sees a brown-eyed child.

'Lana,' says Wiki, pulling away from her aunt and laying her forehead against Te Mara's. 'My girl.'

Kereru wipes her eyes with her apron, reaches down and picks up the child. 'Tena koe, e-Lana,' she says. 'Haere mai ki te kai. Come and eat.'

♛

'Gracious,' says Miss Venson, 'I don't know what this district's coming to.' She puffs up the cushion in the dog-basket beside her desk. 'No, Arthur. Naughty boy. Not on Mr Castle's chair. In your own snuggly bed.'

'Morning, Miss Venson,' says Ted. 'Sorry I'm late. Mrs Castle had another bad night.' He brushes at the dog-hairs adhering to his chair seat.

'I don't wonder.' Miss Venson checks on Arthur. 'What a thing!' She puts on her glasses: her eyes appear to gleam with refracted light. 'What was she called, again, that maid of yours?'

'Flossie.'

'Quite dreadful. And then, the late Mr Castle's terrible accident. Poor Mrs Castle. No wond . . .'

'Look, Miss Venson,' says Ted, wretchedly, 'I really do need the entire Fisher file urgently.'

'I gave it to you already, Mr Castle.'

'You gave me part of it, but there are documents missing.'

Miss Venson bridles. 'I'm sure after all these years as a trained secretary, I'm not likely to be inaccurate in my work. The late Mr Castle always said I gave complete satisfaction.'

♛

Better not to ask where Wiki's been, decides Kereru. No sense in driving her away again.

'You ready to eat, Wiki?' she asks, clucking at Lana.

The baby, sheltering in Wiki's arms, turns away, refusing to respond.

'She's shy, is all,' says Wiki.

'She's home now. You both are. She'll get used to . . .' She stares, horrified, at Lana's arms. 'What's this, Wikitoria?'

Wiki gazes at the floor.

'Well?'

Wiki says nothing.

'Bubba's got pinch marks all over her arms.' Kereru lifts up the shawl covering Lana's legs. 'Here, too.' She turns to Wiki. 'Did you do this to her?'

Wiki shakes her head.

'Answer me. Don't just stand there.'

'No.' Wiki bites back tears.

'Who did?'

There is a silence, then, 'Her dad.'

Kereru strokes Lana's back. 'Bubba,' she says, 'while there's breath in my body, you are never going back to the wicked man who did that to you.' She turns to Wiki. 'And you, neither. Did he hit you too?'

Wiki pushes up the sleeves of her cardigan, revealing fresh and fading bruises. 'He's not all bad, though. Afterwards, when he's sober, he's always sorry for what he did. It was him took me to the hospital, when he split my lip.'

'And what if he comes here to find you?'

'He won't.' Wiki brightens. 'He doesn't want us any more. He found himself another girlfriend. That's why he let us come back home.'

♖

Rosalba has spent the morning scolding Atkinson. 'Come here, Huia,' she demands now.

'In a minute, Mama.'

'When I need you, does it occur to you there may be a good reason why? An emergency, perhaps? I suppose, now I'm a useless widow woman of little account to you or the world, you don't feel the need to . . .'

'You know that's not true, Mama.'

'Stand there,' orders Rosalba. 'Closer. In the light where I can see you properly.' She scrutinises Huia. 'Yes, I thought so. You're developing middle-aged spread.'

Huia flushes.

'Look at that spare tyre.'

Perhaps, thinks Rosalba, I am being a little harsh, but Huia must realise I remain mistress of my own house. Rosalba has seen it before. A widowed mother, a dependent, spinster daughter at home who, little by little, gains the upper hand. Before she knows it, the mother has had her position usurped. Huia must be kept in place.

'If a girl doesn't take care of her looks,' she says, 'they'll fade before she's had a chance to utilise them. All your friends are married. Even that plain Marcia Lomax has caught herself a man.'

'Gwennie's not married.'

'Well, all I can say is you'll end up two old maids together sharing a house with three cats.'

Eru pulls Huia against him. 'Have you decided?'

Huia breathes in the calming coolness of the bush around them. 'Almost.' She leans her head on his shoulder. 'It's going to be so . . . hard. To tell them, I mean.'

'Putting it off's not going to make it any easier.'

It is Te Mara, coming out of the wharenui in the late afternoon, who sees the young man first. A Pakeha, unshaven, with a menacing walk and a scowling face. Instantly, Te Mara knows this is someone to avoid, but the Pakeha comes towards him and blocks his way by standing in front of him. 'You, old man, I bet you know everyone round here. Seen anyone called Wikitoria lately?'

Now Te Mara can smell the drink on him and hear the slurring in his voice. 'Lots of Wikitorias in this pa,' he says. 'Named to show respect for the queen.' His heart is sinking. He fears what is coming.

'Got a little kid. Lana. My little girl.' He sways slightly and Te Mara realises he is very drunk.

'What do you want with this Wikitoria?'

'What do I want with her?' The Pakeha bends down and blows his stinking breath on the old chief's face. 'She's my bloody wife. See? And Lana's my bloody baby. That bitch's got no right to take my kid. I could get the police onto her for that.'

Te Mara says nothing. Shockwaves are spinning round him. So this is Baby Lana's father. How could Wiki have been so foolish?

'You haven't answered me, old man. When I find her, I'm gonna learn her a lesson. Teach her for snatching my kid.'

'What makes you think she is in this pa?'

'I know she's here. A cobber of mine at the Works told me.'

'She is your wife, you said?'

'Yeah. Maori-fashion. Sleep with her, she yours.'

Te Mara bites down his furious reaction. 'I know of no child called Lana,' he says politely. 'It may be your friend was mistaken.'

But at that moment, he sees Wiki, holding Lana, come out of the house and walk unsuspectingly towards them. 'Go back inside to Auntie,' he cries.

'Shut up, old man,' shouts the Pakeha. He lunges towards Wiki. 'You're coming with me, you bitch.'

Wiki stands absolutely still, Lana clutched against her chest.

'You heard me.'

'No,' says Wiki. 'I'm not going anywhere. I'm staying here.'

The man lurches drunkenly up to her and slaps first one side of her face, then the other. 'You'll do what I bloody tell you.'

Red rage rises behind Te Mara's eyes. He flings himself on the stranger and beats at him with his fists. 'Leave her alone,' he roars.

The Pakeha turns and pushes Te Mara in the chest. 'You keep out of this.'

The old man staggers. His cap falls onto the dusty ground.

Kereru comes rushing towards them. 'Help! Somebody help us!'

From other houses people are running.

'Take Bubba, Auntie,' cries Wiki, thrusting Lana at Kereru.

She crashes her fists into the Pakeha's stomach, then into his face. The man sways and sinks to the ground. 'You hurt me, you devil,' he says in disbelief. 'You just blacked my eye.'

'Get out,' says Wiki, kicking him in the groin with her bare foot. 'And stay out!'

Kereru sits her father down in a chair.

'Make him a cup of tea now,' she tells Wiki. 'Bubba's gone to sleep.'

Te Mara waits till Wiki is safely out of the room. 'Pakeha booze,' he says bitterly to Kereru, 'Pakeha food, Pakeha men. No good for Maori women, any of them.'

♛

Ted sits in the office, wrestling with the Fisher account. The only reference on Fisher's file is to a first mortgage, so why does he have an unregistered *second* mortgage in the locked filing cabinet? The mortgagee for both mortgages is shown as Mrs Franklin, widow of a wealthy local landowner. Ted will have to examine her trust account ledger and ask Miss Venson for all the client trust files so he can cross-check them. Better get it over with. 'I'm afraid we need to sort out the filing system, Miss Venson,' he says in the most conciliatory tone he can manage. 'And could you look out the Franklin ledger for me, please?'

Miss Venson stares at him indignantly. 'I'm sure this system was good enough for the late Mr Castle, Mr Castle. *He* never seemed to have any complaint.'

'I'm not complaining. I simply want to make cross-referencing easier so that I can find any files I need urgently.'

Miss Venson bridles. 'That's all very well, Mr Castle, but I'm not sure, at my time of life . . .'

'When you get to grips with it, I'm certain you'll find the new system . . .'

Miss Venson swoops down and snatches from his hand the sheaf of papers he is about to file away. 'No, Mr Castle, not in there. That's the Accounts Only drawer.'

'These *are* accounts.'

'Clients' trust accounts,' says Miss Venson triumphantly, 'have two separate drawers, over here. The only person who ever dealt with those was the late Mr Castle.' She gets up and puts on her hat in preparation for her daily trip to the bakery. 'I'll leave Arthur here with you.'

Ted looks with loathing at the dachshund snoring in its basket.

'I'll get him an Eccles cake. He does so enjoy the raisins. What will it be for you today, Mr Castle?'

'A custard slice and a chocolate éclair, I think.'

Miss Venson glances at Ted's thickening waistline and tuts to herself. 'The late Mr Castle was very strict about that, you know, Mr Castle. He always limited himself to just the one dainty.'

Tonight, Ted stays on at the office, examining the files and ledgers. Mrs Franklin's ledger shows interest payments from Fisher on his first mortgage. None on his second. And what has happened to the principal sum of the second mortgage on which Mrs Franklin's interest should have been being paid? Was it really lent to Fisher? What can be going on?

Hardly conclusive proof of anything, thinks Ted, but irregular enough for me to have to examine, one by one, all the mortgages held by the practice. Blast and damnation. Sure to be only a minor mistake somewhere but, on top of everything else, this is the last thing I need right now. And, he thinks suddenly, since Father was the solicitor for the local tribe, I'll have to look at the trust moneys held for Eru's grandfather's iwi, as well. Just in case.

♔

Were Ted not so preoccupied with sorting out affairs at the office, he might have noticed how distracted Huia seems. Today, as she mixes the hens' mash, she tells herself she will soon have to make some kind of decision. She can feel her life slipping away, lost in everyday tasks, the routine preparation of meals, the ordering of the household . . .

'Hello,' says Ethel, appearing beside her. 'Your mother said you were out here.'

'She's being so difficult at the moment. I keep trying to find outside jobs to do, so I can get some time on my own to think.'

'If I'm interrupting now, I can come back later.'

'No, do stay.' Huia hesitates. 'I'd really like to talk to you.' She pauses. 'It's Eru, of course. Now his sister's back, he's free to leave his grandfather. He wants me to make a decision.'

'But you've decided already, really, haven't you?'

'I think I have. I mean, I know I want to be with Eru. It's just how to manage . . . everything . . . without upsetting Mama.'

'I don't think you *can* do it without upsetting her.'

'Imagine what she's going to say.'

'Well, yes, but once you've gone, you won't be here to have to listen to it.'

'And how will Mama and Ted cope?'

'They'll manage. After all, if you were run over by a horse, or died, or something, they'd have to, wouldn't they?'

'Mama will disown me. And what about Ted? He's been so

odd lately. Whenever I try to talk to him about Papa, he snaps my head off.'

'He's probably under pressure at work.'

'But if I go, who will he have left?'

'You sound like a wife,' says Ethel. 'And honestly, Huia, a sister shouldn't be a wife to her own brother.'

Huia flushes. 'It's not just that. It's . . . everything. What will everyone say? Gwennie and the Bickfords, the Lomaxes, the Middletons – everyone in Castleton's going to know. It'll be a scandal.'

'Only because Eru's a Maori.'

'And *his* family'll be furious, too. They don't want him married to a Pakeha.'

Ethel watches as Huia empties the wet mash into the hens' pail.

'We won't have the courage to go out in public together. Not even to the pictures. We'll be an embarrassment. No-one will invite us anywhere, and how will I cope with all the slights and snubs? And the gossip?'

'You do love Eru, don't you?'

'More than anything in the world.'

'Then, loving him's the easy part. What's bothering you is how to fit loving him into your life, when everyone round you is hostile and disapproving. So Eru's being Maori and your being Pakeha isn't really the problem?'

'It's exactly the problem.'

'No,' says Ethel. 'It's *Castleton* that's the problem. That's what's making things so impossible for you. And Castleton isn't the only place in the world.'

♛ ♔

The path ahead widens, giving onto cleared land with spraying clusters of speargrass, and here and there cabbage trees, their brown dead leaves dangling untidily below new pale, palmy fronds, their rough, ringed trunks like giant moas' legs.

Huia leans against a ponga. 'I've . . . decided.'

'And?'

'I'll come with you. To Wellington.'

Eru puts his arm round her. 'I've got something to tell you, too. When I put in for the transfer from the Masterton office, I applied for Wellington *and* Auckland, and the Auckland one's come through. They want me up there in six weeks. Will you come with me to Auckland?'

♛

The post boy has brought another letter from Cambridge.

Huia knows instantly something is amiss. 'What's the matter? You look awful.'

Ted is silent.

'It's not . . . Daphne . . . ?'

'I . . . well, I expect you'll have to know soon enough. It's . . . Dr Breville, my tutor. They've given my research place to someone else.'

'Look out,' warns Huia. 'Mama's coming. She's in one of her Red Queen moods. Get in first before she starts quizzing you.'

She's right, thinks Ted. He struggles to control his voice.'I've had a bit of a blow today,' he says. 'Dr Breville's given my Cambridge place to someone else. I won't be working with the great Professor Plucknett, after all.'

His mother digests this in silence. Then, 'Breville,' she says, 'who was he again?'

Ted is almost living at the office. As soon as Miss Venson leaves, he pores over the files trying to separate the genuine accounts from the fraudulent. He has unearthed a paper in Mrs Franklin's file that, unlike her other statements, records a post-office box number – for a post office in Wellington – which appears to relate to a safe-deposit box there. But why?

And now, tonight, as he re-examines the Fisher file, he notices a number scrawled on the back of one of the documents.

Pulling out the Franklin file, he compares the numbers. Yes, they are identical. So Fisher's must relate to the same

Wellington post office. What might be in this safe-deposit box? And surely, somewhere, there must be a key to it.

Ted scours the office for possible hiding-places. No sign of a key anywhere. So, even were he to go to Wellington, how could he gain access to the box?

As well as the Fisher mortgages, Ted has found what appear to be bogus files for a Mr Waters and a Mr Lake. But this may be only a fraction of what remains to be uncovered. He will have to examine every account and ledger. Then what? Try to replace the stolen moneys? He struggles to recall what little his Cambridge lectures taught him about accounts. But I am a *lawyer*, he tells himself for the umpteenth time. When I was admitted, Uncle Charles stood as my sponsor and I publicly promised to uphold the law.

He stares at the files for Waters and Lake. Of course! How could he have been so slow? Father, too, would have needed a way to ensure he knew which files were which. Fisher genuinely exists, but the others are fictitious names. And they are all to do with *fishing*.

'Here we are again,' cries Miss Venson. 'Say good morning, Arthur. Isn't that sweet, Mr Castle? He's wagging his little tail at you.'

Ted waits impatiently for her to take off her coat and settle the dachshund in its basket. 'I'll need to take a look at all the iwi papers today, Miss Venson.'

'Oh, you mean the Moana File,' says Miss Venson brightly. 'Everything relating to that is kept in the end filing cabinet.'

Ted stares at her. 'Did you say . . . the Moana File?'

'That's what the late Mr Castle always called it.'

Moana, thinks Ted. The Maori word for a body of water.

He recovers himself. 'I'll need the ledgers as well. Perhaps you could just talk me through them?'

'Gracious, Mr Castle, I've never mastered *double-entry* book-keeping. The late Mr Castle always did all the book-keeping himself.'

Ted opens a ledger. For years, Father controlled the tribe's trust funds and was a trustee, as his father had been before him. Ted, himself, will take over Father's position now. Father is supposed to have been investing funds on the tribe's behalf, including the moneys gained from leasing out the grazing rights on the disputed land gift to the Church. Surely, surely, Father wouldn't have stolen from a friend?

A cursory read of the first few pages appears to show that these accounts, at least, are as they should be. Ted scrutinises the final five entries. Yes, all fine. Then, he sees the very last one. A withdrawal. For five hundred pounds! And, slipped between this page and the next, is a sealed envelope on which is written in his father's familiar flowing script:

Kereru: Could you please pass this on to your father?

Kereru is Eru's aunt. Why would Father be asking her to deliver a message when he, himself, saw the old man on a regular basis?

Should Ted undo it and read what is inside? Yes, considering what he now knows, it is surely better to check every document for himself.

Tearing open the envelope, he takes out a single sheet of paper. It is a letter. Addressed to Eru's grandfather. Wretchedly, Ted reads it.

. . . In order to begin financing works on the proposed school on the iwi land, I shall drop out to the pa tomorrow in the late afternoon with a trust-fund cheque for five hundred pounds for you to countersign. On Friday, I am off to Wellington where I hope to be able to speak to someone from the Church Commission and get things in train . . .

Is it possible, Ted asks himself, that the building of the school is finally to take place? Or has Father persuaded Te Mara to countersign the cheque, and then appropriated funds from the trust for his own use? All that shows in the trust ledger here in the office is that the money was withdrawn. Ted urgently needs to examine the contents of that safe-deposit box in Wellington.

Why, he thinks sadly, would Eru's grandfather not have had complete faith in Father, whom he had known since he was a boy? Te Mara is not a lawyer. Of course he would unsuspiciously sign anything Father put in front of him. Can it be that all the money for Ku's wedding, Mama's clothes, Father's car, Ted's own education, has been stolen?

He looks again at the letter. The request for the cheque is dated one week before his father's 'accident'.

'. . . tomorrow, Ted? Ted!' Huia is standing in front of him. 'You haven't heard a word I've said.'

'What? Oh, sorry, I was thinking. Listen, Huia, if you wanted to hide something – properly, so no-one could ever find it – where would you put it?'

'That depends. If it was something biggish, I might bury it. In the garden.'

Ted thinks briefly of his lucky farthing, probably still lying below the vegetables. So that he could find it again, he'd made a mark on the pepper tree. What could Father have used as a mnemonic for where he had hidden the post-office box key? A key to a key?

'What if you were hiding, say, a key?'

'Well, you wouldn't put anything as small as a key in the ground. You'd never find it again. Maybe in a vase?'

'No.'

Huia thinks for a moment. 'There's a story about hiding things. About a woman who had a secret letter. That's what it's called, *The Purloined Letter*.'

'I'm not talking about a letter.'

'No, but, in the story, the woman has to hide the letter quickly and she puts it somewhere no-one will think to look.'

'Where?'

'In the letter-rack.'

'Not so clever.'

'*Very* clever. The letter-rack was in full view of everybody. Who'd ever think of looking there for a *secret* letter?'

Ted stares at her. 'My God,' he says. 'You might just be right.'

There are six keys hanging on the hook in the scullery: two door keys, the wool-shed key, and the keys to the meat-safe and the gun cupboard. None of them is small enough to fit the lock of a safe-deposit box.

Ted kicks his toe against the scullery wall in frustration. He has come to the conclusion that Father would never have taken the risk of leaving the key to the Wellington post office safe-deposit box in his office in Castleton: it must be here in the house somewhere. But *where*? Think, he orders himself. Think logically.

What had Ted seen that night, not so very long ago, when he had surprised Father in his study? The night they had heard about Flossie? His father starting in alarm; the whisky bottle and glass; the scattered papers, Father's arm flung protectively across them . . . No, not across the papers. Over Grandfather's open wig-box – *Grandfather's wig-box*. Which has always lain in the study. In the left-hand drawer. Which has always been kept locked . . .

Ted races to the study, snatches up the key from the pen-and-wiper tray and slides it into the lock. Yes, there is the wig-box. He lifts it out and places it on his father's desk. Locked, of course. And where is the key to *that*? '*The letter-rack*,' Huia had said. '*In full view* . . .'

Ted tucks the wig-box under a cushion, safe from the Red Queen's prying eyes, and shuts and locks the drawer. Then he returns to the scullery and scrutinises the keys. The door keys he can discard, and Father never would have hidden a key in the wool-shed where Sorenson or the shearers might mislay it. That leaves the meat-safe and the gun cupboard. Not likely to be in the meat-safe either, thank God.

Ted strides down the hall to the gun cupboard and unlocks it. Two shotguns, cartridges, a hunting knife and an ancient pith helmet on the shelf above. But no sign of a key. No hooks in the wall. Ted runs his fingers along the shelf, just in case. Nothing. He is lifting down the pith helmet when the light from the hall catches on something metal lying beneath it . . .

Ted flings back the lid of the wig-box. He scrabbles under the ancient wig, its stiff artificial parting flanked by crinkly white horsehair curls, its little neck-tail tied with faded black ribbon, and feels only paper. Lifting out the stiff topmost sheet, he finds himself gazing at a photograph of . . . of . . . *Eru*. Why on earth would his father keep a photo of Eru locked away in such a secret hiding-place? Ted is cut by jealousy. Why has Father kept no photo of *him*? And this image is of Eru as he is now – not as a child – so Father must have put it there recently.

The old rage rises in Ted's chest: his nose is smarting, stinging. But, as he stares again at Eru, gazing calmly from his studio portrait, he realises he is in uniform, his hair smoothed down in an unfamiliar way, that the photograph is creased and its edges are furled. He tosses it aside, pulls out the wig and rakes deeper through the old papers below it. His fingers encounter something solid . . . cold . . . metallic . . .

'Uncle Charles?' says Ted. 'Something important's come up. I *must* talk to you. Urgently.'

'Fire away.'

'No. Not on the telephone. Can you put me up in Wellington on Friday night?'

'Delighted to. I'll meet your train at the station.'

Ted and Uncle Charles scan the banked rows of metallic silver doors with their numbers stamped beside the keyholes.

'This one,' says Ted, his heart hammering as he slides the little key into the lock.

The door swings open.

Reaching in, Ted pulls out a thick roll of documents, tied with pink legal tape.

'God, what a mess,' says Uncle Charles. 'You poor devil, inheriting all this.'

They are in Uncle Charles's study, 'And not,' Uncle has instructed Aunt Evadne, 'to be disturbed under any circumstances. Not even for fire or earthquake. Nothing.'

'Not even for supper?'

'Please, Vaddy. I'm serious.'

'I could send up a couple of trays.'

'Do that. Excellent idea.'

Mutely, Ted passes a document to his uncle.

Uncle Charles studies it for several minutes. Then he says, 'Not what we'd have hoped for, I realise, but let's look on the bright side. He didn't spend it. The money's still there.'

'But . . . you know what this one means?'

'Afraid I do.'

'Five hundred pounds. The exact amount. It means that Father *did* help himself to that cheque.'

'It does rather seem like it.'

'But the letter to the chief was still there, in the ledger.'

'Not so surprising really. Perhaps he expected to see the daughter and she didn't turn up. Or he forgot to give it to her, and then motored out to the pa anyway. I dare say he intended to destroy the letter, but didn't get around to it before his accident.'

Ted feels that, at any moment now, he will collapse, break down. If only he could wake up and find he is safely back in Cambridge . . .

'Perhaps Father . . .'

'No point speculating. Main thing to keep in mind is how we're going to deal with this mess. Trouble with this sort of thing is the way it snowballs, you see. You start to incur more and more debt and end up with more defalcations to pay past ones which, in turn, generates even more debt. Your father would have discovered that quite early on, I'd say.'

'But how did he manage to . . .?'

'I'm coming to that, old chap. Some of the moneys raised

would have had to go to pay interest on the bogus mortgages. As long as the quarterly interest kept being paid on them, no auditor would have been likely to be suspicious. And moneys had to be kept aside for that. So he needed a bank account, several bank accounts, well away from home. Hence, the post office account in Wellington. He'd have been too well known in Masterton.'

'I just can't believe . . .'

His uncle shrugs. 'He won't be for the first, or the last, to have been tempted in that way. Next step's quite simple. He opens an account in Wellington in the name of Fisher, then another in the name of one of the other bogus clients. And so on. Who were they, again?'

'Lake, Waters . . .'

'Oh, yes, fishing connections, weren't they? Clever of you to spot that.'

'But how did *he* get hold of the money? If he used his clients' names on the accounts?'

'Not difficult at all. He was Mrs Franklin's solicitor, remember, with power of attorney. He simply took the money from her client account, paid it into the fake Fisher account in Wellington, then transferred it from the bogus account into his own accounts. And did the same with all the other false mortgages.'

Ted's earlier distress is superseded by anger. 'But *why*? Why would he do something so . . .'

Uncle Charles puts an arm across Ted's shoulders. 'I can understand how you feel, but I doubt *he*'d have seen it that way. In his mind he was doing this to give you the best possible chance in life.'

'Maybe I'd rather not have . . .'

'Bit academic now.'

Ted slumps in his chair. 'I can't handle this.'

'Look, you're exhausted, and no wonder. Let's sleep on it and, in the morning, we'll see what we can come up with.'

'Father wasn't what *I'd* have thought of as a thief.'

'Technically, and legally, I'm afraid he may have been, but I agree with you.' Uncle Charles sighs. 'Why on earth didn't he come to me? Too proud, I suppose. What a damned waste.' He turns to Ted. 'Now, how are we going to set about sorting this out?'

'I haven't the first idea.'

'Of course we should report it immediately, but I suggest we do it another way. It'll be down to you, though. You'll understand I can't risk being implicated. If we were to be rumbled, we'd be up on a charge of malfeasance ourselves. And for Heaven's sake, don't mention anything to your mother or sisters. The last thing we want is anyone else getting wind of this. Especially that snooping husband of Ku's.'

'I agree.'

'Now, if you take things carefully, you can gradually plug the holes in the accounts. Not strictly legal, but let's keep hold of the broader ethical issues here. Trick is to feed the moneys back slowly and close down the false accounts one at a time over a longish period. Mercifully, old Venson's not up to spotting anything. And keep the defunct bogus files under lock and key at home. Under no circumstances at the office, right?'

'What about the Maori land moneys? That's the thing I feel worst about.'

'You can put that unspent money back into the iwi account immediately.'

'But what if anyone queries the repayment?'

'You simply say the building contract fell through.'

'But where am I going to get the rest of the money to pay back the . . . ?'

'There'll be the insurance from your father's car?'

Ted nods.

'And his life insurance?'

'Yes.'

'And I'll chip in a bit, of course. So you can dribble back most of the moneys without too much trouble.'

Ted puts his head in his hands. 'What I really hate is knowing that Father cheated a friend.'

Uncle Charles is silent. Then he says, 'Have you looked at the date on the largest of all those withdrawals?'

'Yes. Just before I went up. That must've been the "Cambridge fund".'

'He wanted to find the money. Somehow.'

Ted is silent. 'I know he made sacrifices for me,' he says, at last. 'And I kept pestering him for extras. A motor, holidays, rowing gear . . . I had no idea he . . .'

'Wouldn't dwell on that, old man. No way you could've had a clue. And you *could* argue it wasn't morally theft. I've no doubt he intended to pay it all back when business picked up a bit.' Uncle Charles takes up the pile of papers again. 'Have you seen the date on this final transaction?'

'I know. The week before his accident.'

'Exactly. I don't think he could bear the idea of cheating a friend either. He'd never touched that account previously, though in many ways it would be the obvious one to go for. Plenty in it, and the old Maori chief had absolute faith in him. Terrible thing, a guilty conscience. Must have felt under pressure all the time.'

Ted longs to be able to tell sensible, dependable Uncle Charles what he really knows or, at least, suspects about Father and Flossie. 'Yes,' he says. 'Guilt. I think that's what tipped him over the edge.'

Uncle Charles frowns at him. 'What d'you mean "tipped him over the edge"?'

Ted says nothing.

'Steady on,' says Uncle Charles. 'If you're implying what I think you are, take care. You don't want the insurance refusing to pay out on the car. Or his life policy.' He pauses. 'Terrible conditions out there at Drovers' Hill. That sergeant said as much. All those double and treble hairpins. Not surprising, in the dark . . . Better not to speculate, old chap.' He claps a hand on Ted's shoulder. ' "Leave the dead to bury their own dead", shall we? Fighting talk's what we need. Look here, you're a splendid fellow and this is about the worst . . . I want to give you a little something to help you out.'

'I couldn't possibly.'

'You could, you know. Wilson wasn't only your father; he was my brother, too. And I've got something in mind for you. Give you a bit of a lift while you get this thing cleared up.'

'I . . .'

'You can't get around the countryside on the bike or in a trap. I'd already told Wilson I'd thought of getting you a car. Nothing grand, just four wheels.'

'But I couldn't . . .'

'Terribly bad form to refuse a gift. And some might say you've earned it already.'

♛

Wiki pushes Lana back and forth in a webbed canvas swing that Koro has suspended from the beam of the verandah.

Auntie Kereru sits, watching her. 'She's asleep, now.'

'I'll push her for a bit longer to make sure she's really off.'

'Your koro loves that little girl,' says Auntie. 'Reminds him of you as a baby. Best thing that ever happened to him.'

Wiki squats down beside her. 'I wanted to ask you something, Auntie. When Koro wasn't around.'

'He's not around now.'

Wiki studies the boards of the verandah. 'I wondered if you ever told Eru about . . . about our dad's medal.'

Auntie sighs. 'No, and I'm not planning to. Not after all the trouble it caused last time.' She puts an arm round Wiki. 'I shouldn't have told you, either. I'm sorry. Really sorry. If I had my time over, I'd never say a word. Better to keep quiet.'

'No,' says Wiki. 'It's right Eru and I should know. I'll tell Eru myself.'

Auntie shakes her head. 'I don't want your brother turning against your koro, too.'

'But I haven't turned against Koro, Auntie. Not any more. At the time you told me, I was . . . stupid . . . wild. I didn't know who I was or what I wanted. I kept on thinking if I lived with my mum, things'd be different.'

'Different how?'

'I don't know. Better, I think. I didn't seem to fit in anywhere.'

'Seems to me you fit in pretty well here, now.'

Wiki nods. 'I been thinking about things. A lot. Like what do I tell Bubba about her dad? Later, when she asks.'

Auntie doesn't move or speak.

'I don't want to tell her he's a no-good. And it was the drink, mostly. Sometimes, when he was sober, he was quite nice.'

'You're not thinking . . .'

'Of going back? 'Course not. But Bubba, it's not her fault he's her dad.'

'So what will you tell her?'

'That's what I was thinking about. I thought maybe I could tell her he was fine a lot of the time, but, when he wasn't fine, he wasn't so good, so that's why we came back here to live. And to look after Koro. No waka huia box or anything, but the same, in a way.'

'What do you mean, the same?'

'There was nothing in the box really, but, at the same time, there *was* something.' She pauses. 'A sort of . . . picture . . . of our dad. The way Koro wanted him to be for us, not the way he was. That's what I want to do for Bubs. But no medal or anything. And no box, either. No need.'

♛

Castleton, like the rest of the country, is parching in the drought. In town, black ooze leaks from the crusty cracks in the new tarmacadam footpaths, now as soft and springy as turf. Out here, the grass on either side of the road stretches in scorched swathes; the needle-coated earth under the pine trees is amber. The air hangs still. Only Ted's new Austin Seven disturbs the blazing silence.

Though all the windows are down, no breeze freshens the vehicle's interior and Ted's hands are stuck to the steering wheel with sweat. A deep heat-haze shimmers across the loose metal on the road, stretching like a band from verge to verge and blurring his vision. At first, he thinks the figure by the roadside must be a mirage, so perfectly does its corona of sunny hair blend into the landscape. He slows and, peering through the flickering haze, sees it is Ethel Wrench.

I'm hallucinating, Ted tells himself as he pulls up. He leans across and opens the door. 'Can I offer you a lift? It's much too hot to be walking.'

Ethel climbs in. 'Yes, *please*. It's boiling today.'

'Hotter even than last week,' says Ted, covertly taking in her appearance. Why has he always thought her plain? She is no longer gawky and angular. She has grown into her height, and her long legs tuck elegantly under the dashboard on the passenger side. Her wild red hair has been tamed into a pretty curly bob around her face. 'I've never known the sun so strong,' he says, in an attempt to make conversation.

'You're right. I always walk into town, but today . . .'

'Why not use a bike?'

'I don't have one.'

'Do you know how to ride a bicycle?'

'Yes. Huia taught me.' She laughs. 'Quite a long time ago, though.'

'It's like riding a horse. You never forget how.' He pauses. 'We've got a bike you could have. Ku's old one.'

'I couldn't possibly.'

'It's in the wool-shed, just lying there. No-one ever uses it.'

'I must say, it would be a tremendous help. If you're sure . . .'

Her smell of fresh baking and milk is filling the car.

'It'll need air in the tyres and a spot of oil here and there. Why don't I sort it out and bring it over to you?'

'Oh, but . . .'

'I insist.'

Ethel smiles at him. 'You're very kind. Thank you.'

For the first time since he has returned from Cambridge, Ted feels appreciated. 'Let me drop you home,' he says.

'I told Ethel Wrench she can use Ku's old bike.'
'Good idea.'
'You don't mind, do you?'
'Of course not. But it might be better not to mention it to the Red Queen.'
'You do like Ethel?'
'She's very nice.'
'Nicer than Gwennie?'
Huia glances at him. 'What?'
'It doesn't matter . . . I just wondered.'
'Ted,' says Huia, awkwardly, 'there's something I have to tell you.' She gulps in breath. 'I'm leaving.'
'Leaving where?'
'Here. Home. Castleton.'
For a moment Ted thinks she has somehow found out about Father. 'But . . . ?'
'I'm going to Auckland.'
'*Auckland*. Why?'
'With Eru. We're going to be married.'
Ted gapes at her. Has he heard her correctly? 'For God's sake, you can't marry Eru.'
'Why not?'
'You know very well why not. He's a Maori. You can't possibly marry a Maori. You wouldn't have a friend left in the world.'
Huia's voice trembles. 'Eru's more important than my friends.'
'What about Mama? Have you thought what this will do to her?'
'Nobody needs to know right away.'
'And how do you propose to keep it quiet?'
'We'll be in Auckland. Where no-one knows us. Please, Ted, please understand.'
'I understand all right. While I've been slaving away at the office, sorting out the problems of this whole bloody family, losing Daphne, being robbed of my research place, you've been carrying on with Eru behind my back.'

'It isn't like that.'

'It will kill Mama.' He can hear how brutal his voice sounds. 'You know that, don't you?'

'I can't tell her yet.'

'And when do you plan to tell her, if ever?'

'I . . . we . . . haven't decided. Eru says, after we're married, he'll come and speak to her himself. It'll be easier for Mama that way.'

'Easier! This will completely ruin her life. And in the meantime I'm supposed to connive with you in deceiving her.' Fury wells up in Ted. 'Christ, as if I haven't got enough to contend with, without this.'

He feels a trickle slide across his lip; a drop of blood splats onto his shirt front. 'Now, look what you've done,' he shouts.

Huia slips about the house in silent misery. Serve her right! thinks Ted. Somehow, though he knows it is perverse, shunning his sister makes him feel better about Father's dereliction.

Since he gave Ethel a lift, Ted has had to fight down frequent urges associated with the memory of her hair, her smell, her breasts. And now, about to telephone her to say he has fixed up Ku's old bicycle, he finds he is uncertain of what to say to her. Maybe she no longer wants to borrow it. He stares at the Bakelite instrument and realises his hand is trembling. Revolving the silver handle on the side of the wooden box, he lifts up the receiver, puts it to his ear, then hastily replaces it. No doubt Clodagh on the Exchange will earwig on the entire conversation. But why shouldn't he be ringing a neighbour? He has nothing to hide. Summoning his courage, he revolves the silver handle and picks up the handpiece again.

'Exchange.'

'Castleton 503, please.'

'That's the Wrenches' number, Mr Castle.'

'It's the Wrenches I want, thank you, Clodagh.'

'Nothing's happened, I hope, please God?'

'Of course not.'

'Only they don't use the phone much, and after that dreadful business with Major Younghusband, I . . .'

'Sorry to cut you short, Clodagh, but . . .'

'And aren't I putting you through right now, Mr Castle.'

'Hello?'

'Sorry, Mrs Bickford, it's Ted Castle. I'm on a work call.'

'I'll put this down then. 'Bye.'

'Thanks,' says Ted. 'Goodbye.'

'Hello,' says a puzzled voice. 'Are you there?'

'Ethel?'

'Yes. I thought you just said "Goodbye".'

'I did. But not to you. It's Ted Castle.'

Silence. What a fool I am, thinks Ted. I should never have mentioned the wretched bicycle.

'I almost telephoned you,' says Ethel, 'to thank you for the lift home.'

'No need at all. You remember I mentioned the bicycle?'

'Yes.'

'Well, it's ready now and I thought I might . . . drop it over. Is later today all right?'

'Are you sure?'

'It's no trouble. Four o'clock suit you?'

'Yes, of course.'

'See you later, then,' says Ted.

Neither of them hears the pinging of receivers being replaced up and down the line.

The Wrenches' house seems even more dilapidated than Ted remembers. Half-expecting a horde of boys to swoop on his car, he unloads the bicycle. No-one is in sight. He is debating whether to knock on the front door, when Ethel appears.

'This is so kind of you.'

'Not a bit. Where shall I put it?'

Ethel moves closer. 'It's lovely. From the way you described it, I thought it would be positively antique.' She pauses. 'Not that I'd have minded if it was . . . I mean . . .'

'I'm glad you can get some use from it.'

Ethel looks awkward. 'Would you like to come in? I've made some lemon barley-water. And there's fruitcake, if . . . if you'd care for some.'

'Thanks, that sounds very nice.' He follows her cautiously into the lobby, gazing round for the fearsome hound.

Ethel smiles. 'Argus is in the wool-shed. He was so full of moth he should have been burnt, but Mater wouldn't hear of it, so Perse put him out with Pater's chemicals.'

Speeding home, Ted hums to himself as he takes in the landscape. Everything is orange-red. Like Ethel Wrench's hair. He recalls the flash of strawberry-blonde between Flossie's open thighs. Is it possible, he wonders, that Ethel, too, has red hair there?

Huia looks up as Ted comes into the kitchen. 'Dinner's almost ready.'

Ted doesn't answer. He can feel her desperation. Too bad, he thinks.

'Was Ethel pleased with the bike?'

'Try to be a bit more tactful, Huia. Or do you *want* the Red Queen to hear?'

'Ted, please, don't be so . . . so cold. I can't bear it.'

He glares at her. 'And that's *my* fault?'

'Why are you being like this?'

'You know very well why.'

Ethel's delight in the bicycle has somehow led to Ted, over fruitcake and barley-water, inviting her to go for a drive next Sunday. Where on earth will I take her? he wonders as he leaves the office. Hardly decent to suggest the sand-dunes. He smiles to himself. Might give her completely the wrong idea.

'We could go to Masterton,' says Ted, realising too late that someone who knows him is bound to see him driving with Ethel Wrench. Well, why not? It's a free country.

'Whatever you like, really, but . . .'

'There's somewhere else you'd prefer?'

'If it's not too far, I'd love to go to the lake. I've never seen it.'

Everything about the lake seems to please Ethel. She is enchanted by the pukeko chicks staggering at the water's edge; she pokes around among the reeds; she even takes off her stockings and shoes and paddles. Ted watches her sitting bare-legged, drying her feet and wiggling her toes in the sun. She is easy to talk to and interested in everything he points out to her. Being with her is . . . comfortable. He sits down beside her on the rug spread out on the shingly sand.

'It's beautiful here,' she says. 'Much nicer than I expected. I thought it would be darker. And muddier.'

'If the weather's bad it gets dark. And it can be dangerous. People have drowned here.'

'In the reeds?'

'And in boating accidents. I used to come here with my father to fish.'

'I didn't know you were a fisherman.'

'I haven't been out with my rod since . . .' He considers. 'It must be since I came back from England.' He hesitates. 'I hate to ruin things for you but I can't help thinking that somewhere out here is where they found Flossie, our maid.'

'Her being found here doesn't spoil anything. When you stop to think about it, there are bones underneath almost everywhere you go.'

'What a funny girl you are.'

Ethel looks to see if he is rebuking her. 'I suppose it's because Pater was always talking about archaeology. How you think something's one thing and then, underneath it, if you dig a bit, you find it's another.'

'I often think things are different from what they turn out to be,' says Ted diffidently. 'I seem to have quite a bit of trouble getting some things right.'

She nods.

'Like the way people are going to behave,' he rushes on. 'Or what to do in certain situations. It's as if I . . . I don't always understand the rules.'

'I suppose,' says Ethel, 'there often aren't any proper rules. But everything's really only layers, isn't it?'

'Layers?'

'Like archaeology, but digging for people – or what they mean underneath the surface. A sort of human archaeology. And some people are quite happy with just the top layer. Ku is . . . and Lysander . . . and the twins. And then there are people like Perse. He gets to know about things a different way. Through the cows.'

Ted looks at her. 'What about you?'

She flushes. 'I'm like Huia.'

'You're not a bit like Huia.'

'Not to look at. I don't mean that. I mean about things being underneath other things. Not walking across the mounds in the churchyard where the bodies are – that kind of thing.'

'I thought you didn't mind that.'

'I don't. But I'm like Huia because I *know* they're there. Whereas your mother and Ku have never thought about it for a moment.' She hesitates. 'I quite like their being there, if you see what I mean. I like being part of the layers of things.'

There is a pause. Then she says, 'Huia said you wanted to stay in Cambridge for good.'

'Yes.'

'She said you were studying something about hands.'

Ted laughs. 'Not exactly hands. More like tax evasion. It's called Mortmain.'

'What is it?'

'I'm sure you'd find it terribly boring . . .'

'If I do, I'll stop you.'

'So you can see,' says Ted, 'why I felt pretty rotten about not being able to stay in Cambridge.'

'Yes, I can.'

'I didn't want to come back at all.' He pauses. 'And then, when I got home, there was Father's accident and . . . a whole lot of other things . . .' He pauses. 'And Eru's sister running away . . .'

'But that was nothing to do with you.'

'She – Wiki – used to stalk Eru and me when we went out together.'

'That must have been a long time ago.'

Ted can't seem to stop himself from talking. 'She had a bit of a crush on me at one time.'

Ethel says nothing.

'For a long time I thought – I still think, actually – that I could have been nicer to her.'

'That's what Huia thought, too.'

Ted is taken aback. 'That I could have . . .'

'No, not you. Her. She thought the girl wanted to be friends with her.'

'I didn't treat Wiki very kindly. I can't help feeling . . . guilty, I suppose.'

Ethel considers this. 'It seems to me,' she says, 'that there's only any point in feeling guilt about something if it stops you from doing it again. You were younger then. I'm sure you'd be nicer to her now.'

'Well, I . . .'

'And if you still feel bad about it, isn't there something you can do now to make up for it?'

'I'm not sure what . . .'

'There must be something. Just feeling guilty doesn't help anyone.'

A silence falls between them. Ethel picks up a handful of shingly sand and lets it trickle through her fingers. Ted is suddenly aware that she is softly whistling a strange little tune. Where has he heard it before?

Ethel stops whistling. 'Is that why you aren't treating Huia very kindly right now? Because you can't go back to Cambridge? And you feel guilty about Eru's sister?'

Ted stares fixedly at the lake. 'Of course not.'

Ethel takes up another fistful of sand. 'Huia's awfully unhappy, Ted.'

'Some people might say that was her own fault.'

'I wouldn't.' Another pause. 'Would you?'

'Yes, I would,' says Ted, hotly. 'I do. Has she told you what she's planning?'

'That's she's getting married . . .'

'Eru's a Maori.'

'So?'

'She can't marry a Maori.'

'Why not?'

'Because . . . because she'll cut herself off from everyone – everything she . . . She'll never be able to show her face here again.'

'In Castleton, you mean?' Ethel bends forward to pick up a stone: her breasts swing slightly downwards. Through her frock, the outlines of her nipples are clearly visible. 'But you just said it was stultifying here. You didn't want to come back yourself.' She weighs the stone in her hand.

Ted tries again. 'It's different for Huia.'

'I don't see how.'

'All her friends will cut her. She and Eru'll never be received in anyone's house.'

Ethel balances the stone between her thumb and forefinger. Drawing back her hand, she sends it skimming over the surface of the water. 'They had tea with us last Sunday.'

'What? Huia and . . . Eru?'

'Mater thought they made a handsome couple.'

'You mean your mother didn't mind that you – that they . . .'

'Mater invited them.' She looks at him again. Today her eyes are sea-green. 'You're usually so kind, Ted. Couldn't you try, or even pretend, to be nice to her?'

Ted is mute.

'Eru used to be your friend. And lots of people have in-laws they're ashamed of. Look at Pater and Uncle Bertie.' She sighs. 'I'll have another paddle, I think. If there's time before we go.'

'Plenty of time. Ethel . . .'

'Yes?'

'That tune you were whistling before . . .'

Momentarily, Ethel looks embarrassed. 'Was I whistling? Sorry. I didn't realise. I usually do it when I'm happy. It used to infuriate Pater. "*A whistling woman and a crowing hen . . .*" '

'No, it's not that. I just wondered what it was called. I've heard it before, but I can't remember when.'

'Probably when you brought me the bicycle. I've no idea what it's called, I'm afraid. All I know is it was a Boer War marching song. You see, even though Uncle couldn't speak, he'd taught himself to whistle and that was the tune he whistled all the time. It drove Pater crazy.'

Daphne, thinks Ted, as he motors back home from the Wrenches. Strange how he no longer has that sharp ache whenever he remembers her. He recalls her appreciative glances, her warmth, her sweet girlish giggling, but, if he is absolutely truthful, it is Cambridge he misses, not Daphne herself. Would Daph ever even have considered the layers of things, much less discussed them like Ethel? Yes, she was pretty – stunning, in fact – but, if he is brutally honest, she was, well, not terribly intelligent. What had she said when he had tried to explain to her about his Mortmain studies? 'Don't be dull, Teddy darling.'

I'll invite Ethel out again next week, Ted decides. Ask her what she thinks of the notion of moral responsibility . . . About those abbots who, having taken the knights' property into trust, refused to relinquish it after their safe return from the Crusades. One thing is certain. Ethel will have an opinion about it.

Ted groans inwardly as he sees Gwennie Fraser sitting with Huia on the verandah.

She makes a great show of examining her watch. 'Good Heavens! Is that the time? I'm so sorry, I must go,' she cries, not moving from her chair.

Ted sees he has no option but to shake her eager, proffered hand. 'Nice to see you, Gwennie.'

'And you, Stranger,' says Gwennie. 'Where have you been hiding, Teddy Bear?'

'Workload,' mutters Ted. He turns to Huia. 'Busy day?'

Huia looks at him gratefully. 'Not compared with yours, I shouldn't think.'

'Sit down for a moment, Mr Bear,' says Gwennie. 'You look exhausted.'

'No, thanks. I need to wash and change.'

'Not on my account, I hope.' Gwennie gives a tinkling laugh.

'Not at all.'

Huia tries to make amends. 'Why not stay for a quick spot, Gwennie?'

Gwennie again consults her watch.

Why? thinks Ted, since it is obvious she has no intention of leaving.

Ted hands a glass to Gwennie, another to Huia, then settles down with his own whisky and soda.

'We were just discussing the Young Farmers' Ball,' says Gwennie. 'Weren't we, Huia?'

Huia twiddles her glass. 'Yes.'

'We decided we must go and support the cause, didn't we, Huia?'

'Er, yes.'

Ted sips at his drink.

'In fact,' Gwennie again emits her infuriating laugh, 'we were talking about making up a party, weren't we, Huia?'

'Well, you . . .'

Gwennie shoots her a furious look. 'You said you thought it was a super idea.'

'Well, not super, exactly. I said a party of people would make it more fun.'

Ted gulps down another mouthful from his glass.

'What do *you* think, Mr Teddy Bear?'

Ted summons up a hearty laugh. 'You know me, Gwennie. I've got two left feet.'

'It's the usual problem, of course,' sighs Gwennie. 'Numbers. Too many girls and not enough chaps.' She turns a winning smile on Ted. 'So we're just going to have to rake in every available bachelor, even the left-footed ones.'

Panic rises in Ted. When it comes to getting her own way, Gwennie has the same highly developed ability as the Red Queen. 'You'll have to count me out, girls. Too much to do at the office.'

'All work and no play,' coos Gwennie, 'makes Teddy a dull bear.'

Ted has an inspired thought. 'If it's just bodies you're after, what about the Wrenches? Perseus and Lysander. That's two extra men.'

'You can't *possibly* ask the Wrenches! Tell him, Huia.'

'Why not?' says Ted. 'It's a Young Farmers' Ball. They're farmers.'

'Not those sorts of farmers,' cries Gwennie. 'The Wrenches are hillbillies. Hicks from the sticks.'

Ted looks at Huia.

'I know what Gwennie means,' she says awkwardly. 'If the Wrenches did come – and I don't think they will – they might feel awfully out of place.'

'How do you know they won't come, if you don't invite them?'

Gwennie sets her lips. 'Invite them if you like, but better make sure, if you do, you ask Maples as well.'

Ted puts down his glass. 'What's Maples got to do with it? He's hardly a Young Farmer.'

'He's hardly *young*,' says Gwennie spitefully. 'But he's practically engaged to Ethel Wrench.'

Ted sits on the grey planks of the verandah. Somewhere far off a belligerent rook is cawing a hoarse complaint. So Ethel is 'practically engaged' to Maples. Maples! What can she possibly see in the fellow? And why has she been leading Ted on, spending an afternoon with him at the lake, listening to all his private thoughts? Only to help Huia?

Guided by Uncle Charles, Ted has begun to filter moneys back into the plundered accounts, and just when he has started to consider there might be time for a life of his own . . . But why should he think, because a girl agrees to spend an afternoon with him, that he has any long-term claim on her? He knows he is not handsome or tall and athletic like, say, Eru. That he is shy, stolid, balding. Then he remembers how simply Ethel spoke to him, how easy he felt with her, how quickly she seemed to grasp what he was trying to explain. *Maples*? What on earth has possessed her? He must be old enough to be her father. Has she become involved with him by accident, then not been able to get herself out of the thing decently? Surely, surely, she can't be in love with him?

Every evening, Ted dreads returning to Castleton House where the Red Queen, a gigantic spider, waits to trap him in the sticky web of conversation she has spent all day spinning. As he comes in tonight, she pounces. 'I must speak to you immediately, Edward-Wilson.'

'I'll have a brush-up first, Mama, then I'll pour you your sherry.'

Ted passes his mother a glass. 'Here you are.'

She pulls a face. 'Ugh. Dry.'

'Sorry, I'll get you another.'

'No, don't bother.'

Ted settles down with his own whisky and soda. 'Right, Mama, what is it you want to talk to me about?'

'I've been thinking. Heaven knows, since your father's accident, I've had time enough to think.'

'Yes, well . . .'

'I need a change of scenery. Being here, where I'm reminded every day . . .'

'Good idea. Why not go and stay with Ku for a bit?'

'Gracious, no! Unity's so whiney and, anyway, Kotuku's out

gallivanting all the time. She won't take care of a grieving widow-woman. I'm going to Charles and Vaddy. But I thought perhaps Ku could take me shopping. I can't wear black for ever and my skirts are much too long and old-fashioned.' She sighs. 'A little shopping in Wellington with Kotuku might help take me out of myself.'

Ted puts down his glass. 'I'm sorry, Mama. Out of the question.'

'I hardly think,' says his mother, 'it's for *you* to tell me what I can and can't do. I may be a relict, but I refuse to be dowdy.'

'Mama, just at the moment there are no spare funds for shopping. No funds at all, in fact.'

'What are you trying to say?'

'We're all going to have to do a bit of belt-tightening.'

'*You* may tighten your belt as much as you like, but *I* most definitely will not.'

Ted feels the remembered kernel of childhood anger unfurling inside him. 'You'll have to,' he says. 'I can't let you have money that isn't there.'

She rises. 'I see that being in charge of the firm has gone to your head. I shall have to ask your uncle to overrule you.'

Just in time, Ted spots Ethel wobbling precariously on Ku's bicycle on the other side of the street. Quickly he turns towards the bakery window, gagging on the greasy smell of pies. How different this window is from FitzBillies. Ted feigns intense interest in the cake display. No sign of a Chelsea bun – only vivid pink Lamingtons rolled in desiccated coconut, a few asparagus rolls, their yellow-green spears barely visible in the curls of white bread, and slimy orange custard layered between slabs of pastry. At least the Eccles cakes – Arthur's favourites – though sunken, are full of raisins.

In the reflection of the window, Ted watches Ethel park her bicycle against the library wall.

Turning, she sees him and walks across the road. 'Hello.' She indicates the bike. 'You've no idea what a help it is.'

'Oh, good,' says Ted stiffly. 'I'm glad it's useful.'

Ethel looks at him in concern. 'Are you all right, Ted?'

'Fine.'

'You don't seem very fine. Is it Huia?'

'Is what Huia?'

'She told me she was leaving soon.'

Ted stares at her. 'She hasn't mentioned it to me, yet.'

'She's frightened to tell you.'

'I'm the one who'll be left to deal with Mama.'

Ethel smiles. 'Pater used to bait Grandmater by telling her the saints had an over-inflated view of their own suffering.'

Ted is hurt. 'You think I have?'

'I didn't say that.' She looks at him mischievously. 'Do you remember that time you had the nose-bleed in our lobby?'

So this is what she thinks of me, Ted tells himself. Pathetic. Weak. Terrified.

'Pater,' says Ethel, 'was fiercely opposed to any form of religion. He thought it was all irrationality, you see. But Mater's father had been a vicar, so she used to sneak off to St Edmund's on high days and holy days. Pater had no idea. Grandmater had gone over to Rome, and her room was littered with tracts and concordances and lives of the saints. I used to love all those gory pictures of the martyrs.'

Ted is astonished. 'Really?'

'You must admit, they *are* excitingly bloodthirsty. St Sebastian with all those arrows, St Laurence on the grill, St Lucy with her eyes on a plate, St John the Baptist's head . . .'

'Oh,' says Ted faintly.

'So, when I saw you gouting blood all over the lobby . . .' She laughs. 'I thought it was the stigmata.'

Despite himself, Ted laughs, too.

'I had this notion,' says Ethel, 'you were some kind of saint marked out for glory.' Momentarily, she looks uncomfortable. 'I used to watch you, spy on you, I suppose . . . To see if it would happen again.'

'I'm sorry to disillusion you, but they were just boring old nose-bleeds.'

'I know that now. But then, I suppose it livened things up to think I might see an actual martyrdom.'

She seems so friendly, so pleased to see him . . . Ted recovers himself. 'You must excuse me,' he says, moving away from Ethel towards the bakery door. 'I've got a couple of purchases to make.'

♔

'I feel bad about Gwennie,' says Huia as she and Ethel trot into Castleton in the trap. 'I keep having to pretend I'll be here for the Young Farmers' Ball.'

'You haven't told her about Eru?'

'Gwennie? Gracious no. I mean, she's a friend, but . . . she wouldn't approve at all. And she's not very good at keeping secrets.'

But I am, she thinks, and I'm Ethel's best friend, so why hasn't she told me about Maples? 'Are you . . . has . . . anyone asked you to the Ball?' she says aloud.

'I can't think of anyone who would,' says Ethel.

♕

Ted is home early. Miss Venson was in a better humour today, and Father's insurance payouts have finally come through. Things are looking up. If only Ethel . . . thinks Ted as he parks his car in the wool-shed.

It is such a perfect evening, he decides to make a circuit of the garden before going inside. Swaying gently in the mild breeze, the pepper tree throws its shadow over the lawn. Ted surveys the vegetable garden. Somewhere here, near the base of the tree, close to Mrs BanTam, his lucky farthing is still buried.

The moon is rising over the wool-shed. Soon the daylight sounds will be smothered in the stillness of night. Faint bleats drift from the paddock behind the wool-shed and a morepork mourns in the distance. In front of him, teetering across the grass, its wings folded like arms behind its back, a solitary rook lowers its head to the ground, scanning the earth for fallen walnuts. It looks so like a don, pacing, engaged in deep thought, that Ted cannot help smiling to himself.

The rook raises its head, cocks a beady eye at Ted and emits a harsh, scolding cry. Like me, thinks Ted, suddenly. Admonishing Huia. Cawing my judgement at her. Rook. Castle. Rook. '*A thieving bird who destroys the nest of other, smaller, birds.*' How Father had lived up – down – to his name. And now, I . . .

I am not . . . likeable, he thinks. What had Ethel said? '*Is that why you aren't treating Huia very kindly right now?*' '*. . . you just said it was stultifying here. You didn't want to come back yourself.*' But why should I care what Ethel Wrench thinks? Ted asks himself. If she considers me all, she's probably decided I'm a dull sort of fellow. Because, he realises suddenly, I *am* dull. What else had she said, when he had been unable to stop himself from telling her how guilty he felt about Wiki? '*You were younger then. I'm sure you'd be nicer to her now.*'

But would I? he asks himself. Just because I'm older, am I so very different? I am still cold and punishing to Huia, my own sister. In all my life, he thinks, I've never put a foot out of place; I've been good, done my duty, never taken any risks. Except for that once – only that once . . .

Somehow, he cannot get the memory of Wiki out of his head. The only time he can ever remember being swept by, not love, but . . .

Passion, he thinks suddenly. I am a man without passion.

All these years I have blamed Mama for favouring Ku and Huia, but what a snivelling, greedy creature I have been – a jealous thief of a child, stealing his bright scraps, storing away his crumbs. No, I am not dull, he thinks, I am worse than dull. I am a miser.

He hears Ethel's voice. '*. . . there's only any point in feeling guilt about something if it stops you from doing it again . . . Isn't there something you can do now to make up for it? . . . Just feeling guilty doesn't help anyone.*'

And Wiki? Ethel's right, thinks Ted. There *is* something I can do to make amends – for me *and* for Father. It will take a while to sort out, but I can start it tomorrow, speak to Uncle Charles . . .

And what was the other thing Ethel had said, that day at the lake? *Human archaeology*. That was it.

I'll dig up my farthing, decides Ted, and take it to show her. And, I'll be kind – I'll try to be kinder – to Huia. I'll prove to Ethel I'm not irredeemably dreary. And not wallowing in guilt. True, she's engaged to Maples but I can still have a friendly chat with her, surely?

Before long, the soft darkness of twilight will close in. The first few stars are already low in the sky, and the sun is setting rapidly over the grazing paddock. As Ted gazes at its orange disc, he is reminded of Ethel's copper hair. So, Ethel *had* been watching him all those years ago. He remembers her head protruding from behind the haystack. Her bright red curls. Like Flossie's. He has a fleeting recollection of Flossie, her skirt raised – of himself . . .

Flossie! Of course. *That* is where he has heard the strange little tune Ethel was whistling at the lake. Flossie, whistling as she tried to touch him for a threepence. '*Clever, eh? Bet you can't do that? Me beau learnt it to me.*'

My God, Father is off the hook! Wilson Castle couldn't whistle a tune to save his life.

♔

Ethel shifts uneasily on the chair in Ted's office. 'I didn't know who else to come to.'

'Look,' says Ted, 'if we talk about it here, I'm more or less obliged to pass on anything . . . relevant to a police inquiry. Why don't we drive over to Masterton and talk it over in a tea-shop? As friends.'

'You don't know how much I'd appreciate that, but I . . . it's much too . . . private for a tea-shop. Or any public place.'

'No difficulty with that. I wonder, since it's such a lovely day, what would you say to driving out to the lake again? No chance of being overheard there.'

Ethel hesitates.

Ted decides to show her he can be magnanimous. 'Of course, if you want to bring Mr Maples along, that's fine with me.'

Ethel gapes at him. '*Maples*. You mean the grocer? But whyever would I want to involve *him*?'

'I thought, since you're practically engaged . . .'

'*To Maples?*'

'You mean, you're not?'

'No, of course not.'

'I think,' says Ted, 'I may have been being a bit of an obtuse idiot.'

'Don't worry,' says Ethel. 'So have I. You'll realise when you hear what I have to tell you.'

'It was while you were away in Cambridge. Uncle Bertie . . .'

'A horrible accident. I heard.'

'But you see, I always wondered exactly what made Uncle – why they found him like that . . . After all, he'd smoked for years. What made him suddenly, that day . . . ? And then, Huia said Flossie had gone. Of course I was suspicious. But who could I have talked to about it? And, anyway, it was only a suspicion.' She breaks off. 'I expect you think I've got a very mistrustful nature. My own uncle.'

'No. Not one bit. I . . . well, sometime, I'll tell you.' He stops. 'Sorry. Do go on.'

'The locket was Grandmater's. And, just before she went off to Rome, it went missing. There was the most terrible hullaballoo. We all searched everywhere, but there was no trace of it. Pater was convinced she'd been duped into giving it to the Church, and she was certain Pater had melted it down to use in his experiments. Poor Mater, she was constantly standing between them. And then, after Grandmater died, everyone rather forgot about it. But the locket they found with Flossie is definitely it. I'd recognise it anywhere.'

'And your mother? Would she recognise it, too?'

'Certainly. But if it's humanly possible, I don't want to involve poor Mater. Because you must know what it means, Flossie's having the locket.'

'She could have stolen it.'

'How? She never came anywhere near our house. No, there's only one way Flossie could have got that locket. I think you know it, too.'

'Your uncle gave it to her?'

Ethel nods. 'And you see, when he died, there were scratches all over his face and hands. They said it was from a barbed-wire fence, but . . .'

Silence.

'So,' says Ethel, 'what do you suggest I do?'

'You've got a choice,' says Ted. How extraordinary, he thinks. Just like I had. Aloud, he continues, 'You can tell the police your suspicions, but, after all this time, what can they possibly do? Any evidence will be long gone. You and your family will have to appear at the inquest and every newspaper in the country will take up the story. And at the end, the coroner will sum up solely on the basis of probability. Or . . . you can do nothing. Nobody will be any the wiser. Nothing can bring Flossie back now. And you don't know for sure.'

'I *am* sure. Well, fairly sure.'

'Fairly isn't absolutely.' He pauses. 'I wasn't going to say this, but now you've brought it up, there's something I ought to tell you. Do you remember that tune you were whistling last time we came here? From the Boer War, you said.'

'Uncle's tune?'

'I told you I'd heard it before.'

'Yes.'

'It was Flossie whistling it. She said her sweetheart had taught it to her.'

'Oh no. So it was Uncle. What do *you* think I . . . ?'

'I think you should leave well alone.' Briefly he recalls talking to Uncle Charles. ' "Leave the dead to bury their own dead," I'd say. And shall I tell you what else I think?'

Ethel looks at him.

'I think,' says Ted, 'you're the most astounding woman I've ever known. If I spread out the rug here, would you – shall we – sit down a bit more comfortably?'

'Ted?'

'What is it?'

'The locket. It was meant to go to Mater. Since Pater died, I do have a little bit of money. Do you think there's the slightest chance I might be able to buy it from Mrs McPhee?'

'Every chance, I'd say. I'll speak to Reilly.'

♛

Walking through the bush tracks in the Domain is like entering another world, hushed and green. As they brush against the hoheria and spicy-scented pittosporum, Ted and Ethel are wet by drops of rain from this morning's shower. Ted picks up a piece of bark from under a ponga fern. 'See the patterns on the inside.'

'Like carving.'

'Maybe that's where the Maori patterns came from originally.'

'Have you heard from Huia?'

'She phoned me at the office yesterday.'

'They're married?'

'Yes.' Ted sighs. 'She'll never be able to come back to Castleton, of course.'

Ethel stops. 'Why not? This is her home. Eru'll be back. And not just for his grandfather. This is his . . . what's it called?'

'Turangawaewae. A standing place. Somewhere he truly belongs. Every Maori has one.'

'Not just Maori,' says Ethel. 'Everybody has a place like that.' She takes off her coat, spreads it on the damp ground and sits down. 'Pai bo kai kino tan gan.'

'What on earth does that mean?'

'It's Greek. Something Pater used to quote all the time. From Archimedes of Syracuse.'

'The one who shouted "Eureka" in his bath?'

She nods. 'It means, "Give me a place to stand and I will move the earth." Just like Eru's turangawaewae.'

'Can I join you on your coat?'

'Yes, there's plenty of room.' Ethel moves over. 'That's what I meant when I said you should go back to Cambridge.'

Ted snaps a dry pine needle between his fingers. 'You think Cambridge is my standing place? I don't agree.'

'You see,' says Ethel, 'that was the trouble with Pater. He never belonged in New Zealand. His real home was always Gawminsgodden and, when Uncle Archibald inherited, there was no place for him any more.' She wraps her arms around her drawn-up knees.

'Well, I can see that Eru's ancestral home is here in Castleton.'

'And so's your mother's.'

Ted digests this. 'So is mine then. There's the practice and the house and . . .'

Ethel shakes her head impatiently. 'No. That isn't it at all. For most people, their real home is a house or a town or a place. But then there are other people like you – not so many – and where they really belong isn't some*where* but in some*thing*. I didn't mean you should be based in Cambridge, I meant in the Mortmain Statutes.'

'The Mortmain Statutes? They're not a place, they're . . .'

'I know. But studying them, being immersed in them, was where you felt most comfortable. Where you felt completely yourself.'

'That's true,' says Ted slowly. 'But what about you, then?'

'My turanga-whatever-it-is can be anywhere.'

'You're dodging the question.'

'No, I *can* live anywhere. Because of what I told you that day at the lake. About the layers of things. Wherever I am, I know that no matter how neat and tidy the surface is, underneath are all the levels, stacked on top of one another, where dozens – hundreds – of people, have lived before . . . and I like that. That's my "territory".'

Ted puts his arm round her. 'I've never met anyone who thinks the way you do,' he says. And he kisses her.

'I should tell you,' says Ethel, as Ted helps her put on her coat, 'I'm going to get a job. Probably in Wellington.'

'A job?'

'Why not?'

'But what will you do?'

'I've got Greek and Latin. Very good Greek and Latin. I'll easily get a job teaching in a girls' school.'

'But I . . . why Wellington?'

'Once I'm working, I'm going to save up to go back to England and see it again for myself. Not the way Pater and Mater used to talk about it. The way *I* want to see it.'

'Wellington . . .' says Ted, in dismay.

Ted watches Ethel as she paddles at the edge of the sea. What was it Mama used to say? 'Ethel Wrench. A real fish out of water.' But, thinks Ted, it isn't the fish Ethel resembles, it's the water. She is like a wave perpetually flowing the wrong way, a silent stubborn undercurrent pulling in her own direction. One of those smaller rip-tides that drags itself along, regardless of the wash and swell of the larger breakers, bumping and rippling sideways across the rollers crashing to the shore. Ethel Wrench, forever managing to keep afloat in deep water.

And, if she is an errant cross-wave, what is he, Ted Castle?

His life has foundered in shallows; he is a pool left behind by the tide, stagnant water stranded further up the beach, away from the ocean. I have missed the boat, he tells himself, been left high and dry, beached and abandoned in this backwater.

Ethel sits down beside him on the sand. 'Have you thought about what I said?'

'A lot.'

'You *could* go back to Cambridge.'

'Too late for that, now.'

'Why?'

'There's the firm, the house . . . There've been Castles in Castleton since it was founded. Somebody has to stay on. I couldn't let down Father, Grandfather, Great-Grandfather . . .'

'They're all dead,' says Ethel. 'What you do makes no difference to them.' She considers for a moment. 'Do you remember, at the lake that time, when you told me about the Mortmain Statutes?' She draws a pattern in the sand with her big toe. 'What you're saying's exactly like that. You said it was mostly churches. The dead hand stretching from beyond the grave. The institution that never dies, but goes on living in perpetuity.'

'Gosh, you do have a good memory.'

'I can see why it fascinates you. Because, in a way, you're like that, too. Only in your case the dead hand's your family, your name. But it's different for you, as well. You're not like the Church. You could sell up. Get away.' She looks at him searchingly. 'If that's what you really want.' She smiles. 'Unless, of course, you only want to go back for the Chelsea buns.'

Ted makes a mock-swipe at her, then becomes serious again. 'I was thinking about it while you were paddling. I've missed the boat.'

'Not yet,' says Ethel. 'But almost. This is your last chance. Sink or swim.'

Ted takes in Ethel's tangled hair, her bare feet, her earnest expression; then, pushing her back on the rug, he lies on top of her, stroking the curls back from her forehead. 'If I decided to swim, would you swim with me?'

Ethel smiles up at him. 'I might.'

'Promise me?'

'I promise.'

'You won't change your mind?'

'Never.'

'But before we swim off anywhere,' says Ted, 'there's something important I have to do here.'

'What?'

'I'll tell you just as soon as I've sorted it out.'

♛

Eru takes Ted's proffered hand. He is wary.

'Nice to see you,' says Ted carefully. 'How's Huia?'

'She . . . well, as a matter of fact, she's expecting. We're not telling anyone yet, but she won't mind your knowing.'

'Wonderful.' Ted can hear how forced his voice sounds. 'Congratulations.'

'She sends her love.'

'Look, you're probably wondering why I asked you to meet me here. But it's . . . I . . . I've got a bit of news myself and I thought it would be more professional to tell you in my office.'

'News?'

'Yes. I saw Wiki the other day, in Castleton with her little girl, and she told me your grandfather's fading.'

'He's got very frail since Kuia passed on. And now he's just slipping away.' Eru pauses. 'He's given me his chessmen.'

'Does he know about you and Huia?'

Eru shakes his head. He is visibly relaxing now that he realises that Ted is making an effort to be friendly. 'No point in upsetting him now. Auntie knows. And Wiki. But not Koro.'

'Do you remember,' Ted pulls a sheaf of papers towards them, 'that business about the iwi land being given for a school? Only no school was ever built?'

Eru grins. 'Has any of us been allowed to forget it?'

'Well, I've been . . . going through the iwi papers and I realised that, if the trustees and the iwi agree, part of the land could be sold to finance the building of the school. It's subject to approval from the Church Commissioners, too, of course, but my uncle in Wellington's already spoken to them informally and they say they can see no possible grounds on which to object. In fact, with things the way they are now, they'd look on it very favourably. It'd create a significant number of new jobs. So, what do you think?'

Eru says nothing.

Disappointing, thinks Ted. I'd hoped he'd be at least a bit jubilant. Then, he realises. Eru is fighting back tears.

'I can't explain how much this means,' says Eru when he is finally able to speak. 'To all of us. But especially to Koro. There's nothing I can say to thank you properly.'

'No need.'

Eru hesitates. 'You'll find this a cheek, but . . . could you possibly tell Koro yourself? If it comes from you, he'll believe it.'

♛

Fragile and thin, Te Mara sits propped among cushions in a chair, Auntie Keruru hovering beside him.

'Kia ora,' says Ted.

'Kia ora,' says the old man. He takes Ted's outstretched hand. 'Eruera has told me. Is it the truth?'

Ted nods.

Briefly, the chief shuts his eyes. 'So, at last, there will be a school. And when I am reunited with my koro . . .' He opens his eyes and looks directly at Ted. 'Put your head here. Against mine.'

Ted lays his brow to the old man's papery forehead.

There is a long silence, then Te Mara says, 'You are a fine man. Like your father. And you and my Eruera will be friends always. Like your father and me.'

♖

Rosalba Castle lays her trug on the verandah and pulls off her gardening gloves. 'Atkinson!'

Atkinson shuffles out from the kitchen.

'A glass of cold water,' says Rosalba, mopping her brow with a violet-scented handkerchief. 'And, Atkinson, now that Miss Huia's decided to stay on in Auckland, you'd better give her room a thorough clean. And put out the mattress. It's ideal airing weather.'

Atkinson's eyes narrow. She can perfectly well judge airing weather.

'But make sure it's out of sight by this afternoon. Mrs Bickford and Mrs Fraser are coming to tea. And Miss Gwennie. She'll be driving them. Such a comfort to have a daughter at home. And she's so attentive to the older ladies. Which reminds me . . .'

Silently, Atkinson waits.

'Bridge sandwiches, I think,' says Rosalba. 'And shortbread fingers. One can never go wrong with shortbread fingers.'

Glossary

Aotearoa	the Maori name for New Zealand
haere mai ki te kai	come here and eat
haere ra	goodbye
hapu	pregnant
Heke	Maori warrior chief, Hone Heke, fought against the British in the 1840s
hongi	Maori greeting – pressing noses together
huhu	small edible grub of the huhu beetle (*Prionoplus reticularis)*
huia	wattle bird (*Hetralocha acutirostris)*
iwi	tribe
kai	food
kauri	New Zealand hardwood tree (*Agathis australis)*
kia ora	greeting – hello *(lit. may you have health)*
kit	bag of woven flax
kohine	girl
koro	sir, old man, grandfather
kotuku	white heron (*Egretta alba modesta*)
kuia	old lady, grandmother
kumara	sweet potato (*Ipumoea batatas*)
kuri	dog
mana	integrity, prestige, high status

manuka	New Zealand native tea tree (*Leptospermum scoparium*)
marae	central meeting area of tribal village
mimi	urine, urinate
moa	large flightless bird (*Dinornis giganteus*), now extinct
moana	lake, sea, body of water
mokopuna	grandchild
nikau	palm (*Rhyopalastylis sapida)*
pa	Maori settlement
Pakeha	non-Maori, European
paua	shellfish (*Haliotis spp*), abalone
ponga	New Zealand native tree fern (*Cyathea dealbata*)
pukeko	swamp hen (*Porphyrio melanotus*)
tangi	Maori funeral practice
taniwha	mythical water monster
tapu	sacred, forbidden
tena koe	a Maori greeting, addressed to one person
toe-toe	pampas, sharp-leaved sedge grass (*Cortaderia splendens*)
tohunga	priest with sacred knowledge
totara	large New Zealand native tree (*Podocarpus totara*)
turangawaewae	domicile, home (*lit. standing place*)
utu	revenge
wahine	woman, wife
wairua	spirit, soul
waka huia	storage box for treasures, including sacred feathers
whare	house
wharenui	tribal meeting house

Acknowledgements

The quotations on the three part title pages are taken from the Statute of Mortmain, enacted by King Edward I of England in 1279.

This book was written during my time as the inaugural Royal Literary Fund Fellow at the Courtauld Institute, and with financial assistance from the Society of Authors' Literary Fund, and the help of a Hawthornden Fellowship and a Visiting Scholarship at Lucy Cavendish College, Cambridge. I am most grateful to them all.

I am indebted to Peter Rowe and Jon Corballis, and to Prof. Jim Evans, formerly of the University of Auckland, for invaluable help with the passages about the law. Jim directed me to Frederika Hackshaw's paper, 'Nineteenth Century Notions of Aboriginal Title and their Influence on the Interpretation of the Treaty of Waitangi' in H. Kawharu (ed.), *Waitangi: Maori and Pakeha Perspectives of the Treaty of Waitangi* (Oxford University Press, Auckland, 1989).

My thanks for much-appreciated assistance are also due to the following: Harriet Allan, Zöe Carroll, Tony Corballis, Eleanor Crow, Jillian Ewart, Vivien Green, Mandy Greenfield, Phillip King, Rob Lorch and the Model T Ford Register of Great Britain, Winifred Lynch, Nicolas Pilavachi, Neil Tuckett, Rose Walker and, most particularly, to Ronda Armitage, Sue Brill, Roger Cazalet, Penelope Hoare, Witi Ihimaera, Hilary Spurling and Rose Tremain.

J.C.